Chinese Cooking
for Diamond Thieves

Chinese Cooking
for Diamond Thieves

DAVE LOWRY

A Mariner Original • *Mariner Books* • *Houghton Mifflin Harcourt*

BOSTON   NEW YORK

2014

For information about permission to reproduce selections from this book,
write to Permissions, Houghton Mifflin Harcourt Publishing Company,
215 Park Avenue South, New York, New York 10003.

www.hmhco.com

Library of Congress Cataloging-in-Publication Data
Lowry, Dave.
Chinese Cooking for Diamond Thieves / Dave Lowry.
pages cm
ISBN 978-0-547-97331-9
1. Cooking, Chinese—Fiction. 2. Gangsters—Missouri—Saint Louis—Fiction.
3. Suspense fiction. 4. Humorous fiction. I. Title.
PS3612.O928C48 2014
813'.6—dc23
2013050977

Book design by Chrissy Kurpeski
Typeset in Dante

Printed in the United States of America
DOC 10 9 8 7 6 5 4 3 2 1

For Christopher Bates: colleague, friend, xiong di

Chinese Cooking
for Diamond Thieves

Rule #10: *Keep focused on the broad perspective and don't get distracted by minor stuff—like, say, graduating from college.*

"Da-da-da-dadadada-da-da-da / three's company too."

I'd been going over it for at least the last hour. The last cold, dark hour. And over it. The stupid theme song was gunning its tinny engine in my head, revving up and grinding around and around and not going anywhere. That was bad enough. What was even worse, much worse, was that no matter how many times I repeated it, no matter how many times it kept replaying in my brain, again and again, I couldn't pull up that line. It was maddening. If I'd had a gun handy . . . I'm not saying I would have killed myself. I might have clicked the cylinder around a few times just to stare at the business end of the bullets, though.

Part of it was that I was still, as my grandmother would have put it, a "touch feverish." For a couple of weeks now, I'd been pretending a case of flu was just a bad cold. I'd been pretending so long, I was getting fairly good at it. I was past the "I'd really like to roll over, but if I move I may just die" stage of the flu that I was pretending was a cold. I was going to live. Probably. A week ago, concrete had been shoveled into my nose and had seeped up into my sinuses and hardened. By now, it had loosened up. Some. I no longer felt like my eyeballs were slowly frying their way out of my head. I was improving. I wasn't going to jump up and qualify for the Olympic track trials any time soon. I wasn't getting exhausted by those seven long steps I had to take from the bed to the bathroom, though. I was just feeling a little shaky and a little hot still. I'd self-diagnosed my condition. My medical expertise wasn't entirely reliable, but it did have the advantages of being cheap. And not requiring me to sit in a doctor's waiting room. I had prescribed for myself some cough syrup and went on the assumption that if a single dosage of the little plastic jigger that fit over the cap was good, a couple of them would be even better. So maybe that was making me a little squirrelly too.

Feverish or squirrelly, I didn't have a good excuse for not remembering the stupid third line. I'd heard it sung five times a week, every week, all last semester. Toby Ingersoll, my roommate at Beddingfield College, had gone on this weird kick, watching a cable channel in our room that played TV shows from the seventies. Every afternoon when I got back to the dorm after sitting through another ninety minutes of American Literature: A Postmodern Perspective, Toby's butt, along with the rest of him, would be plopped in his beanbag chair. He'd gotten it—the chair, not his butt—from a senior last year who didn't want to drag it home. The TV would be tuned to a channel where it was still the seventies and where comedies and dramas from that decade played twenty-four hours a day. Toby never missed an episode of a show about a guy who had to pretend to be gay so he could share an apartment with a couple of attractive girls. I think that was it. I wasn't as involved in the particulars of the show as Toby was. I should have paid more attention. I wouldn't be in the mess I was in right now, sleepless at 2:30 in the morning and fixated on that idiotic third line and unable to get my mind out of neutral over it. Tucker's Rule #12: The more trivial the problem, the more it will be distracting.

To be honest, though, that was not my biggest problem.

Two days before, I'd said my goodbyes to Toby and to all those kooky, zany TV hits from the years of the Carter administration. Aloha to that divorced woman who worked at a diner somewhere out in TV land, the one with the uproariously funny customers. Adios to the cop show that took place in a gritty TV urban jungle. And now that I thought about it, arrivederci to Beddingfield College, a comprehensive, very exclusive, but accommodating first-class liberal arts institute dedicated to secondary learning since its founding by Philander Beddingfield in 1857; to its gracious, tree-lined campus located in Lancaster, New Hampshire, right between the banks of the scenic Connecticut River and the even scenic-er Great North Woods of the aforementioned Great State of New Hampshire. *You have,* I said to myself, *moved on.* I was just going to skip some of the assorted festivities and—uh, accoutrements. Like a cap and gown. And a diploma.

I don't usually talk too much to myself. Usually I get out most everything I need to say to me fairly quickly. And lucidly. But there was that lingering touch of fever. And the fact that I was sleeping—or trying to—on a futon at Chris Langley's place that smelled like his Irish setter, and it smelled that way because that's usually where Langley's Irish setter *did* sleep. I had asserted evolutionary privilege and staked out my claim, at least for that evening. The dog was curled up beside me on a ratty old quilt of Chris's. So mostly I just lay there in New Hampshire's winter dark, kicking off the heavy sleeping bag over me, then groping to tug it back up a while later as I went from sweating to shivering and let that theme song—the first two lines of it, anyway—run through my head. And in between the Quest for the Lost Stanza, I thought about what my parents were going to say when they found out I had parted ways with Beddingfield College in what was supposed to have been the triumphant and rewarding semester of my senior year.

There was some stuff I didn't think about that night. Understandable, since it hadn't happened yet. But also because, to be uncharacteristically honest, I really didn't have the imagination to think that some of it *could* have happened to a guy like me. Like, for instance, what happened after the cops in St. Louis found that body.

Rule #17: *Sometimes what you really need in life is nothing more complicated than a lot of cough syrup and twelve hours of sleep.*

It was two nights before the night I stayed up and thought about those lines from the TV show.

"You never seemed the type," Chris had said to me, after I slid across from him into the booth at Spencer's Grill and told him that the pedagogical institution of Beddingfield and I were going our separate academic ways. Spencer's Grill was the closest place the village of North Lancaster had to the diner like that one in the seventies TV show Toby watched. The customers weren't as funny or clever as in the TV show. Although they had their moments. Once, back during hunting season, a deer hunter came in carrying the field-dressed corpse of a buck he'd just shot. He propped the buck up in a booth, sat down opposite it, and ordered a beer for both of them. Mostly it was a place where the locals hung out. Along with the beer they served to customers, including recently deceased antlered ungulates, Spencer's put out burgers and sandwiches. Maybe the best dill pickles in the state. It was where the kids from Beddingfield went when they got sick of the food at the school's cafeteria.

"The type?" I said.

"The type to get kicked out of school," Chris said. His plate was empty except for a tumble of lonely-looking fries.

"'Kicked out' is a little strong," I said. "Let's just say I decided to pursue the self-actualization of my educational potential in more varied directions."

"And the dean agreed with you," Chris said.

"Exactly."

"And you both concluded this right after the . . ."

"Correct," I said. I really didn't want to go into it. "Here's the thing," I added. "I need a place to stay for a couple of days. I've cleared out of my dorm and I'm headed south."

"Where's your stuff?" he asked.

"Back of the Toyota."

"How far south you going?" he asked. He ate one of the fries, leaving the others looking even lonelier.

"Back to my parents' place," I said. "Massachusetts." I didn't add that I was forming a plan, slowly. And so far vaguely. I was only going to be in Andover, where my parents lived, long enough to drop off what I didn't need from my dorm. My plan wasn't all that detailed yet. I didn't want to sound like I was completely clueless, though. Which I mostly was.

"Think the Toyota will make it that far?" he asked.

"Are you kidding?" I said. "I'm still just getting it broken in." I'd stood over too many pans of splattering, skin-searing oil; sweated off too many pounds in steamy, stifling restaurant kitchens; collected too many scars on my forearms from the blistering edges of woks to make enough money to buy that car. Four summers' worth. Four summers spent in sauna-hot, airless kitchens listening to singsong Cantonese, understanding only about one word in every six, and Mandarin, which after a long time I could finally manage not only to understand but use to get across my own opinions from time to time. The Toyota had a few thousand miles on it when I bought it, true. Actually a hundred and sixty thousand of them. But it was a Toyota. Had to be good for at least another K, or even two. I just had to remember to put oil in it. It was drinking oil lately like I'd been swigging cough syrup the past week.

Chris smiled and shook his head. The spring before, the University of New Hampshire had conferred upon him a degree in environmental engineering. It turned out the environment did not need nearly as many able-bodied engineers as one might have expected—particularly if one was among others who were listening to the ambitious predictions of teachers in that department at UNH. I didn't think Chris tried too hard, however, to find a job in the field. The summer after he graduated, he went almost directly to the environment of the Ammonoosuc River outside North Lancaster. He engineered the rehabilitation—to the degree he could actually move into it—of an old summer shack his uncle owned and never used anymore, out on Germantown Road. He moved in, along with an Irish setter named Gork and a girl named Gretchen. By the end of Chris's first winter in a place heated with a wood-burning stove and an open-air outhouse, Gork was still there. The only sign of Gretchen's tenure was a toothbrush still dangling from a hook over by the dry sink. Chris eventually took a job with the Forest Service Ski Patrol, rescuing hikers and skiers and the assorted kinds who managed to get themselves lost on a regular basis all over the North Woods that covered this part of the state. During the winter, he taught kids to ski over at Bretton Woods.

January in New Hampshire is cold. Which is like saying the surface of the sun is hot. The cold doesn't just sit there over New Hampshire during the winter. It's active; silent but lively—and vicious in its own sneaky way. You might not be consciously thinking about the cold in a New Hampshire January. Ignore it too long, however, and it will make you pay. January in New Hampshire wasn't so much an experience of trying to find a way to stay warm; that wasn't happening. It was a matter, instead, of trying not to be too cold.

Chris had two kerosene heaters he moved around the cabin for places that were too far from the wood-burning stove's tropical spell. One was in the bedroom where I was sleeping, hissing gently, putting out a warm, orange glow from the coils near the bottom. My sleeping bag was a thick one, suitable for temperatures close to freezing. So I was holding on okay. I'd been there two nights now. This was the last. It would have been nice to have gotten a good night's sleep. I was satisfied not to be hypothermic. In fact, with something like a plan for my future forming slowly, if I could have just pulled up the third line to that song, I would have been almost perfect. I pressed the button that illuminated the dial on my watch. I thought it might have said 2:30. But before I could check again to be sure, I was sound asleep.

It was bright when the dog started whining and woke me up at what seemed like about a week later. I glanced at my watch again. It was already past two in the afternoon. I'd managed to sleep twelve hours. I pushed my way out of the bag and found it wasn't damp with my perspiration. And I wasn't shivering. And my left nostril was actually taking in the chilly air of the cabin, free and clear. Cough syrup is magic. It could probably cure cancer, I thought. I let the dog out. Chris hadn't come home last night. He had been trying very hard to date a Dartmouth girl who was taking the semester off from school to work for the ski patrol. I assumed he'd succeeded—if not in dating her, at least in sharing some quality time with her.

I looked around his place. Chris had a sort of laissez-faire approach to housekeeping. It didn't seem likely that *Elegant Interiors Monthly* was going to be showing up to do a photo spread anytime soon. Even so, I straightened things up, trying to hit that fine balance between saying, by my housework, "Thanks for letting me stay; I'm picking up around the house to show my appreciation" and "Jeez, you're such a slob I couldn't leave here without doing major domestic surgery." I dusted, using what was either a very well-worn T-shirt or the dog's toy. I washed dishes that appeared to have been in the sink most of the winter. My homemaking instincts satisfied, I packed up my stuff. I worked slowly, enjoying the sensation of moving around without feeling achy. My head felt like it was assuming normal proportions again. It didn't take long for me to be ready. When I pulled out of Chris's driveway and turned the nose of the Toyota south, though, the sun was already snuggling down into the upper branches of the hemlock trees all around. Sleeping late, then cleaning house had cost me a day's driving time, true. But by sleeping in, I'd found a lot of my energy again. I wished I could say the same about the third line of that theme song.

3

Rule #19: *Never pick up strangers at a highway rest stop unless they speak Mandarin.*

The entire city of Lancaster, New Hampshire, may have assembled to wave goodbye as it disappeared entirely behind me when Highway 2 took a long, smooth curve off to the right. I wouldn't know. I didn't feel any need to look back. I passed through Lunenburg, then Dalton, then Gilman, and then, off to my right, I went by the long black, spruce-lined pool of the Moose Reservoir. I wasn't in any real hurry. I didn't dawdle either. By the time I made it to St. Johnsbury, where the two-lane road connected with I-93, the daylight was just about played out. It wasn't quite there; only a few more moments until the time of the evening when you consider that it's dark enough to contemplate turning on the headlights. I realized I hadn't eaten in a long time.

When it comes to eating on the road, some people like to make a big deal out of those little Mom-and-Pop places along the highway that serve good old-fashioned home cooking. Blue-plate specials. Meat loaf. Swiss steak. Chicken pot pie. I don't have anything against Mom. Or Pop. When I'm traveling, though, going from one place to another and not just rambling around on some kind of road trip vacation but actually trying to get to a destination, I don't want to get off the highway and scout around trying to find a place that has the best corned-beef hash or pan-fried chicken. I just want to eat and get back to driving. I wasn't in the mood for anything much, anyway, even though I was breathing now through both sides of my nose. There were road signs for half a dozen different franchise joints. They didn't sound appealing. What sounded appealing were cinnamon buns. Ever since I'd thought about making either a late lunch or an early dinner back at Chris's and deciding not to, I realized, I had started thinking about those sugary iced, cinnamon-dusted buns that come in pairs, wrapped in cellophane. The cinnamon buns that are available only in the finer, high-quality gas stations and twenty-four-hour convenience marts of the land—and, I was hoping, at highway rest stops. Like the one I was approaching, outside Littleton. I pulled in. My mouth was actually watering. I told myself to be realistic. Chances of striking dispenser-machine cinnamon-bun gold out here on I-93 were fairly small. I might have to settle for a fried fruit pie. As with much of the rest of life, I tried to keep my expectations low. Tucker's Rule #52: Never ignore the strategic advantage in embracing low expectations.

She was sitting on one of the benches inside the rest stop. Other than her, the place was empty. She had a road map of New Hampshire spread out on her lap. A big dun-colored satchel-like duffle bag was beside her feet. Her pea coat, black, looked like it belonged wrapped around a sailor on deck for the dogwatch in the North Atlantic. She looked up when I came in, then dropped her eyes back down to the map.

Luck was on my side. The buns were right there. Sitting and waiting for me behind the glass of a snack machine. A bubbling water fountain that sprang up from the desert in the middle of Death Valley wouldn't have been more welcomed for a guy crawling across the sand. Push a dollar bill into the slot, press C4, and—with a whir and a click and a satisfying thump—dinner was served. Wrapped in their shiny cellophane sleeve, the buns looked glossy and ripe with life-giving sweetness. In another machine were plastic bottles of orange juice. Could it get any better? I doubted it. Between the buns and the juice, I would pretty well satisfy my growing body's need for simple and complex sugars for the next week or so. Moments later I was doing just that, slowly savoring one bun and licking a piece of icing off my upper lip while I stood and read a poster mounted behind a plastic frame about the history of that part of the Granite State. I learned that Littleton, New Hampshire, was originally called Chiswick, which is a Saxon word meaning "cheese farm." I wondered why the Saxons needed a word for that. I learned that if you were living back around the beginning of the twentieth century and you wanted a stereoscope—and who wouldn't have?—you could get one made at a factory right here in Littleton. I learned that there was a restored gristmill nearby. And a candy store right in town that was reputed to have the longest candy counter in the world. I wondered who kept records for that kind of thing. I finished the second bun, tossed the last of the juice down.

I heard a buzz behind me. I turned around and looked at her. She was wearing jeans faded at the knees, sneakers, and that bulky pea coat, unbuttoned, with a bulky knit sweater, brown, underneath. Her black hair was hanging straight down from a gray stocking cap, and she was bent over the map, studying it, so her eyes were hidden by her bangs. Still not looking up, she fished into the pocket of her coat and came up with a phone. She glanced at it, then put it to her ear and spoke.

"*Wèi*," she said. And then, again in Mandarin, "Yes, yes, I'm okay. I'm in New Hampshire." She repeated, "*New Hampshire. Yes, I know.*" Silence, while the other person was obviously talking, then, "Three friends who were going skiing here," she said. "Yes, I got a ride from them." Silence. "Because it was the fastest way out of town."

Well, I thought, momentarily distracted from contemplating the deliciousness of my recently finished meal, *this is interesting.*

"I don't know," she said. "They dropped me off, and I'm some-

where in New Hampshire right now—I can't find it on the map."
She looked down again at the map spread out on her knees. "But,
yeah, I'll get there. I just don't know when yet." She looked up,
out the glass doors of the rest stop, into the nightfall. "Or how."
Another pause, then she nodded into the phone and said, "Yes, I
will be. See you soon." She ended the call and stuffed the phone
back into her pocket.

I thought about it. Not long. Not long enough, anyway, to
make any kind of wise, well-contemplated decision. About 1/100
of the time I'd devoted the night before trying to remember that
third line of the TV theme song. About 1/10,000 of the time I'd
thought about the Saxon need for a word for "cheese farm."
Which probably says more about me than I'd like to admit. And
if the men's room had been in the other direction, I might have
turned that way and just kept going. She was sitting, though, between me and the place where, now that I'd slugged down all that
juice, I needed to be. I was going to have to walk right by her. And
it was just the two of us, in that official New Hampshire Department of Transportation Rest Area, in the middle of Nowhere,
New Hampshire (somewhere close to Cheese Farm). In late January. Almost dark. Dark enough that the trucks and cars passing
by outside were all wearing their headlights now, cutting beams
through the shadowy dusk that was seeping in and sucking out all
the light that was left of the day. I walked up to her.

"So," I said in Mandarin, "come here often?"

She didn't look up. She kept studying the map. I couldn't really
think of a clever line to follow up what I thought was, all things
considered, a fairly amusing and effective opener.

Then she spoke, still not looking at me. "You speak Mandarin as beautifully as a monkey playing the cello," I thought she
said back. I got most of it. I caught the word *"erhu,"* a kind of
two-stringed cello-like Chinese instrument. I knew that because

a month or so earlier I'd read a review of a Chinese movie, and the movie's composer used a lot of *erhu* music. I was pleased with myself at having that little bit of wisdom tucked away.

"Monkey played well enough for you to understand the piece, though, didn't he?" I smiled.

"Yeah," she said in English, still not looking up. "But I took a whole semester of Understanding Bad Mandarin." Her English wasn't accented. She'd learned it in her pumpkin seat. But Mandarin had been in there too. She'd learned both the words "cello" and "*erhu*" right about the same time in her life probably. If she had some kind of regional accent in Mandarin, I didn't think I'd be able to pick it out. I couldn't pick out her regional English either, except it sounded just a touch broad and flat and Canadian. If I could get her to say "about," I'd have a clue.

"Not to be rude," I said, "or intrusive. But do you need some help?"

"Yeah," she said again. She looked up from the map on her knees and lifted her eyebrows. Her eyes were blacker than her hair. "I'm a fragile China doll, and I'm sitting here hoping a big, sensitive, but manly American guy will come along and take care of me in my moment of distress."

"Good luck with that," I said. I pulled my hand from my coat pocket and glanced at my watch. With my other hand, I felt my keys. The Toyota was calling to me. Miles to go before I slept. "Next manly American guy's scheduled to be coming through here in about thirty minutes. Might be a little late, what with the winter weather and all."

I figured she needed some time to think about that. So I went into the restroom. When I came out, she'd folded the map and put it on top of the bag at her feet. She was gazing out into the evening, watching the traffic. There wasn't much. I thought about the situation again. This time not so long.

"Look," I said, "I was kidding about the next scheduled sensitive but manly American. And I assume you think I'm a Wally Reed and all."

She wrinkled her forehead. She did make eye contact, though.

I kept going. "And if I were you and looking for a ride, I'd think a long time about accepting one from anyone, least of all from some guy alone out in the middle of nowhere. If I were you, I'd be thinking this is scene three from a slasher movie, and everyone in the audience is watching you and begging you not to be stupid enough to get in the car with what looks like a 'troubled loner.'"

She smiled, just a little bit, at the "troubled loner" part. I kept going. "But if you don't have some other plan for this evening, it's going to end one of two ways: either you are going to have an actual troubled loner come in here, and you're going to be in some kind of danger, possibly serious danger, unless you're concealing a Glock under that coat and know how to use it. Or two, the highway patrol is going to come by, and you are going to be picked up for—excuse me, nothing personal intended—'solicitation' or for not having any visible means of support or some such thing, because they understand that nothing good's going to come from having a girl sitting out here all alone."

She didn't say anything for a moment, as if she was thinking it over. "Could you repeat that in Mandarin?" she asked finally.

"I'll give you the highlights," I said. But I didn't. I just called her a "big egg." It's a slang expression in Mandarin. It means a "stupid person." And I told her it was dangerous, very dangerous, to be sitting there. She sat there anyway, staring out at the highway, where the traffic was cutting sharper beams of light through the twilight that had completely closed in. In January in New Hampshire, night doesn't fall slowly. It drops in like a piano falling out of a tree.

She sighed. "What are the odds a slasher slash troubled loner would be able to speak Mandarin?" Then, before I could say anything, she added, "Bad Mandarin."

"Long," I said. "Long odds. Though not impossible."

"I'm going south."

"I know," I said. "It's a divided highway. If you were going north, you'd be in the rest stop on the other side of the road."

"What're the odds a slasher slash troubled loner would also be logical in drawing deductive conclusions?" she asked.

"Okay," I said, "I *am* a troubled loner. But that means if you get in the car with me, your principal threat will be boredom from my dramatic angst and morose self-pitying and not from exsanguination."

She reached over and took the strap of her duffle and stood up. "Fine," she said. "But I'm accepting a ride from you not because I believe a word you're saying but because I just think it's unlikely I'm going to be in danger from anyone who uses a word like 'exsanguination.'"

She followed me out to the lot behind us, tossed her duffle into the rear of the car, and sat in the passenger seat, clicking on her seat belt.

"Where are you going?" she asked.

I backed out of the spot and threaded through the parking lot to the exit back out onto I-93. "St. Louis, Missouri," I said, "by way of Massachusetts. How about you?"

"Buffalo, New York. By way of any way I can get there."

I was curious about why anyone would be going to Buffalo in January. Or to Buffalo, come to think of it, in any month of the year. I didn't really want to go into why I was going to St. Louis, though. No reason not to go into it. It wasn't a secret. It just seemed a little complicated and, if I thought about it too much, a little too "undefined." So I didn't pursue the topic. Before I'd even gotten the car up to highway speed, she tilted her head back onto the seat rest and closed her eyes. I drove south.

4

Rule #3: *Incredibly beautiful, exotic Asian babes are almost never psycho ax murderers.*

"Wally Reed?" she asked.

I glanced over at her. She'd been sleeping, her breathing slow and deep and steady, for over an hour. It was night now. Full-on dark. Snow had started falling not long after we'd left the rest stop, snow that had begun to alternate with a sleety, freezing rain that peppered the top of the car with a soft patter. We were stopped, along with the five sets of taillights I could see in front of us. Beyond them flashed rotating wheels of red that I assumed had a state police car under them. The dashboard lights lit up the side of her face as she turned to me. The rest of it was in shadow. She hadn't taken off her knit stocking cap. "You said I thought you might be a Wally Reed."

"Yeah, Walter Reed," I said. "You ever hear of him?"

She paused and thought for a minute. "The doctor? The one who went to Cuba or someplace back during the Spanish-American War; discovered the cause of—" She stopped. "Ohhh. I get it."

It was quiet some more. "That's a good one," she said finally. "Yellow fever."

"Sure," I said. "What do you call them?"

"Gee-Gees."

"Gee-Gees?"

"Acronym," she said. "Stands for 'Geisha Guys.' Guys who

have a thing for Asian girls. Guys who have, as you put it, 'Yellow Fever.'"

"A trifle creepy."

"We still haven't established that you aren't one of them," she said.

"I haven't asked you to give me a massage."

"Or to pour you some sake."

"Are you hungry?" I asked.

"Nope," she said. "You?"

I shook my head.

"Yeah, given that banquet I saw you indulge in back at the rest stop, I can see why not," she said.

"A sound diet is the cornerstone to a healthy life."

She rubbed her face briskly, with both hands. "Why are we stopped?" she asked.

"Moose would be my guess," I said.

"Moose?"

"Moose. Somebody probably hit one crossing the road."

"Does traffic stop for the funeral?"

"Ever see a moose?" I asked.

"Not that I know of."

"You'd know it," I said. "They're big. Hit one with a car and you'll take him out, pretty messily, and do about the same to your car. The combined mess of moose and machine tends to shut down the road until they can get a tow truck out to haul off the car and the moose."

"Where are we?" she asked, covering an impressive yawn.

"Getting close to New Hampton," I said. "You were asleep all through the middle of the White Mountains."

"Were they scenic?" she asked.

"Spectacular," I said, "though arguably not so much when it's pitch-black."

From behind our car, from our right, I saw more flashing, moving slowly off on the side of the road, that came close and turned out to be another highway patrol car. It slowed, then stopped beside us, and I leaned over when my new friend rolled down her window. The patrolman had lowered his as well.

"Moose?" I asked.

"Moose." Then he added, "Road's starting to ice up too. Going far?"

"Mass," I said.

"Why?" he asked.

I grinned. There was not a lot of love lost between Massachusetts and New Hampshire. People in the latter tended to regard people in the former as thoughtless littering jerks who used New Hampshire as their backyard playground. On the other hand, people in Massachusetts, too many of them, were famous for thinking of New Hampshire as, well, their backyard playground.

"Hauling a load of the trash they left back down to dump on their lawns," I said.

He grinned back. "Good," he said. "But you might want to take a break. Salt trucks are coming this way. Be easier driving after they're through." He waved. The line of traffic in front of us had started moving. There was enough snow and ice on the road that I could hear it crunching beneath the tires. We passed the moose—its mortal remains anyway—that was on the side of the road next to a pickup truck. Given the shape of the front panel of the truck, the moose had done some customizing work on it.

"Wow," she said. "They are big." She yawned.

When she yawned again, I asked, "Tired?"

"Yep," she said. "I was mostly pretending to sleep, waiting to see if you were going to try to molest me."

"Same here. Only I was just pretending to be driving. Next rest stop, do you mind if we pull off and sleep for a while?"

"Oh, *now* it gets weird."

"Only if you can contain your natural impulses to throw yourself on the first sensitive but manly American guy who picks you up at a rest stop in the middle of nowhere," I said. "Besides, you heard the highway patrol guy. If we wait until the salt trucks come through, the road'll be in better shape."

I slowed and eased off the highway and came up the ramp that led to the rest stop parking lot. There were separate spaces for trucks and cars, and I wanted to park as far away as possible from the row of throbbing diesels idling in the truck lot. But I didn't want it to look like I was driving us off into the shadows too deeply, away from all the other cars and trucks. That could have seemed a bit weird. So I nosed the Toyota up against the curb close to the restrooms and the covered pavilion that held the snack and soda machines.

"You go first," I said, pushing my chin toward the restrooms. "I'll stay with the car."

She opened the door. "There are some snack machines over there," she said. "Want me to get you another course in your banquet?"

"Pass."

When she returned, I took my turn. I washed my hands and face in the sink and brushed my teeth. Time to tuck myself in for beddy-bye. At an interstate rest stop. Alongside what was basically a hitchhiker I had picked up randomly. At another rest stop. I didn't think this was taking me in exactly the sort of life direction my counselor back at Beddingfield would have approved of.

We pulled the levers to make both front seats recline back as far as they could, which is, in a Toyota, nowhere near comfortable or conducive to sleep. I offered her the sleeping bag. She took it, unzipped it, and tossed it over herself. I had on a pair of silk underwear I used to ski in, heavy corduroy pants, a cotton shirt, and a knit sweater. I threw my parka over me. It was full of some fluffy material guaranteed to keep me warm on most of the mountain slopes of the Himalayas and to wick away moisture like a sponge. It didn't, however, have much going for it in the way of bedclothes. As long as I was warm, though, I'd be able to sleep. I burrowed my way into the seat and rolled onto my side. The trucks hadn't gotten any quieter.

"How do you know I'm not a psycho ax murderer who's going to castrate you in your sleep?" she asked me, after we'd both rustled around a bit and found what seemed like the most comfortable places to be and had been still for a while. I could tell from the sound of her voice that she'd pulled the bag up around her head.

"Be a clear violation of the rules," I said.

"Rules?"

"I have some rules," I said. "They're pretty dependable."

"Which rule covers this?" she asked. She'd sat up.

"Number three," I said, rolling over. "Rule Number Three is that incredibly beautiful, exotic Asian babes are almost never psycho ax murderers."

"Oh," she said. She lay back down. It was quiet, except for the rumbling engines of the trucks in the lot beside us and another going by on the highway right then that changed gears with a throaty growl.

"I'm curious about what Rules Number One and Two might be," she said.

"Stick around," I said. I rolled back again and faced the door handle and closed my eyes. I'd figured, with the combination of the truck noise, the sodium lights in the parking lot casting sickly yellow shadows, and the oddness of having a complete stranger lying next to me, that it would take time to go to sleep. I was wrong.

I woke up to a truck horn blasting and, simultaneously, the sun coming up just enough to edge over the side of the car and hit me right in the eyes. I tried to burrow deeper into my parka. My arms had twisted around and wadded it, and it wouldn't go any higher.

I kicked around a couple of times before giving up and rolling over onto my back. She was already awake, sitting up, looking at the frosted interior of the windshield. All the windows in the car were covered in an icy rime. It was the view beer must have from inside a frosted mug.

"Exotic?" she said.

"Huh?"

"Last night you described me as—I think I am quoting you correctly here—an 'incredibly beautiful, exotic Asian babe.'"

"So you're objecting to 'exotic' but not to the other stuff?" I asked.

"I did find the 'Asian babe' reference to be simultaneously sexist and racist," she said.

"I can't tell you how deeply sorry I am," I said. "I'm very poor at apologizing for the inherent racism of my breed. I can only blame it on our natural genetic superiority."

"Yeah," she said. She rubbed her face with both hands and pulled her hair back. It was longer and a glossier black than it had seemed last night. "Whatever."

"Did you sleep okay?" I asked her.

She nodded. "You?"

"I tossed and turned a little bit," I said. "I was trying to figure out how you could use an ax to castrate someone."

"Likely there would be a lot of collateral damage in the process."

"I prefer not to think about it," I said. "I'd rather think about breakfast."

She polished the window on her side of the car with her fist, clearing a little, golf ball–size hole through some of the frost. She peered out.

"I'm guessing room service is out of the question," she said.

We opened the doors and stiffly stepped outside. It hadn't gotten any warmer. The morning air was so sharp it seemed brittle.

Our exhalations exploded in clouds of steam. The snow and sleet had stopped. There was just a dirty white crust on the ground. I could see a long hump of snow out on the side of the highway. The plows must have come through while we slept. There was a kink in my neck that wasn't going away soon, and a sore spot on my right hip where I'd laid on the loose seat belt buckle part of the night. I had never spent the night in a car. I wasn't looking forward to doing it again.

"Think this part of the New Hampshire interstate might have some places where we can get a bowl of *zhou* and a side of crispy *youtiao?*" I asked her. The thought of a classic Chinese breakfast of hot soupy, fragrant rice with toasted bread sticks made my stomach grumble.

"I'd settle for waffles," she said.

"Wow," I said. "You *are* exotic."

Rule #60: *You can go home again, although the place might be slightly dusty.*

We stopped at a gas station, where we took care of the Toyota's dietary needs and then walked across the lot to fill ourselves at a restaurant. She glanced at the menu after we sat down. "Would you order for me?" she said. "I need to—uh—'freshen up.'" She told me what she wanted and disappeared in the direction of the restrooms. I ordered. Waffles for her. With blueberry syrup. Scrambled eggs for me. I looked out the window. The sky was a bright blue bowl. The sun was harsh, with a chilly light. Cars pulling out of the gas station belched out wisps of steam from their mufflers. I rubbed my hand over my cheeks and felt the stubble. I'd shaved last at Chris's place. I needed to again.

She came back to the booth and saw me brushing my fingers along my chin.

"You could use a little freshening up yourself," she said.

It was an odd thing to say. But I was distracted. It was the first time I'd seen her with her hair combed, without the stocking cap. Her hair was blue-black, long and straight. She wasn't pretty. She wasn't anything like the China doll she'd mentioned last night. She wasn't ugly, either. Or even homely. Her face was long, with high cheekbones. She didn't look like a Han, the most common ethnic Chinese. She looked a little Mongolian. I realized I didn't know her name. I decided not to ask. She hadn't exactly been a fount of information about herself. Maybe she had her reasons. If she wanted me to know, I concluded, she'd tell me.

"We'll be in Andover before noon," I said. "I'm thinking of freshening up there, with about a one-hour hot shower."

"What's in Andover?" she asked.

"It's where my parents live," I said. "It's where I grew up."

"So now that we've slept together, you're taking me home to meet the folks," she said. Which I also thought was a weird thing to say.

"The folks won't be there," I said. I told her about the trip. My parents and two other couples they'd known since their college days had been talking, ever since those days, about a sailing cruise around Indonesia. They finally decided if they didn't do it soon, they weren't ever going to. So they did. They rented a fifty-foot ketch and the captain who came with it, and they became the crew. They would be on the high seas until spring or until, as my mother said, they were taken captive by Indonesian pirates.

We crossed the line between New Hampshire and Massachusetts a little after ten. I didn't get off the highway until we were at Methuen. My passenger was quiet, watching the scenery.

"Ever been to this part of Massachusetts before?" I asked. She shook her head.

"Ever been to Massachusetts period?"

"Nope."

"Pity," I said.

I pulled off just outside Andover and went to a market at Shawsheen Village. At the meat counter, I got a plastic-wrapped chunk of pork belly. Most people in this part of Massachusetts use pork belly, chopped into bitsy pieces, to flavor clam chowder. So lots of stores carry it. I added some knobs of fresh ginger, two heads of broccoli and one of garlic to my basket. Unless my parents had raided my stash in the pantry, I was fairly certain I could find whatever else I needed there. She followed me around, hands in her coat, watching, not saying anything.

"You need anything?" I asked.

"I'll meet you at the checkout," she said.

When she did, she put a package of tampons on the check-out conveyor belt. She could have separated from me when we came in the store and bought them discreetly. But she didn't seem embarrassed or shy about it. Maybe she was just doing it to— what?—shock me? I'd seen girls do that before: deliberately use language "nice girls" weren't supposed to use or whip off a shirt in front of you to change—stuff that seemed like it was meant to prove some kind of point. I thought this was sort of like guys in school who take up smoking because they think it makes them look older or tougher. On the other hand, maybe she just needed the tampons and she didn't really care one way or the other.

It's funny how you don't see your house the same way other people see it. I'd grown up there. It was my home. I never thought much more about it than that. I knew it was bigger than some homes. It sure wasn't a mansion, though. We pulled into the driveway. I heard a low whistle beside me.

"Nice how you've obviously got the slave quarters out of sight of the main house here at the plantation," she said.

"It's not a plantation," I said. "It's a cross-gabled Victorian. With shingle siding."

"What it is," she said, "is big. It's also beautiful," she added quickly, like she thought I might be offended at being accused of growing up in a big house. I wasn't.

"Do your parents own the Internet?" she asked. "Or some small country? Like Denmark?"

"My parents," I said, "specifically my mother, specifically her great-grandfather, worked on the Boston & Maine Railroad, as a conductor. He had a lot of time on his hands while the trains were running, so he hung out in the mail car. He came up with a way that made it faster for trains to transfer mail from the mail car to the station. The train didn't even have to stop to make the transfer. He came up with some hooks and poles so they could just switch out as the trains came running by. He sold the idea to the train company. He sold it to a lot of other train companies. He made a lot of money. He built this house, back in the twenties. My mother inherited it."

"So will you inherit it?" she asked.

"Probably." Although after the way I'd left Beddingfield, maybe the will would be changed.

"Maybe this is a little forward of me," she said, "but would you consider marrying me?"

"Maybe later," I said. "First let's go inside and make sure the domestic staff haven't been stealing from our Rembrandt collection again."

Rule #21: *It's not quite as weird if the person doing your laundry knows your name.*

My parents didn't own any Rembrandts. We had a couple of Fitz Hugh Lane landscapes hanging on the walls—or seascapes to put it more accurately. In one a long schooner tilts across the horizon sailing out from Rocky Neck Beach over in Gloucester. In the other, a ship hull lies on its side, careened at Brace's Rock. I liked the way Lane had captured the light in his paintings. It looked like it was coming from inside the paintings themselves. I used to study them when I was a kid. I finally narrowed down the times of the day they had been painted, just by looking at the color and the slant of the light. Mostly, though, there were family photographs on the walls. Nothing had been disturbed. No one had been in the house for at least a couple of weeks, not since my parents had left.

We dropped our stuff in the hallway between the kitchen and the living room, and I took her upstairs to the extra bedroom.

"I'm going to get to work on dinner in a minute," I said. "Make yourself at home."

"I will," she said. "I'll do some laundry if that's okay. You have anything that needs to go in?"

"Just my entire wardrobe." I showed her the laundry room in the basement and left her with the intimidating pile of clothes that had accumulated since I'd left the dorm at Beddingfield. Walking back upstairs, I thought about all my dirty underwear in that pile. It wasn't *that* dirty. It wasn't gross. Nothing organic was actually growing on anything. Or at least if it was, it wasn't flourishing. It was just that no one except my mother and I had ever done my laundry before. I turned around at the top of the basement stairs and went back down until I was near the bottom. She was squatting over two piles she'd made of both our stuff, sorting it by color. She squatted like a lot of first-generation Chinese, flat-footed instead of on the balls of her feet like a Westerner would.

"Listen, I said. "If you'd prefer not to do my laundry, I can get to it later." She looked over her shoulder at me. "I mean, it's a little personal, I guess, having someone I just met doing my laundry. Especially considering I don't even know your name."

"Okay."

I retraced my steps back up the stairs and went into the kitchen. As I was pulling the rice cooker off the shelf in the pantry, I heard her come up to the top of the steps. She stuck her head around the doorway.

"My name's Corinne," she said. "Corinne Chang. So now is it okay if I do your laundry?"

"Absolutely."

Cooking, after I hadn't done it for a while, was like slipping into a warm bath. It was that relaxing. Maybe in some ways even more relaxing than a soak. My cold rolled-steel wok was still sitting on one burner of the stove, just where I'd left it when I'd been home for Christmas. My parents never used it. I think they left it out on the stove, though, to remind them of me. It had a deep, rich black patina from having been used so long. I turned on the burner. I found my cleaver in the knife drawer, the blade tucked inside the cardboard sheath I made to protect the edge. The round slab of a tree trunk that functioned as a cutting board was on a shelf under the cupboards. I chopped the broccoli for steaming, then shredded the onions and sliced the ginger into pa-pery slices that gave off a sharp perfume I realized I'd missed. I wished Corinne was here to watch. It isn't easy to slice ginger thinly with a big Chinese-style cleaver. I was cutting the slices so finely that light would have shown through if I'd held them up to a window. I'd spent a lot of time perfecting that skill. But appar-ently she'd finished packing the washing machine and had gone into the library. When I glanced in there, she was curled up in my father's overstuffed chair, looking at a book on early American marine painting.

I sliced the square of pork belly into two pieces, then used butcher's twine to tie them like little birthday presents, with a bow around each. The wok was starting to send up thin drifts of smoke. I drizzled oil into it and swirled it around, then slid the porky presents in. They burst into a satisfying sizzling hiss; clouds of smoke and steam billowed up, reminding me to turn on the overhead fans before the fire alarm was triggered.

While the pork was browning, I found my clay pot. Its sandy outer surface was chocolate dark with use; inside there was a creamy smooth finish that came from having cooked so many meals. Its handle felt in my hand just like the cleaver had. It was like shaking hands with an old friend. I got a couple of clumps of rock sugar from the pantry and tossed them in the pot, adding a gurgle of light soy sauce and another of the dark, and a generous dollop of Shiaoxing cooking wine. The pork had tanned nicely by now. The surfaces of both pieces were crispy, golden brown, with little delicious-looking bubbles forming. The sweet scent of hot pork fat filled the kitchen, mixing with the starchy aroma of the rice from the automatic cooker. I drained the pork, then added it to the clay pot, along with the ginger and onions; put the top on; and set the whole thing on the burner, turning the flame down to low. Done. All it needed was about three hours in the pot. What

I needed was a shower to wash off the accumulated grit of every-thing between here and Beddingfield. And maybe a nap. Tucker's Rule #39: There's usually time, if you plan life well enough, for a nap.

I was never an overachiever. Even so, I managed to get in both.

7

Rule #14: *Knowing what you don't need to know is at least as important as knowing what you do need to know.*

The diary's right there. Somebody left it. You'll get it back to them, of course. But take a look first, skim through a few pages? Peek in the medicine cabinet when you're using the bathroom in someone's house? It's just natural curiosity. It isn't like you're prying into state secrets. What are you going to find out? The diary's author has a crush on someone? You suspect that anyway. The owners of the house are using some kind of birth control? Does that really come as a surprise?

You're just taking a harmless peek into someone's private life. That's the sort of thing you tell yourself. Just before you open the diary. Or the cabinet door. Except me.

I don't tell myself any of that to justify any snooping I might contemplate. I don't look at other people's stuff. It isn't that I'm not curious. I am. More than most. It's just that I read Nathaniel Hawthorne's short story "Young Goodman Brown" when I was a freshman in high school. Goodman's a trusting young guy, believing the best in everyone, and then, wandering around out in the woods one night, he comes across some kind of kinky cult, where all the town's upstanding citizens, including his own wife, are about to start a bizarre ritual. And suddenly he's waking up, all alone out in the woods, and he doesn't know if what he saw was real or just a bad dream. And he spends the rest of his life bitter and cynical. It made a big impression on me. That's when I came up with Tucker's Rule #14: Knowing what you don't need to know is at least as important as knowing what you do need to know. And Rule #14a: It might even be more important.

That's why, when Corinne's cell phone started buzzing, I didn't have the slightest intention of answering it. An hour had passed since I'd gone down for the nap. Before I did, I'd heard the door to the room I'd shown her close just as I was drifting off. I assumed she'd gone in there and done the same. She was still in there.

Buzzzzz.

Showered clean, wearing my best Boston College sweatpants and a fresh shirt, and feeling much better after my nap, I was walking right by it when it went off. Corinne's phone.

Buzzzz.

It wasn't exactly one of my rules, more like a Tucker's Rule addendum, but I always figured I wasn't going to get into any kind of trouble by *not* answering a phone. Especially when it wasn't my own.

Buzzzz.

Minding one's own business is an often-neglected, little-appreciated quality in a person. As I said, I pride myself on not sticking my nose where it doesn't belong. Yeah. Sure. You bet. Which is why I'd approached Corinne in the first place, back at that New Hampshire rest stop. And why she was now sleeping in my parents' house. And why I was taking her a couple of hundred miles without knowing the reason why. Mind. Your. Own. Business. Words to live by.

I picked up the phone and hit RECEIVE.

"I know where you are," the voice said in Mandarin. "You and I need to have a little talk. You know what it's about."

There was silence. The voice was obviously waiting for Corinne to answer. I answered instead with a sickly sweet politeness that's almost impossible to duplicate in English. I answered as if I were a court eunuch receiving a visitor to some princess at the imperial court in the Forbidden City.

"I'm sorry," I said. "I regret to inform you that the young lady is not at this moment receiving calls."

"Who are you?" the voice snapped, like a dog growling when you get too close to its food bowl. "You need to tell the woman who owns this phone that she's in a lot of trouble, and it's not going to get any better until she's talked to me!"

"Might I inquire as to the nature of your business with the young woman in question?"

"Who are you?" the voice repeated.

"I am her social secretary and confidant," I said. "Might I inquire as to your name and your position?"

"My name? My name?" He wasn't sounding any friendlier. "My name is this: I'm the guy who has some questions she'd better be answering if she knows what's good for her."

"I see." My mind was racing. Hard to tell how old the voice was. My first thought was Corinne must have some seriously screwed-up boyfriend.

"If you will leave your name and number," I said, "I will alert her, at the earliest opportunity, to your efforts to contact her."

"I'm not leaving you shit," the voice said, "except this: If you're involved with her, you're in trouble. You like trouble? You think she's going to be worth the trouble that's coming?"

I didn't say anything.

"You hear me? You still there?"

I was. But then I pressed END. I just stood there, phone in hand. The guy sounded like a jerk. Just as I could sound more obsequious and slimier when speaking Chinese than I could in English, it was also possible for him to sound even jerkier speaking Chinese. The intonation, the way the words are put together—you can come across like an arrogant ass in Mandarin if you want to. This guy sounded good at it. It irritated me. I didn't know why. Maybe it was because I was only a couple of steps away from putting together a really great meal and I didn't want the mood spoiled. Maybe it was something else.

I still assumed he was some boyfriend. Ex-boyfriend. In a couple of seconds, staring at the phone in my hand, I'd worked out a scenario. She'd dumped him. I could understand why. Maybe when he got angry, he got violent. Maybe she was trying to make a clean break. That's why she was out on the road. Starting over. That's why I'd overheard her talking on her phone back at that rest stop, telling someone she'd had to get out of town fast. Maybe I was so far away from minding my own business, I wasn't thinking clearly. I opened the menu for the phone. Then I deleted the record of the call.

I set the kitchen table with ceramic bowls and stabbed a bamboo paddle into the rice maker, splashing the paddle under the tap first so the rice wouldn't stick. Then I laid out napkins and plastic chopsticks. When I lifted the lid of the clay pot, the aroma was so overwhelming that my stomach gave a quick, sharp squeeze of anticipation. I carried the pot to the table and set it on a hot pad; then I brought in a bowl of the broccoli I'd steamed, tossed with sesame oil, and sprinkled with sesame seeds. I filled both bowls with rice and gave it all one last look, making sure there weren't any spills or smears on the side of the serving platter. In a Western restaurant kitchen, it's called "plating," making sure the whole presentation looks clean and neat just before the waiter takes it out to the dining room. In a Chinese kitchen, it's called "pecking the nest," because it looks like a mother bird using her beak to clean out any debris from her nest. I started for the stairs to wake Corinne. When I turned around, though, she was walking through the hallway into the kitchen. She had changed clothes. She was wearing jeans and a gray sweater. She was thinner than she'd looked in her traveling clothes. Not skinny. Actually, she was pretty nicely built. I assessed this information without lingering on it.

"Dinner is served," I said.

She sat down. I took the chair on the opposite side of the table.

"*Dongpo rou,*" she said, studying the square of pork on her plate.

"Yep," I agreed. "*Dongpo* pork. Tell me what you think."

She lifted a slice of the pork belly. It was soft enough now that it separated into layers, each with its own portion of chewy tender meat and glistening, succulent pork fat.

"You didn't deep-fry the pork first," she said.

She glanced up, a piece of the pork poised between her chopsticks.

"That's what a lot of restaurants do," I said. "Cuts the cooking time way down."

"But it makes the meat greasy."

"It does."

We ate. We didn't talk. I was thinking about the jerk on the phone. I was thinking about telling Corinne I intercepted the call. I was thinking that might be a bad idea. Especially since I'd deleted the call. It had been a long time, though, since I'd eaten good Chinese cooking. So after a couple of bites, I decided that the jerk was either going to call back, in which case there was no reason for me to tell her he'd called the first time. Or he was going to think maybe she had a new boyfriend, someone who knew her well enough to have answered her phone, and he'd give up. In which case there was also no reason to tell her. After that, I just concentrated on the pork.

After dinner Corinne did the dishes. I went to the basement and transferred our clothes from the washer to the dryer. Her bra and panties were both black, matching. As with her body in the sweater and jeans, I didn't dwell on it. At least I tried not to. When I came upstairs from the laundry, the dishes were done.

"I think I'll turn in," she said.

"See you in the morning," I said. She'd reached the first step of the stairs when I said, "You know, last night, when we slept together?"

She stopped and half turned, her hand on the rail. She looked at me. Her eyebrows went up.

"Was it as good for you as it was for me?"

She pursed her lips, looked up at the ceiling for a second, then she said. "It was every bit as magical as what I'd imagined sleeping in a Toyota at a rest stop would be like."

"Great," I said in English. "Every girl's dream." Then I said good night in Mandarin and went to bed.

8

Rule #50: *There are a lot of amazingly wonderful things in life, but if they involve lifelong celibacy, that's almost always a dealbreaker.*

I was planning to leave the next morning. Considering the choking blitz of traffic we'd have faced if we'd left any earlier, though, I was just as happy when I finally woke up and rolled over and looked at the clock beside my bed and saw we were well past the morning rush. I was still getting dressed when I heard Corinne go downstairs. She was standing in front of the kitchen table, my mother's laundry basket in front of her, taking our clothes out and folding them. She'd folded my shirts into neat packets like they do at the dry cleaners. I thought that a remark about Chinese and laundries was too easy. And maybe a little dated. I let it go. It was midmorning when we packed the Toyota and locked up the house.

I never liked leaving home. That's not entirely true. I liked to travel. I'd enjoyed my time at Beddingfield, being on my own. I just always liked the house where I grew up. I had a lot of good memories there. I knew the time was coming, was probably already here in some ways, when this place wasn't going to be "home" anymore. It was exciting, but it was also sad in a way I couldn't exactly explain, not even to myself.

We cruised across western Massachusetts on I-90 and ate lunch at a burger chain in Stockbridge.

"Not as good as the pork last night," she said.

"Few meals can be," I said. Then I asked Corinne if she'd ever heard of the Shakers. She hadn't.

"Are you in any hurry to get to Buffalo?" I asked. She wasn't.

Instead of getting back out on the interstate, we drove through Lenox, past Tanglewood, the famous music camp and performance center, and on up a few slow and winding miles lined with maple woods and neat stone-fence-lined fields on both sides of the road to the Shaker Village at Hancock.

I gave her the abbreviated tour of the village-size museum: the sprawling round stone barn; the dairy; the Brethren's workshop, still filled with eighteenth-century tools, looking as if some Shakers might be showing up for work any minute to make their famous flat brooms and chairs. My parents had first brought me to this place when I was still in grade school. A lot of the original buildings in the Shaker community were still here, restored and rebuilt to re-create the village that was home, back in the early nineteenth century, to more than three hundred Shakers in western Massachusetts. I was only about eight or so when I visited the first time. I didn't know anything about it or the Shakers who'd lived there. My parents just told me it was an outdoor museum when they took me out there one summer day. I could remember wandering around. At that age, I didn't get entirely what the Shakers were. They seemed like some kind of cross between a back-to-nature cult and the Amish. What I did know, as soon as I walked into one of the buildings, was that in some way I didn't fully get—and still didn't get more than twelve years later—the place was speaking to me. The buildings; the things in them; the perfectly simple, spare architecture; the long, low range of the emerald Berkshires that spread out all around—being there was like tuning into a radio station that, in the middle of static on the dial, suddenly came in, clear and strong. Some people need to go to the mountains to feel renewed. Or to the woods. I needed this place.

The Shakers were a sect, I explained to Corinne. One that got started in the middle of the 1700s and lasted for about a century. They were a part of the Great Awakening, a huge religious revival that swept across the whole country. The Shakers decided to get away from what was then modern society, to live in communes and support themselves with farming, furniture making, and other kinds of crafts.

"They didn't waste a lot of money on decorations," Corinne said. We were walking by the main village dormitory. At this time of the winter, there weren't many tourists. We had the place to ourselves. Bare walls, plain planked floors, simple, clean lines. There wasn't a single piece of unnecessary furniture, not one superfluous angle of architecture. Only what was needed to get the job done and nothing more. I'd asked to come back here every summer since that first trip, and I still never got tired of it, of wandering around. It almost felt like I was breathing in the beauty, the peacefulness of it all.

"You know all those temples and palaces in China, all painted brightly, decorated over every square inch with dragons and phoenixes and all that stuff crawling all over them?" I asked her. "That's pretty much the antithesis of Shaker architecture. Pretty much the antithesis of everything they were about. The Shakers wanted things bare-bones. Function created beauty for them. Anything that wasn't necessary they didn't want. You get to that kind of simplicity, and it has a lot of beauty in it."

"You like that," Corinne said. It was a statement.

"I like things simple," I said. "That's Tucker's Rule Number One: 'Keep it simple.'"

"Okay," Corinne said. "Gee, I've got numbers one and three now. 'Keep things simple' and 'Don't expect Asian chicks to be serial killers.' Weren't you supposed to save Rule Number One for a more dramatic moment? Didn't you kind of ruin the big workup to revealing it?"

"I didn't think it was fair to keep you in suspense."

"So will you fill me in on Rule Number Two so I can have all of the first three in the set?"

"'When you're making dough for *jiaozi* dumplings,'" I said, "'use cold water, so the wrapper stays soft and chewy. When you're making the same dough for *guotie* pot stickers, use boiling water.'"

"Really?"

"Really," I said. "The hot water helps release gluten, so the dough doesn't get dry and crack when it's sizzling on the side of the hot wok."

"No, I mean 'really,' as in that's *really* Rule Number Two?"

"Yep."

Out in front of the round stone barn, we watched a little spaniel-like dog herd a flock of woolly black-headed sheep while his trainer shouted commands. The village had its own flocks of sheep and cows, and gardens that were brown and empty now, the raw dirt frozen into furrowed clumps. The dog nipped at the hind legs of a dawdling sheep, fat and thick in its winter coat. The sheep unleashed a kick, then jumped and pranced to join the rest of the flock.

"Back at the dorm, you showed me the two staircases that led to the women's and men's quarters. So where did the married couples live here?" Corinne asked.

"The Shakers were celibate," I said. "They didn't believe in marriage."

"Yikes."

"Or sex."

"Again," Corinne said, "yikes. You ever think about becoming a Shaker?"

"They're all gone now," I said. "But I thought about it."

"What kept you from it?" she asked.

"Weren't you just listening to that celibacy thing?"

Before we left, I took Corinne to the white clapboard-sided meetinghouse, the closest thing the Shakers had to a church. It was here they met for services, to sing and to move about when they became possessed with spirits, bobbing and dancing, which is how they got their name. The angle of the sun coming through the windows was low. Shadows were crisp, so sharply defined they looked etched on the walls and wooden floor. The air inside was still enough I could hear my heart. The benches usually lined up inside had been removed so the floor could be cleaned. The floor planks had that kind of glow that can only come after hundreds of years and thousands of feet polishing them with use. I just stood and drank it all in. Corinne seemed to sense I wanted to be alone. She murmured that she was off to find a restroom. I stood some more and closed my eyes. It was something I'd done since my first visit here. Each time I came to the village, I tried to take a little time to think about how much had happened, how much had changed in my life since I'd been there last. This time, I thought about how much might happen before I came back here again.

It was early evening when we left and crossed over into New York. We got to just the other side of Albany when I suggested we stop for the night at a motel.

"You want a separate room?" I asked.

"We're not Shakers," she said.

We were not. I asked for a double, though. We got into the two beds and turned on the TV and watched a show about sharks until I asked if it was okay if I turned it off and she said yes. As I did, she reached over and clicked off the table lamp, and the dark closed in for a few moments until the lights from outside gave us a soft glow. It was quiet.

"You do this a lot?" Corinne asked.

"Nope," I said. I was relatively sure I knew what she was talking about.

"You do this ever?"

"Nope."

"Oh," she said. "So you've never spent the night in a motel with a girl?"

"I've never spent the night with a girl in a motel or anyplace else."

"Wow," she said. I heard her roll over on her side to face me in the dark.

"Wow?" I said. "What's that supposed to mean? You're surprised that someone with my looks and my—let's face it, frankly, irresistible personality—wouldn't have had a lot of motel dates?"

"Wow," she said, "as in, 'Wow, I can't believe a guy would actually admit he's never slept with a girl.'"

"Lots of guys my age haven't slept with a girl," I said.

"Not a lot of guys admit it."

"We're fragile creatures," I said. "If we say we've never slept with a girl, we're afraid people might think we don't have any sex appeal or that we don't have the social skills necessary to successfully woo a girl."

"'Woo'?"

"Good word," I said. "Too under-utilized nowadays."

"Maybe that's because it sounds like it comes from the era of the Shakers."

"Possibly. Although they would have had little chance to put it to good use."

"Good point," she said. "Or maybe if you tell a girl you've never slept with one, it'll cause her to think of you as a challenge. Reverse psychology. You come across as innocent and vulnerable and in need of a good—wink, wink—'teacher.'"

"You Asian babes are pretty canny," I said.

"Inscrutable too," Corinne said.

We both lay there for a while.

"So," I finally said. "If a guy did tell you he'd never slept with a girl, would you take it as a challenge or would you assume he didn't have the right stuff?"

"Not sure," she said. I heard her roll over and punch the pillow. "I guess I'd have to look at the whole woo package."

9

Rule #25: *Some places are less destinations than they are*
accidental arrivals.

We were following the path of the Mohawk River, which slices
right across the center of New York, almost the length of the
whole state. Outside the Toyota, it was bright, a sharp January
light. A scatter of fluffy clouds coasted slowly across the sky, moving sluggishly in the cold. The river, flowing in the other direction
all along the New York State Thruway, was flat and silvery and
floating a few flat, crusty, car-size chunks of ice in the sluggish
current. The trees were naked and black, and when we dipped
down below the hills, the sun started flickering through them,
creating a strobe effect. I always worried when I was driving in
this kind of light that I might be an undiagnosed epileptic or sus-
ceptible to some bizarre illness and I was suddenly going to have a
seizure or a fit. To distract myself, I kept poking the SCAN button
on the radio, keeping the volume low. The FM listening selection
in western New York is a treasure if you like hillbilly music or
hourlong discussions about the future of corn prices.

Corinne had been napping. I thought she was still asleep. She
had her hands clasped together, pushed between her knees. She
was leaning against the car door, with her coat jammed in between it and her head like a pillow.

"Okay," she said, after a while, without moving or even opening her eyes. "I give."

"You give?" I glanced over. She nodded, still not opening her
eyes.

"Who the hell are you?" she asked. "How did you learn to speak Mandarin?"

"You mean bad Mandarin?"

She ignored the question. "How do you know so much about Chinese food?"

"You're assuming I'm not just a Wally Reed, coursing the highways of the country, looking for exotic Asian babes, and hoping to impress them with my language and culinary prowess?"

"It's still a reasonable assumption," she said. "I was willing, though, to go way out on a limb in hoping there was a little more to your story than that."

"Everybody's got a story," I said. "How many of them have you heard that are even vaguely interesting?"

"Not many."

"Then mine would be in the majority category," I said. "Not all that interesting but way, way too long."

"Tell me anyway."

"You sure?"

"No," she said, "but I'm willing to bet it will sound better than what's on the radio."

"My grandfather was in China right after the Second World War," I said. "It was some kind of secret spy-type stuff. He was with an organization like the CIA. He never talked about it that much. He did talk a lot about China. He really liked it. He liked the food. When I was just a kid, still in grade school, he started taking me to Chinese restaurants in Boston. Not to the ones that catered to non-Chinese. He knew about the ones that had authentic dishes, the stuff they wouldn't put on the menus. You had to know to ask for it."

"So you were a grade school connoisseur of Chinese cuisine."

"Not quite," I said. "Starting in second grade, I met a guy, Langston Wu. We got to be friends about fourth grade or so. His uncle owned a Szechuan restaurant in Andover. We started working weekends there, washing dishes, doing odd jobs. By the time we were in high school, we were both cooking there. All through high school, I did what the French call *commis*. It's sort of apprenticing, at different Chinese places around Boston. So you could say I grew up in a Chinese restaurant kitchen."

"You liked it?"

"Still do," I said. "It's really all I ever wanted to do."

We kept driving. Corinne seemed to be thinking it over. Or maybe she was just bored. Finally, she said, "A *da bi zi* whose dream is to become a master Chinese chef."

Da bi zi—literally "big nose"—was a fairly common derogatory term in Mandarin for a non-Chinese.

"I resent the racist appellation," I said. "But, yeah, that's my story."

"Well," she said, "I've heard stranger ones." After a long pause she added, "But not many."

We made it to Buffalo. Which, I thought, could be considered either a destination or a consequence of some poor decisions. Corinne explained that she had a friend living there. She had to call twice to get directions to the friend's apartment. It turned out to be a loft in a neighborhood near the University at Buffalo. We got there after dark, parked the Toyota on the street, and climbed the stairs and rang the buzzer. Corinne's friend had a bleached white streak down one side of her hair and a very tiny nose ring. She was wearing a short-sleeved T-shirt over a long-sleeved one that read, "Sarcasm is just one service I offer." She grabbed Corinne by both elbows as soon as she opened the door. Her eyes were shiny with excitement, and I could tell they were friends, even though Corinne didn't show much emotion. She did smile. I hadn't seen that before. There'd been a few smirks. But no full-on smiles. The smile looked good on her. Corinne introduced her friend as Ariadna Liu. Ariadna said hello to me, then lapsed into

Mandarin to speak to Corinne. I caught the word "handsome" and the question "your boyfriend?" before Corinne interrupted to tell her I spoke Mandarin.

"How well?" Ariadna asked me in Mandarin.

"I'm mostly *shuashuai*," I said. It meant I was basically just a poser, someone who thought he was cooler than he was.

Ariadna laughed. I hauled Corinne's bag from the car back up to the apartment. Then I sat around and listened to them talk. They lapsed back and forth from English to Mandarin. I learned more about Corinne in a couple of hours than I'd found out in the three days we'd spent together. She and Ariadna met at a gemological school they'd attended together in Toronto. After they graduated, Corinne had worked for a jeweler in Montreal, sorting diamonds. If there was a subject I knew less about than diamonds, I would have been hard-pressed to name it. Corinne and Ariadna explained to me how the business works.

"Diamonds come out of the ground," Corinne said. "You know that much?"

"Check," I said.

"They only come out of the ground a few places in the world," Ariadna said. "Mostly in Africa. And only a few companies control it all. The diamond trade, that is. They take the rough diamonds to, again, just a few very tightly controlled other places, where the gem-quality stones are processed, cut, or ground into shape."

"And those places add a little to the cost of the diamond?" I asked.

"Oh, yeah," Corinne said. "That's one reason—probably the major reason—diamonds cost as much as they do. They go though all kinds of steps and pass through lots of different hands. You've got the guys who grind or cut the raw stones, guys who polish them, companies that buy them in bulk and then distribute them to retail markets. And everyone along the way gets a piece of the diamond."

"They end up in an exchange, called a bourse," Ariadna said. "Of which there are fewer than thirty in the whole world. Bourses sell to wholesale and retail diamond businesses. So a big diamond store or a wholesaler will get a bunch of loose stones we call a 'lot.'"

"That's where people like us come in," Corinne said. "We look at the diamonds while they're still loose stones and evaluate them for their retail value."

"So you decide how much of his annual income some poor schmuck's going to devote to a ring meant for the finger of Miss Mary Lou Marrying-for-Money?"

"Romantic way to put it," Corinne said. "But not exactly accurate."

"We tell the owner of the jewelry shop or diamond store or wherever it is we're working," Ariadna said, "how much the stone is worth. How much they charge the schmuck is up to them."

"And you learned to do that at the gemological school?" I asked.

"In Toronto," Corinne said, nodding.

"After we graduated, I got a job here through a friend," Ariadna said.

Corinne said she got hers the same way in Montreal. It turned out that Corinne was a U.S. citizen, working for a Canadian diamond wholesaler; Ariadna was a Canadian working for a U.S. business.

"So how come you're in Buffalo now," I asked Corinne, "instead of back in Montreal sorting diamonds?"

"I'm taking some time off," Corinne said. I studied her face when she said it. She didn't make eye contact with Ariadna. Ariadna developed a sudden interest in her feet. It sounded like one of those conversational comments that are tossed off casually. I didn't know much about Corinne. I did know she didn't indulge in a lot of casual comments.

Later that night, in fact, stretched out in my sleeping bag on the floor of Ariadna's living room, I made a checklist of everything I knew about Corinne Chang.

I knew she wore black underwear.

I knew she didn't talk a lot, but she listened better than most people I had been around.

I knew some guy was looking for her and didn't seem like he was very happy about it. And that she'd had to leave town quickly — which is never a good sign.

I knew she made little puffy, airy noises when she was asleep.

I knew — I didn't know how I knew, but I knew — that when she said she was "taking some time off" from the diamond-sorting business, Corinne Chang was lying.

10

Rule #8: *Hitting people is often bad, but if it's necessary, it's necessary to hit first—always.*

I spent two days in Buffalo. The Toyota had been getting harder and harder to start, so I drove it to a shop a couple of blocks from Ariadna's apartment. It took them a day and a half to decide I needed a new battery. Oh, and that it looked like it was using a lot of oil.

"They're thorough, aren't they?" Ariadna said. Fortunately, she'd showed me a map of the University Heights District, where she lived, that highlighted local bookstores. While I waited for the car, I wandered around Main Street there and spent a lot of time at the Talking Leaves Books, which was one of the better used bookstores I'd ever visited. They didn't seem to mind if you sat around in one of the chairs and read, which I did. I read a book about the ins and outs of cruising under sail, which was something I'd never done but which sounded kind of nice and gave me some ideas about the life my parents were leading right about then. I looked at some Chinese cookbooks and made a few notes on substitute ingredients they suggested. I read a book about the diamond trade.

The day I left Buffalo, Corinne and Ariadna were going downtown so that Ariadna could introduce Corinne to some of the other people at the diamond place where she worked. Ariadna told me to feel free to sleep in and just to be sure the door was locked when I left. It was a little awkward saying goodbye the night before. Ariadna told me to come back any time I was in

Buffalo again. Which, aside from going back to that bookstore, I couldn't see as a very distinct possibility.

Corinne said, "Thanks for the ride."

I nodded.

"And for the *dongpo* pork," she said.

I nodded again.

"And for the visit to the Shaker place."

"You bet," I said, because I was tired of nodding.

"And for not being a troubled loner when you picked me up back in New Hampshire."

"Any time," I said.

"You mean that?" she asked.

"Absolutely," I said. "Any time you find yourself stranded at a highway rest stop and need a big, sensitive, but manly American guy to rescue you, I'll be there."

We looked at one another. When I'd first seen her, I'd thought she was pretty, though not in the conventional sense. She still wasn't, I thought, looking at her there in Ariadna's apartment in Buffalo. But she did look *something*. I hunted around for the word. I couldn't find it. The best I could come up with was that she was intriguing. Especially when she smiled. She looked even better, I noticed, though, when she wasn't smiling, when she was sober and serious. Like she was now. Then she went into the bedroom she was sharing with Ariadna. I shook out my sleeping bag, then turned out the light and got in it.

The next morning I was awake, curled in my bag, when they left. I pretended to be asleep. Mostly I just didn't know what I'd say to Corinne if I let her know I was awake. I got up leisurely and packed, which consisted primarily of rolling up my sleeping bag. On my way out, I made sure the door locked behind me, checking a third time that I had the car keys, then I went downstairs and tossed my stuff in the car. It was cloudy, with a quick, hard breeze. The cold felt damp. I didn't know how far we were from Lake Erie, but the musty smell of lake water was in the air, faintly.

"Hey," a guy said from across the street. He was almost as tall as me. He was wearing a dark green nylon warm-up suit. The shiny kind that made that *slick-slick* sound when you're walking. Which he was doing. Walking. What he was also doing was being Chinese. About my age, maybe a couple of years older. He'd shaved his head so smooth it glistened, even in the cloudy light. He was walking, not too fast, but fast enough to show he meant business, that he had something that needed to be done and quickly.

"Hey back," I said.

"You a friend of Wenqian's, yeah?" he said. He was only about ten feet away now. He bounced lightly and came up over the curb onto the sidewalk just a few steps away. He had a quick, jerky way of speaking. That, and the way he chopped up his words, made him sound, even speaking English, like he might have come from Hong Kong.

"Who?" I asked.

"Oh," he said, nodding. "You a ass-smart too, yeah?"

"It's 'smart-ass,'" I said. "Not 'ass-smart.'"

"Yeah?" He seemed excited. His eyes had a feverish shininess. It was like he was trying to pump himself up. I had a feeling, suddenly, that whatever that something might be, it was probably not in my best interest.

"Yeah," I said. "And I'm just a semi-smart-ass." I didn't have any idea what he was talking about. I knew he was closing the distance as he talked, still smiling. He kept his hands in his pockets. He probably thought I was going to be cautious. Maybe I was supposed to think he might have a weapon in one of them. The way he was talking, he was either mentally screwed up some way, or he was trying to fluster me. My guess was the latter. My father spent some time with me when I was in high school, talking about the way you can get into trouble on the street.

"Bad guys aren't as stupid as most people would like to think," my father said. "They are good, very good in some cases, about picking a target or a victim. They size up their targets, look for any weaknesses, and they try to get as close as possible if they are going to attack. It cuts down on the intended victim's chance to run away." He explained bad-guy strategy in these situations. When they start to speak to you, so low you can't hear them, you tend to automatically lean forward or even take a few steps closer to try to hear them. Every step they can get closer to you, the target—like every step a lion can manage to sneak in on an antelope—narrows any chances you have to make a getaway.

The Bald Warm-up Suit was expecting me to play the part of the antelope. Or at least to be caught off-guard and confused. I wasn't. I didn't say anything. I came closer, walking directly at him. But I came a lot faster than he expected. The lion was still in the middle stages of his stalking, and the antelope was suddenly coming on, suddenly right on top of him. The lion wasn't prepared for that. I stepped in close. He stopped. I didn't. I kept my forearm parallel to the ground, my fist vertical, and I moved my body with the motion of my arm. He whipped his hand out of his pocket to try to intercept it. He was too late. Didn't matter. My forearm was going to slide over his arm no matter what he did to try to stop it. I hit him right in the solar plexus, squarely. Not hard. Hard enough, though.

Just like getting robbed or assaulted in real life usually isn't like it is in the movies, hitting someone isn't usually like it is in the movies. Most of the time if you try to hit someone, unless you've done it a lot before, either the bones or the ligaments or the tendons in your hands are going to give. Maybe even break. Or your wrist is going to collapse. I'd done it a lot, though. I'd hit a big heavy swinging bag so long and so often that my wrists weren't going to give. Unless I got unlucky and hit a hard spot, a bony place, or unless Baldy was wearing a suit of armor under that warm-up jacket, nothing on me was going to break either.

He staggered back. He doubled over at the waist, trying to raise his hands up to his midsection. He was trying to get his breath, with even less success, making soft breathy noises. In a combination of sitting and falling, his butt landed on the pavement.

"Hurts more than you'd think it would, doesn't it?" I said in Mandarin. "Try to straighten up." I switched to English since I didn't know the word for 'diaphragm' in Chinese. And if he was a Hongkie, chances were good that he might not understand Mandarin anyway. Most people from Hong Kong speak Cantonese. "Your diaphragm is spasming," I said. "You have to straighten up to stretch and relax it."

He looked up at me, still bent over. His eyes were a little gauzy. His lips were chalky.

"In a little bit, after you get your breath back," I said, "you're going to feel a real deep need to go to the bathroom."

"Huhhh?" It wasn't so much a statement as a groan. Even so, it sounded more coherent than the whooshing noise he'd been making.

"I don't know why," I said. "I don't know what the exact physiology is. But trust me, you will. Probably ought to get going to try to find one."

He looked up at me, still stunned. Whatever he'd planned, he hadn't planned for it to go this way. But he wasn't giving up.

"You shit-dumb," he said.

"Dumbshit," I said. He didn't seem to hear me. Or maybe he didn't appreciate my impromptu lessons on proper English usage of the vulgar vernacular. He straightened a bit more. But he was still breathing gingerly, from high in his chest—I could see him heaving under his warm-up suit—and his voice was wavering.

"Shit-dumb," he repeated. "You think this all going away? You think she going to get away with this? We just forget about it? We not go easy now. Somebody die? We no care! You die, shit-dumb? We no care."

He suddenly put his hand on his abdomen. I could see his face flush.

"Like I said, you're going to need a toilet." I didn't know what else to say. I was such a shit-dumb I couldn't figure out what he was talking about.

Down the street, a corner a couple of blocks away, I saw a patrol car slowly make the turn and head toward us, cruising leisurely along.

"Those cops will probably know where the nearest restroom is," I said. I pushed my chin in the direction behind him. "Why don't you hang around here a minute and ask them?"

He glanced up at the car, still a block off, then back at me. He was as confused as I was. I still didn't have a clue why he'd been coming at me. The difference was that his stomach hurt a lot more than mine did. He started walking away, as quickly as it looked like he could—still a little stiffly and still a little bent over—and disappeared around the corner behind me.

It wasn't the first time I'd hit someone. It was the first time I'd hit someone and wasn't exactly sure why. Some guy asking me if I was a friend of Wenqian's. Which is a Chinese girl's name. A guy who was coming toward me with some intent that wasn't in my best physical interest, I was pretty sure. Sure enough to have jacked him first. And then all the stuff about "her" not "get away with it," about not giving up, about "not go easy now." And especially the part about somebody dying—and more specifically "you" dying. Which was directed at me. It *was* the first time I'd had that experience.

I glanced up the street. The cruiser had paused. The driver was talking to a woman who leaned over to hear what he was saying.

I put my back against a phone pole. My knees felt like they didn't want to lock, no matter how I tried to make them. The muscles in my thighs were suddenly quivering. If it wasn't for the pole, I'd have been sitting down about where I'd put Mr. Bald Warm-up Suit just a few minutes before, on the sidewalk.

The woman stepped away from the cruiser and waved to the cop. He kept driving down the street toward me, then eased up and stopped. The passenger's window rolled down. I stepped away from the pole and took a couple of steps toward the car. I was happy my legs seemed to be holding me. And a little surprised they were.

"That your Toyota there, Massachusetts?" the cop in the passenger seat asked me. He jerked his head in the direction of the car's tag.

"Yes, sir," I said. I'd picked it up the day before.

"You're parked in a limited-time spot. You got someplace you can move it?"

"I do, officer," I said. "To St. Louis."

11

Rule #70: *Snow fungus and white wood ear are the same—and, yes, that is important.*

I could have called Langston Wu before I got to St. Louis. It would have been polite. I was planning to stay with him, after all. Maybe even move in, if he had the room. On the other hand, Langston showed up at my house unannounced one afternoon back when we were juniors in high school. He brought a bag full of live eels with him. My mother, I thought at the time, was actually considering killing him when she came into the kitchen and there was Langston dumping a dozen squirmy, slimy gray eels into her granite sink. Langston was the sort of guy who appreciated the spontaneous. I couldn't think of anything much more spontaneous than showing up at his front door in the middle of the morning, asking him if he'd like a roommate. Immediately.

That's where I was, twelve hours, more or less, after I'd left Buffalo. At his front door. Langston opened it at my second round of knocking. He was wearing a sweatshirt inside out and a pair of running shorts. His black hair stuck up at a bunch of odd angles all over his head, like a collection of exclamation points, like he was a cartoon character drawn to express only surprise. Which, at that hour of the morning, he was.

"Tucker?" He rubbed his hand over his hair and made it stick up even more. "What the hell are you doing here?" He looked sleepy. I assumed he was working in a Chinese restaurant. I couldn't picture Langston doing anything else. If he was—if he was working in any kind of restaurant—he was keeping late hours. People who've never worked in eating places, and who go there just for meals, don't realize how much of the work goes on after the last diner has left for the evening. Restaurant workers keep vampire hours. A restaurant doesn't just shut down, not even after the last dish has been washed, the last stained, wrinkled linen whipped off the table and tossed into the laundry hamper. There is always something else to do: prepping for the next day, scrubbing a sink, worming a piece of wire into the gas port of a stove to clear out the gunk that accumulates inside. Then there's the decompression hour, where workers gather someplace to nibble and drink and complain about their jobs. By the time most chefs and other restaurant workers get to bed, it's closer to morning than to anything like night. It was already past nine now. For a working chef like Langston, that would have been the best part of his sleep.

"You know," I said. "Happened to be in the mood for some fish maw soup and realized I was out of snow fungus. Thought I'd pop over here and borrow some."

"Don't have any," Langston said. "Got plenty of *bai mu er,* though." He stood aside and gestured for me to come in.

I did.

"You eat yet?" he asked.

I shook my head. I followed him into the kitchen. He took a plastic tub of rice from the refrigerator and dumped some into a pot, then poured in water and set it on the stove, lighting the burner underneath. He filled a kettle with water and lit another burner. I sat at the table. He sat across from me and folded his arms across his chest. I could see scars, old burns and a couple of new ones, on his forearms. Cooks in Western restaurants have scars like thick red smudges where their arms come down accidentally on the side of a pan. Chinese cooks like Langston—and me—have kitchen scars that are fine ribbons, either scarlet or tan, depending on their age, where our forearms have encountered the thin, searing edge of a wok. I had my own collection, most of them healed into shiny streaks by now. It had been a while since I'd gotten any new ones.

He pushed against the table so he was balanced on the back legs of the chair and looked at me. "You're on."

I told him the story of my life, skipping the parts he knew. Since we'd known one another since second grade, that meant I could leave out most of it except the past week or so. I left out the part about Corinne Chang. I thought that part might be superfluous. I still wasn't sure what it was all about anyway, and I didn't feel like going into it, even with someone like Langston, who was a good listener. He sat and did just that and didn't interrupt.

"So," I finished, "not having any other immediate prospects educationally, socially, or professionally for the moment, I thought I'd come out here and see if there were any restaurants looking to upgrade their kitchen staff."

Langston nodded. "And you, being a *laowai* with pretensions and a deep, probably neurotic need to try to be a part of a culture that neither needs nor wants you in the club, thought I might get you in the kitchen door of some place."

"Exactly," I said, reflecting on the fact that was the second time in less than a week I'd had ethnic slurs used to my face. Corinne had called me a "big nose." Which was mildly offensive but was really just an old term for Westerners, who, when they first appeared in China, seemed to have bigger noses than the Chinese were used to seeing. Langston was calling me a *laowai,* an "old foreigner." I'd never known why it had become a standard Mandarin term for a Caucasian. It could be an insult. It usually was. But sometimes it was just a description. And even when it was used insultingly, a lot of my Chinese friends and coworkers like Langston used it more to tease than anything else. Any way it got used, it didn't bother me. If you were going to be a white guy hanging out in Chinese kitchens, you had to put up with a certain amount of cultural insensitivity.

The rice was bubbling in the pot now, thick, viscous enough that a pair of chopsticks would stand up in it. Langston leaned into the open refrigerator and pulled out a bowl of leftover chicken stew studded with feathery knobs of silver jelly-like fungus and stirred it into the rice. He poured the hot water from the kettle into a teapot. I found a couple of bowls in the cupboard and put them on the table with two teacups. Breakfast was served. *Zhou*, rice porridge that we both liked Cantonese style, with a sprinkle of pickled and slivered bamboo shoots Langston retrieved from the refrigerator. It was the breakfast I'd mentioned to Corinne that first morning back in New Hampshire. It was even better than I'd imagined it then.

"Good snow ear," I said, using the Mandarin word for the fungus, *xue er*. "Tastes like it's from Dongxiang."

"It is," Langston said. "Only it's *bai mu er*."

This was our old, not particularly funny routine. Back in high school, cooking at his parents' house one day, we got into an argument. I insisted "snow fungus" and "white wood ear" were the same; Langston said they weren't. I turned out to be right. I never let it die.

After we finished, we cleaned up our breakfast dishes, and Langston showed me the apartment. The place he was renting was on the top floor of a brick apartment building built back around the time of the World's Fair in St. Louis, in 1904. More than a century later, it was near enough to Washington University to appeal to students looking for a cheap place to live. The landlord, Langston explained, was a local Chinese businessman. He'd figured out Chinese restaurant workers were just as able to pay rent as students and, unlike the students, didn't leave for three months every summer. If they had parties, they kept things quiet enough that neighbors up and down the street didn't complain. The entire apartment building, all three floors of it, was filled with Asians. Most were Chinese, either fresh immigrants or ABCs—American-born Chinese. Some were Vietnamese or Cambodian, Laotian, or Thai. Most worked at various Chinese restaurants within walking or biking distance. Langston's place was divided into his large bedroom in the rear, a small kitchen, and a living room with a fireplace that looked like it hadn't seen a fire since the World's Fair. Facing out onto the street was a front room that must have originally been some kind of parlor or sitting room. We were standing in the middle of it now.

"All yours," Langston said. "We can put up a sheet or a curtain right here"—he gestured—"and block this off so you can have some privacy and sleep in late as I know you're accustomed to doing."

I unpacked the Toyota and hauled my stuff upstairs. There wasn't much. Langston had a folding frame with a futon on it in the front room he'd told me was, for the foreseeable future, mine. I spread the futon on the wooden floor and put my sleeping bag on it. I arranged my clothes on a bookshelf built into one wall. I looked around. That seemed to be it, in terms of my personal property. I sat on the window ledge that looked out on the street below. Crusty mounds of snow the color of ashes were heaped along the curb. A couple of girls walked by, both in quilted parkas and very ugly big fur boots. A crow cruised by in a long glide. He landed with a single flap of his inky wings on the branch of a sycamore tree across the street. He was eye level with me. He glanced over my way, looking me over. Apparently I passed his inspection. He shrugged, shivering his black feathers, then settled down, watching, waiting. He looked like he was not intending to stay all that long there, but he was taking it all in, looking around to see what might be interesting for the time being. I knew how he felt.

12

Rule #31: *Beginnings offer more options in life than do endings.*

Langston used to cook at a place called the Eastern Palace. He'd gotten the job the way all Chinese cooks got them. His cousin knew a guy who was the brother-in-law of a woman who'd worked once at the Eastern Palace. Something like that. There was an expression: "Jangling the wok." It meant that if you asked any one person in a Chinese restaurant to bang their metal spatula against the side of their wok if they knew or were related to any other person, chances were good the noise would commence and just go on and on.

Langston took me to the Eastern Palace the next afternoon. It was only about a block from the restaurant where he was now cooking, in a section of St. Louis ambitiously called Chinatown. It was more like China Street. The neighborhood was a section of street at the western edge of the city, about half a mile long, lined on both sides with Asian restaurants, grocery stores, and acupuncture clinics. Two different Chinese newspapers. There were cramped shop fronts selling insurance and cheap jewelry, and a couple of auto repair shops, where, according to handwritten signs that appeared stuck in the windows, Chinese was spoken and understood.

The Eastern Palace, Langston told me, catered to non-Chinese diners at lunch. There were enough businesses and offices within walking or quick driving distance to make lunch the real moneymaker. The Eastern Palace, along with a dozen other similar joints, served standard Chinese American lunch fare to everybody from accountants to shoe sellers. Dinner, on the other hand, when most of the lunch customers had returned to homes out in the suburbs, comprised almost exclusively Asian diners. There were two different menus for dinner: one in English, the other in Chinese. I'd worked in Chinese restaurants like this. I was always irritated by the two menus. A lot of Chinese restaurants were still treating non-Chinese customers as if they were eating back in the sixties, when moo goo gai pan and chop suey were considered exotic. There were dishes on the Chinese side of the menu that weren't included in the English version. I thought there were a lot of non-Chinese diners who would have been adventurous enough to try some of the authentic stuff, if it was offered to them. On the other hand, I hadn't seen many Chinese restaurants go broke. So maybe the owners knew something I didn't. Nobody in management had ever asked any of us in the kitchen how to run their places. That was probably for a reason.

We went in the rear door off the alley, into the kitchen of the Eastern Palace. It was, like the kitchens of every Chinese restaurant where I'd worked, small. The average American living room was bigger. Under the soft buzz of fluorescent lights, three guys were working. One was scrubbing a wok the size of a kid's sledding disc. Another was turning a chunk of beef into mouthful-size strips. The third was clattering a spatula against another wok where a thick cloud of steam was boiling up. I'd never been here, of course. But it all looked familiar.

Langston introduced me to Jao-long, who told me to call him Jim; and Kuo, who told me to call him John; and to Li, who said I might as well just call him Li since he couldn't figure out any way you could Americanize a name like that to make it easier. Then Langston took me into the owner's office and introduced me to Ting Leong, who didn't tell me to call him anything. As we stood at its door, he sat in his office, peering at a shopping list like it was the directions for defusing a bomb strapped to his own waist. His attention on the task was completely focused. Finally, he looked up at us. He was skinny, in dark pants with a short-sleeved white cotton shirt and under it a white wife beater. A long strand of silver and black hair was thoughtfully swirled over the bald spot on the crown of his head. His glasses were so smudged I didn't think he could see me all that well. Apparently he saw I wasn't Chinese, though. He turned to a woman, and the Cantonese was so rapid it was hard to even make out words—and it wouldn't have done me any good if I had been able to catch them. I heard *gwai lo,* the Cantonese equivalent of *laowai,* except instead of "old foreigner" it mean something like "foreign devil."

"You look for work?" he said to me in English once Langston had introduced us. He was in his late forties, I was guessing. He crossed his skinny arms and absently rubbed both elbows with his palms.

"Exactly," I said.

"You wash dishes?"

"I do," I said. And I did. Or at least I was about to. Leong wheeled his chair around and reached to a shelf behind him. He tossed me an apron and pointed back through his office door into the kitchen toward the sink.

"Knock you-self out."

I washed dishes all through the noon and dinner shifts. I must have done okay; Mr. Leong told me to show up the next day. I did. And the day after, and about 2,768 dirty plates later, rendered clean and sparkling under my ministrations, a week had gone by and I had enough money to pay Langston for my half of the rent with a little extra left over. It wasn't something I'd want to make a career of. Still, it was nice to be back in a Chinese restaurant kitchen again. Being in a Chinese restaurant kitchen for me was like going back to my bedroom in my parents' house in Andover. I'd spent a lot of time in both. I was comfortable there. I felt at home.

There are Chinese restaurants in almost every city in the United States. Places the size of a public restroom that are exclusively for take-out, with steel grates and bulletproof-glass-fronted counters—all in dark places. Places that are giant, extravagant halls, with indoor streams and opulent architecture and menus that are pages long. I've never been to any of them, but I'm betting there are little prairie hamlets in South Dakota and tiny burgs in the swamplands of central Florida and wide-spot-in-the-road towns in the New Mexico desert that all have Chinese restaurants. Szechuan and Cantonese and Hong Kong style, and even some places devoted to the more esoteric of China's cuisine—Hakka, Honan, Fukien. Americans, millions of them every day, eat Chinese food made and served in these restaurants. With all those thousands of restaurants and millions of people eating in them, it's kind of interesting to consider that very few of those people have been in a Chinese restaurant kitchen. No reason why they should, really. If it's a choice between a trip to Epcot Center or a visit to a Chinese restaurant kitchen, go with the Epcot option. Still, a Chinese restaurant kitchen is a different world. And sure, most diners don't go into the kitchens of any kinds of restaurants where they eat. It's just that a typical Chinese restaurant kitchen is different from, say, a French restaurant kitchen. Or an American diner's kitchen.

All restaurant kitchens have their own setups and layout. They have their own specific rhythms, their own slang; they have their own customs and hierarchy. Right now, in that hierarchy in any Chinese kitchen, I was a *sheng shou,* a "new hand." That meant, more than anything else, I kept my mouth shut. I watched while I worked. I learned how things went on in that particular kitchen. I listened to the guys talking. Chinese cooks never shut up. In

some restaurant kitchens—I'd talked with enough cooks and restaurant workers to know—the energy comes from smoking or
from a snort of something or a shot of something with a century-
plus proof. In Chinese kitchens, the energy is most often supplied
by talking. Chinese chefs rag one another. They rag until they
run out of things to rag about. At least for the moment. Then
they start talking aloud to themselves. Then they regroup and rag
each other some more. It helps the time pass. It keeps everybody
engaged. Nobody has time to daydream or drift off.

I didn't join into the talk at the Eastern Palace. I wasn't a cook,
at least not in that kitchen. Not yet. Dishwashers don't rate. My
second night there, I was joined by Thuy, a JOB—"Just Off the
Boat"—immigrant from Vietnam who'd come over, he told me
in broken but understandable English, after his father lost their
Saigon business in a dice game. Unless Thuy or I fell behind and
caused the three chefs to run short of plates or bowls, they didn't
even notice we were there. If we did run behind, they noticed
right away. Not in a good way. I knew that from experience. I'd
done my own share of yelling at dishwashers. So I didn't say
anything. And I kept up. During the lulls, I watched Kuo ("Call
Me John") cook. He was the head chef, the most senior in the
kitchen, and he answered only to Mr. Leong. Even Mr. Leong
was respectful when he spoke with Kuo. In a Chinese kitchen, the
owner might be the guy who pays the bills and the salaries, hires
and fires. The head chef, though, runs the place.

As a chef, I came to the conclusion fairly quickly that as a fellow chef, Kuo was okay. I was better.

13

Rule #81: *Between substance and appearance, know when to focus on which.*

I'd been sharing the apartment with Langston for a week. We slept in the first morning we'd had off on the same day. We made a leisurely breakfast, then Langston said, "Okay, big brother. We've put it off long enough. Let's see what you've still got."

"Isn't so much what I've still got as how much you've lost," I said.

We changed into sweatpants and a couple of layers of long-sleeved shirts. We went downstairs and out into the alley behind the apartment building. My breath came out in a puff of steam that hung in the still, cold air. The sky was the color of an old nickel. The wind dragged torn clouds slowly over it. It was a winter sky that threatened snow. I stood still, sinking down to get my balance, letting my knees relax, trying to center the mass of my body over the spots right behind the balls of my feet, the spot traditional Chinese medical anatomy calls the "gushing spring." Then I began dribbling a pair of imaginary basketballs, faster, faster, until the palms of my hands were just a blur. It forced the blood to begin to circulate, along with my *chi,* my energy. I felt my arms tighten with the movement, then slowly start to relax. I stopped shivering.

For a while we stretched, bending over, swooping down, cranking our trunks in big circles, making wide patterns with our swinging arms, just moving gently, carefully. Then, still working separately, we moved slowly through the basic forms we'd both been trying to perfect for almost ten years. Splitting, drilling, pounding, exploding, and crossing, stepping in straight lines, shifting back and forth, weaving, always moving ahead, always taking territory from an opponent, then turning, and going back the other way. We moved deliberately, exaggerating the actions, punching, slapping, dropping our bodies close to the ground, then coming up again, always attacking. We weren't trying to stretch and loosen our muscles so much as we were trying to get our ligaments and tendons to respond. Chinese fighting arts are divided between *waigong* and *qigong:* external and internal arts. External arts, like *gungfu,* emphasize the same kind of physical movement and training that Western sports like boxing and wrestling do: the muscles, the "red." Internal arts, like the *xing-i* Langston and I did, worked on strengthening the "white," the ligaments and soft tissue. Instead of contracting muscles to make power, the idea is to relax, to be soft and pliant, right up until the moment of impact. It's like the difference between getting hit with a sledgehammer and getting hit with a whip.

I took my time. I worked slowly as I went through the fists. I felt the creakiness working its way out. I felt all those miles sitting behind the wheel of the Toyota across the country, then standing and washing dishes for what felt like about twenty-five hours a day. Within twenty minutes or so, my legs were trembling just a little with the effort. Being relaxed is harder than it sounds.

After an hour of solo work, we faced off. Langston was puffing, I noticed. His face was flushed, even in the cold. We started stepping back and forth together, facing each other. It looked like we were dancing. Only instead of dancing, we were launching attacks, receiving them, shifting away, then countering. Langston punched, exactly the way I'd punched the guy back in Buffalo, fist pounding in vertically, his elbow parallel to the ground. I slid back and brought my open palm down in a sweeping motion before he could connect with it, pulling his punch and his arm toward me, pulling him off balance just enough to take the power out of the attack. He scraped his back foot up to compensate and simultaneously drove his other fist up in front of him, almost like he was making an uppercut to his own chin, then arcing it out, aiming for my nose. We had a few misconnections. It had been a while since we'd trained together. He nailed me once with a fist that glanced off my cheek when I didn't move as quickly as I should have. I hooked his ankle and swept him, intending to catch him before he went down, but I missed grabbing him to stop the fall. He landed hard on his shoulder, and I heard his breath go out in a *whoosh*. We slowed to correct our rhythm, then sped up gradually as we got more comfortable with each other's timing and sense of space again. After about fifteen minutes, we were moving together like a pair of machines. All the gears clicked between us. It didn't take long to make our strikes and our shifting back and forth start to fall into a long, polished groove. We'd done it before. Lots.

Almost ten years before, one evening the summer we both turned twelve, we were hanging out on the front porch at Langston's parents' house in Andover, when his uncle came out and got us.

"Let's go, guys," he said. Langston's uncle, when he wasn't working as a real estate lawyer, practiced *taiji,* which he told us was too complicated for us, and *xing-i,* another Chinese fighting art he said was also too complicated but that, if we caught him in the right mood, he told us, he might show us. Apparently, that evening he was in the right mood. He led us to the backyard. He showed us how to stand: much like the way a person would in the prow of a canoe going through swift water. My forward foot was pointed straight ahead, the rear foot out at an angle for balance, my weight centered. He put my left hand up in front of me, open, fingers pointing up. My right he had me hold in front of my belly, open, so the thumb pointed back at me. It seemed simple. It wasn't. He corrected our posture. He made me round my shoulders. He pulled my head back so my chin wasn't sticking out. He pushed my butt in to straighten my posture. He shaped and molded both of us until we were exhausted just trying to stand as he wanted us to. That was my introduction to *xing-i*. An hour and a half in the humid heat of a Massachusetts summer, spent just learning how to stand.

Now it was almost ten years later and instead of a summery Andover backyard under the shade of the maples, Langston and I were in an apartment alley, with the wind whickering around the corner of the building, snipping at us. It didn't matter. We didn't feel the cold much. We were both perspiring. We moved together until we were too tired to do it anymore, even though neither of us wanted to admit it. Finally, Langston said, "It's no use. We both still reek."

We didn't. We looked okay, considering we were both out of practice. I didn't argue though. "No point in wasting more time on this," I said. "It's a lost cause."

On Monday Kuo, the head cook at the Eastern Palace, quit. Word was that he was recruited by another restaurant. Leong wasn't happy about it. Leong was not particularly stoic when he was unhappy.

"I bring these guys here. I teach them to cook, teach them how to run a kitchen," he ranted. He was standing there in the kitchen, hands on his hips and taking up space, while I was in the process of turning a pile of dark green peppers into neat, chopped squares. When the dishwashing was slack, he'd had me cutting vegetables, doing prep work. "What they do then?"

He didn't wait for me to tell him what they do then.

"They leave!" he said. "Up, go, gone!" Mr. Leong was steamed. He'd run his hand through what was left of his hair, and the carefully swirled circle of thin strands that had been so artfully and inadequately covering his bald spot drooped off the side of his head.

I didn't say anything. I was enjoying the feel of the cleaver in my hand, working it, feeling it slice cleanly through the peppers. I liked watching the pile of emerald squares growing next to my cutting board. I was in a nice rhythm, the cleaver moving exactly as I wanted. It felt like doing *xing-i* with Langston.

"I hear you think you can cook," Leong said suddenly. Out of the corner of my eye, I saw him put his hands back on his hips. "How about you show me? We need cook now. How about you make cashew chicken for me? You show."

"Nope," I said. I kept chopping. The blade of the cleaver made a satisfying crunch as it sliced through the peppers.

"Hah?" he said. I stopped and looked at him. He'd probably never had a dishwasher say that word to him before. It was almost like it didn't register.

"I cook Chinese food," I said. "You want somebody to make cashew chicken or beef and broccoli or pork fried rice, you can find twenty of them around here. I'd rather wash dishes."

That wasn't true. Not even slightly. I was getting sick of washing dishes. Really sick. It had reached the point where prepping, cutting up carrots or onions or the green peppers I had in front of me, was like a vacation compared to the dishwashing. I felt like a jockey who was spending his time mucking out stables instead of cantering on the back of a horse. I was ready to ride. And if getting into the saddle meant turning out orders of General Tso's chicken and egg rolls, I was ready to do it. I just wasn't ready to admit that. Not to Leong, anyway. Fortunately, I didn't have to.

"Okay." He still had his hands on his hips. He reached up with the right one and became suddenly aware of the thin curtain of hair hanging off the side of his head. He hoisted it delicately and started trying to smooth it back in place. "Okay," he said again.

"You make something Chinese, you smart guy. You show me how it done."

I did. First, I asked Li if it was okay for me to use Kuo's wok that was sitting cold on the burner. Technically, he was the senior man in the kitchen at the moment, with Kuo's defection. I wouldn't have gone near any wok without showing him the courtesy and respect of asking first. Li shrugged and nodded. It was too early for even the earliest of the lunch crowd to be around. The dining room was empty. I checked the cooler. I found chicken thighs and chopped them into bite-size pieces, leaving the bones in. I mixed soy sauce, sesame oil, and rice wine with the chicken and tossed it all into a clay pot, a bigger version of the one I'd cooked the pork in for the dinner with Corinne back at my parents' house. I put the cover on before setting it on the stove and clicking on the gas burner. While the chicken cooked, I added a gurgle of rice wine to a couple tablespoons of fermented black beans, put them in a small *dim sum* steamer, and set them over a low flame in a metal pot with water. I heated Kuo's wok. When it started to smoke, I tossed in a handful of the green pepper pieces I'd prepped, searing them against the side of the wok. When they got a little char, I flipped them and added a scatter of chopped green onions, soy sauce, and rice vinegar. Then I tilted in the dish of steamed black beans.

Leong was sitting at a table near the kitchen door, making out a shopping list. His wife was with him, with a laptop in front of her, going over the books. I brought the chicken in to the dining room, to their table, still in its pot, then came back with green peppers. I stood off to the side while Leong opened the clay pot. The steam came up in a small perfumed cloud. He sniffed it.

"*Sanbeiji,*" he said. He tried to hide it, but I could tell he was surprised. Sesame oil and soy sauce, mixed with the alcoholic smack of rice wine, together with the fragrance of slow-cooked chicken—not much coming out of a Chinese kitchen smells better than three cups chicken. The smell alone is enough to set mouths watering.

"Where you learn cook Taiwan food?" he asked.

"Nowhere," I said. "That's not Taiwanese. It's the original version, the one that came from Ningdu, in Jiangxi." He looked at me again. The expression on his face was a combination of surprise and confusion. I'd seen it before. A lot of Chinese are astonished that any non-Chinese can name a city in China other than Beijing. "The Taiwanese version is almost always made using Shiaoxing wine. I used straight *mijiu*. Gives the chicken a crispier texture."

"You know what the story is about where this dish came from?" his wife asked. She was at least two feet shorter than her husband, plump, with an oval face, her hair in a curly perm that the waitresses had told me she had done regularly at a Korean hair salon a couple of blocks away. A lot of Chinese women in the United States think Koreans have some special hair-care secrets. Korean hair stylists are for a lot of Chinese women what reliable bookies are to gamblers: carefully cultivated and kept happy, they are considered an invaluable asset.

"You know that story?" she asked again.

It would have been hard to say just how much I enjoyed being able to say that I did.

"Story is," I said, "that Wen Tianxiang, back in the Southern Song Dynasty, was in prison, getting ready to be executed. The jailer supposedly came up with this recipe because it didn't need a lot of pots to make."

I handed them each a pair of chopsticks. They poked into the pot and lifted out pieces of the chicken. Tendrils of steam came off. The smell made me hungry. Mrs. Leong took a bite; then Mr. Leong did the same. Then they tasted the green peppers.

"Kuo made this," Leong's wife said.

"Kuo didn't make it this well," Mr. Leong said.

"He didn't steam the black beans in rice wine," I said. "That's the trick. Brings out all their flavor."

"He should be cooking for us," Mrs. Leong said. She spoke English. She was from Fujian, which had its own dialect. She spoke Cantonese okay, I'd observed, but it was slow between her and her husband, and so when they really needed to communicate, they tended to switch into English.

"He's a *gwai lo*," Mr. Leong answered. I was accustomed to this too. Sometimes Chinese would start talking about me, right in front of me, even though I was standing there speaking to them in Mandarin. I assumed they knew I understood—but that I didn't really *understand*.

"He'll work cheap," Mrs. Leong said. "He won't know how much we're paying the others."

"He knows exactly what you're paying the others," I said. "He speaks English, just like you're doing now. See? Hear him speaking it to you?"

They ignored me. "Nahh," Mr. Leong said. "He can speak some Chinese. We don't treat him like the others, one of the other places around here will swipe him."

"Again," I said. "I'm right here." It could be maddening if you let it get to you. I didn't. After all these years, I tended to think it was just funny.

"Hire him," Mrs. Leong said.

I started cooking at the Eastern Palace that night.

14

Rule #9: *You're unlikely to regret much of what you don't say.*

"They said I'd find you out here," the woman said. "You must be Tucker."

We were out in the alley behind the Eastern Palace. There was a lull between the lunch and dinner crowds. I was caught up on prep work and taking a break. I had been going through some slow stretches. I was finally getting re-accustomed to the long hours of standing doing kitchen work. The dishwashing had been a good way to break back into it. Now that I had been cooking there for a couple of weeks, at least I was moving around more, leaning over to grab ingredients, bending down to get something on the kitchen's low shelves. I was still a little achy, my hamstrings tight. I had just straightened back up out of a squatting stretch to relax them when she came through the kitchen door.

I must be, I considered saying. But I didn't. It was a pretty good line, I thought. It didn't seem like a pretty good idea, though. That's because the woman—in a blue knee-length skirt, a crisp yellow blouse, and a dark blue jacket that matched the color of her skirt—was dressed either like an MBA graduate or a plain-clothes cop. I couldn't think of any reason an MBA grad would be hanging out at the rear of a Chinese restaurant kitchen and asking for me by name. I couldn't think of any reason a cop might for that matter. I just assumed it was the more likely scenario. I went with it.

"Yes, officer," I said. "I am he." I may not have graduated Beddingfield, but I did not leave Ms. Kresge's third grade English grammar lessons without some benefit.

Her eyes widened. Then she smiled. Her dark red hair was cut short, close to her face. She was short too. And athletic looking. She looked like she'd played field hockey in college, which looked, too, like it hadn't been all that long ago. She was smiling. It was a good smile. Not the kind of smile that said "I'm just a friendly sort." It was a smile that showed she didn't take herself too seriously. But seriously enough. I'd seen that kind of smile before.

"How did you know I was in law enforcement?" she asked.

"I've been around a few law enforcement officers."

"That's right," she said. "Your father works for a national security organization."

I nodded. I didn't say anything. It was a game. I recognized it right away. It was a game that cops and other people in law enforcement like to play. They like it because it's a good way to establish their presence and to take the initiative and to put you on the defensive. They also like to play games. I knew that from being around my father and a lot of his friends. One reason they liked to play games, mental games, was that because from their perspective, dealing constantly with suspects and with people from whom you want to get information, it was also just a lot of fun. Trying to throw someone off balance mentally was something a lot of cops and law enforcement people enjoyed. It made the job more entertaining. She was already pitching 'em high and hard to me. I was supposed to be confused and wondering who she was, how she could know my name, how she knew my father's occupation. I'd managed to connect with only one pitch, getting out ahead of her by letting her know I knew she was a cop. It wasn't much. But it did make me feel good. It made me feel even better to say, "Do you have some mutual friends in the agency?"

I didn't say which "agency." I figured she knew. I was going to make her volunteer that she did, though. I could tell she liked that.

"I'm more in the domestic end of things." She pulled a thin, black leather wallet out of her purse. She flipped it open. I knew she'd done it before. More than a few times.

"Wow," I said. "FBI."

She nodded. "Do you have some idea why I'm here?"

I sat on a pile of plastic boxes that had once contained fat pale green heads of napa cabbage and that were now stacked to be picked up by the supplier.

"You really like our beef with broccoli?" That was pushing it a little. She seemed, though, like the type who wouldn't take it as insolence or any kind of smart-assery.

She shook her head. "I'm trying to go vegetarian. Guess again."

I pursed my lips. "Illegal immigrant roundup," I said. "You got a tip I'm here without a green card, just off the boat from Hong Kong, and you're here to take me in."

"That'd be Immigration's problem," she said. "But I'll be happy to drop a coin to them and give them the tip."

"Then I'm all out of guesses," I said.

"Do you know a girl named Corinne Chang?"

I raised my eyebrows and looked up at the sky. Today it was clear, deep, almost flawlessly blue. A couple of skinny ribbons of darker purple were skidding along the western horizon. Winter was still in that sky. There was a hint, though, of spring. My expression was about as close to inscrutable as I thought I could get. Guys from Andover, Massachusetts, might be good at a lot of things. Being inscrutable isn't one of them. I was playing for time.

Unless you count growing up in a house with an agent of the NSA—that was the "agency" my father worked for—I didn't have a lot of firsthand experience with police. Toby, my now-ex-roommate back at Beddingfield, probably knew more than I did about how to behave around cops from watching all those seventies police shows on the retro channel. One thing I did know was that it was usually pointless to lie to them. You should always assume, my father told me, that cops have more information than you—or at least they can give that impression better than you. You should also assume, he told me, that even if they didn't have that information, they can—and will usually—get it eventually. Then they'll come back and your lie will be out there and you'll look stupid. And suspicious. Even if you are neither.

Right now, sitting on those crates behind the Eastern Palace, I'd worked the raised-eyebrow and looking-at-the-sky thing for just about all it was worth. I dropped my head back down and looked at the woman.

"Yes," I said. "I have met Corinne Chang."

"I'd like to meet her too," the woman said. "Is there someplace more comfortable where we can talk about her?"

"How do you know Miss Chang?" she asked me. We sat at a corner table of the Eastern Palace. She had introduced herself as Jill Masterson, special agent assigned to the Midwest region of the FBI. She wore her short red hair pulled back, held in place with a barrette. It wasn't tight enough to make it look like her eyebrows hurt, like some professional women do. It was just enough to give the sense that she meant business. Mr. Leong was standing in the doorway of his office watching us. Chinese of his generation, many of them, haven't had a lot of Officer Friendly interactions with cops, either back in China or here. They tend to react to cops the way they'd react to a rabid dog staggering through the door. Worried, wary, hoping not to do anything that might attract its attention. I was willing to bet, too, that Mr. Leong must have had some other worries. I was one of his employees, so he wanted to protect me. On the other hand, I was a non-Chinese, just like the cop. So where did his loyalties lie? He gave me a long look, thinking it over. I lifted my palm and fanned my outstretched fingers at him, waving him off. He took that as an okay, shrugged, and turned and went back into his office. Whatever it was, he seemed to have figured it wasn't his problem.

I was caught up with the dinner's prep. That's why I'd been out in the back, stretching. I'd already gotten tonight's chicken stock on the stove. An eighty-quart aluminum pot was filled with water, knobby thumbs of ginger, half a dozen chicken carcasses, and the secret ingredient of chicken stock in most Chinese restaurants—a couple pounds of pork bones. All this was at the *yunyong* stage: bubbling up so slowly, it looked like lazy summer clouds forming on top of the liquid. That was pretty much all I needed to do until the first dinner orders would start coming in, in an hour or so.

"I know Miss Chang because I gave her a ride," I told her.

"From where to where?"

"New Hampshire to Buffalo," I said.

"So this young woman just appeared in your life out of nowhere needing to get to Buffalo, and you just happened to be going to Buffalo?" Ms. Masterson asked.

I nodded.

"That happen a lot to you? Women just appearing in your life, and you just coincidentally able to help them in their time of distress?"

I shook my head. "Not as often as you might expect," I said, "given these dimples"—I touched my forefinger to my right cheek. Ms. Masterson nodded and ran her own forefinger over her mouth, like she was trying to wipe the smile away before it took hold. I took some satisfaction in that. I also knew I was pushing it a little.

"That's very interesting, Tucker," she said. "And it's awfully amusing sitting here with you and listening to your wit. But here's the thing." She paused.

I waited.

"I'm an FBI agent," she said. "And I'm in the process of an investigation. That investigation includes ascertaining the whereabouts of a Miss Corinne Chang. I have a reasonable suspicion, abetted by your own admission just now, that you may have some idea where she is or how she might be found."

Oh, yeah. I'd been right about the hair pulled back. Not too tight. But firm. No stray fingers of it trailing off. Ms. Masterson wasn't the severe, humorless librarian type. She wasn't a sentimental romantic, either.

"I have answered all your questions," I said. I took my time. This was the part where things might get a little bit uncomfortable. More advice I remembered from my father: When you are dealing with any kind of cop, whether it was a local guy stopping you for a broken taillight or a federal agent like Ms. Masterson, if things were going to get uncomfortable, it was a reasonable bet they would get uncomfortable a lot faster and a lot harder for you than for the cop. So I wanted to take it slowly and carefully and not have to regret or rethink anything that came out of my mouth. "And I've thrown in the wit at no extra charge," I added. "If I can be of any help in your investigation, I will absolutely do it. And while I might be a little bit of a smart-ass, probably most of that is because, well, take a look around."

Ms. Masterson raised her eyebrows. *Right again*, I thought. The hair was loose enough that the eyebrows still had a little play.

"I'm a twenty-one-year-old college kid," I said. "An upper-middle-class college kid. Kids like me interact with law enforcement personnel when we get stopped for speeding. Or when we get tagged because we stole a stop sign or threw eggs at somebody's house. Kids like me get nervous if we're out driving and a cop car is behind us. Kids like me have only seen the inside of a jail in movies, and from those we're pretty sure jail isn't someplace we'd like to spend any time. Kids like me are naturally worried and scared when we're dealing with any kind of authority more authoritative than a high school counselor."

Ms. Masterson didn't say anything. She was listening, though.

"And here I am, sitting here with an FBI agent, who's asking me questions about a girl I picked up and gave a ride to—to whom I gave a ride," I corrected myself, and thought briefly again about Ms. Kresge's third grade class, "and I'm wondering what the hell's going on. Is Corinne in trouble? Is she dead or hurt? Is she making some allegations against me?"

Ms. Masterson pushed out her lower lip to show she was contemplating what I was saying.

"Can you see," I said, "where I might be a little antsy about all this? And while we're at it, would it be out of line for me to ask how you managed to find me and how you know I had some connection to Corinne?"

"Yes," she said, "in answer to your first question. I can see why you'd be a little antsy. And, no, it wouldn't be out of line for you to ask how we know you'd met Miss Chang." She paused. "And in answer to your other questions, 'Maybe,' 'No, I don't think so,' and 'No, she hasn't.'"

I sat back in the booth and folded my arms.

"No, Ms. Chang hasn't made any allegations against you," Ms. Masterson clarified. "Not so far as I know. No, she isn't dead or hurt, so far as we know. We just don't know where she is right now." She paused. "She may be in some trouble. We need to locate her to find that out. We traced her cell phone. She made two calls to Buffalo, from your parents' home in Andover. We found out your parents are on a long cruise somewhere in the Pacific. So we traced your phone since you are also a resident at that address.

And we discovered you were making calls—and presumably stay-ing—in St. Louis."

I nodded. "I dropped Corinne off at an apartment in Buffalo. I don't remember the address, but I can probably give you direc-tions to it. Unless you can track the phone there too."

"Whose apartment?"

"It was a friend of hers, she told me."

"You believe her?"

"No reason not to," I said. "They told me they went to school together in Toronto. They told me about their time together there. I stayed at the apartment a couple of days while my car was worked on. Then I came here."

"Yes, you did, and I'm curious as to why," Ms. Masterson said. "What's a white guy from Andover, Massachusetts, doing work-ing in a Chinese restaurant in St. Louis?"

"The Chinese restaurant part and the St. Louis part are both because I have a friend who had a job at another Chinese place here, and after I left school at midterm, I decided to come out here to see if he could get me a job."

"And obviously he did," Ms. Masterson said.

I nodded.

"And you," she said, "the aforementioned white guy from An-dover, Massachusetts, waltzed into the Eastern Palace here, and they turned over kitchen—wok, stock, and spatula, so to speak—to you?"

"Excuse me a second, please," I said. I was looking forward to this part. I was looking forward to it the way I'd looked forward to serving that three cups chicken to the Leongs. I went back to the refrigerator in the kitchen and came back with a small bowl that I put in front of Ms. Masterson, along with a pair of chop-sticks.

"Give it a try."

She did, using the long plastic chopsticks awkwardly, like a lot of non-Chinese: held too far down and bending her elbow instead of her wrist when she brought the food to her mouth. She took a bite, chewed, then looked up at me.

"Wow," she said.

"Precisely."

"Wow," she said again. "That's really, *really* good. It's some kind of cucumber, right?"

"Szechuan pickled cucumber," I said. "With sliced ginger and Szechuan peppercorns and rice vinegar. It's a side dish usually, but I added dried tofu skin to give it more body and texture. And protein . . . for you vegetarians."

"I was just kidding about the vegetarian thing," she said, taking another bite. "But, boy, this is good. And you made this?"

I nodded.

"So do you think my wondering what a white guy from Andover is doing cooking in a Chinese restaurant might be a despicable racist assumption on my part?" Ms. Masterson asked.

"Absolutely."

15

Rule #4: *When you shouldn't hesitate, don't.*

Three days later, I was prepping for the dinner rush again. The Eastern Palace kitchen was starting to feel more comfortable, more like a place where I belonged. It helped that the kitchen had basically the same layout as every other place I'd worked. There were three wok stations along the side wall. They were all the same: a heavy aluminum countertop with three holes cut into it to fit the big rolled-steel woks we used. The woks were fired from below, where butane jets flashed a wicked roaring ring of blue light that looked more like it was coming from the turbines of an F-15 than something to cook on. Want to know why the Chinese food you make at home never tastes as good as in the restaurants, no matter how closely you follow the recipes? One reason is because you probably don't have the BTUs in your stove to launch a medium rocket into low-level orbit like those restaurants do. These flames could roast the flesh on your arm like a leg of lamb if you reached across them the wrong way. I'd seen it happen. Lift the wok out of its ring to pour the food into a bowl or onto a platter, and the oil that ran down its smoking hot side would hit the flames below and send up yellow gouts of fire. With all three woks going, tilting food out or turning them for a quick scrubbing, it looked like a troupe of demons opening and closing portholes to Hell.

Behind the woks, against the wall, was the stainless steel backsplash that kept the kitchen wall from spontaneously bursting into a conflagration. That's where the swiveling, long-necked spigots that we used to rinse the woks out between courses came out of the wall. It wasn't spacious working quarters. I'd never been in a Chinese restaurant kitchen that was. It was fairly confining. That was actually a good thing, though, mostly. If I was in front of my wok, I only had to pivot around to the table that stretched nearly the whole length of the kitchen right behind me to get all the ingredients we needed under shelves that held platters and bowls. On either side of the wok stations, barrel-size aluminum pots simmered, bubbling, filled with stocks and soups. Make any arm movement too big or dramatic, and the sides of these pots would leave a blistering brand on an elbow. Not only had I seen that happen; I'd felt it too.

When I started cooking at the Eastern Palace, I knew to go, without being told, to the station nearest the door into the dining room. That's where the junior chef always works, turning out simple stuff. Shrimp fried rice or juicy scorched dumplings that can be scooted out to the dining area quickly. It was also the most cramped, with stockpots on either side. I'd cooked in that position before. It was part of the game.

Taking the low end of the wok totem pole didn't go unnoticed by my two fellow cooks. Jao-long and Li took it as a sign I knew how to behave in a kitchen. They showed me their appreciation almost immediately. They started calling me *bai mu*, slang for "stupid," which they thought was amusingly even more appropriate in my case since it literally meant "white eyes." In a Chinese restaurant kitchen, insults — constant barrages of insults — are not just the approved medium of communication. They are the *only* form of communication.

And not just insults or vulgarity. The kinds of trash guys talk in the locker room? The language oil derrick workers use? That stuff's like the affectionate baby talk a mother makes with her toddler compared with what comes out of the mouths of typical Chinese cooks.

If Jao-long needed a steamer basket close to where Li was working, he could have just asked for it. That would have been completely unthinkable for Jao-long. Or any other Chinese chef.

"Hey, *ba lan jiao!*" he'd yell at Li. "You, the guy with no discernible genitalia!"

Then, having gotten Li's attention, he'd ask for the steamer.

Li would toss the steamer to Jao-long, along with the advice that Jao-long ought to have sexual intercourse with his mother's ancestors.

I didn't jump in on these exchanges right away. I stayed quiet for a while until I figured I'd done enough time there to make my presence known. One evening, when we were busy, I spun and reached for the well in the tabletop behind us that was supposed to have held chopped green onions. It was almost empty. It was Li's job that night to be sure those wells were filled. In a voice just loud enough for everyone in the kitchen to hear, including the two waitresses who were there at the time, I told Li he masturbated and didn't wash his hands afterward. In the rich repertoire of Mandarin insults, it's an oldie but a goodie. He looked up at me, mildly shocked. Then he went to the cooler where we kept the chopped green onions, refilled the well, and told me to *"Qin wo de pigu"* — "kiss my ass."

I was fitting in at the Eastern Palace.

All the shouting — along with the roar of the gas jets under the woks, the splashing of rinse water, and the clanking of spatulas and metal spoons — made the kitchen sound like it was continually being picked up and shaken. I kept my phone on vibrate. No way could I have heard it, even from my front pants pocket. It buzzed while I was in the middle of putting together a meal that one of the regular customers had ordered. He wasn't just a regular. He was a very wealthy regular. What's known in the Chinese restaurant trade as a *feide yourou,* a "fat fish." Fat fish, when they became regulars, provide enough income for all of us to eat well.

He was from Nanjing. The waitress from his table told me he wanted to be surprised that night. I was making his table a classic from that city, a delicate soup made of a light gingery broth and fine potato starch noodles and thin slices of congealed duck blood. It wasn't a difficult recipe to prepare. If the blood's added when the broth is too hot, though, it melts and ruins the whole dish. So I was taking my time to get it right. The customer was someone who would know immediately if I didn't. Half an hour later, the soup on its way to the table, the duck blood still beautifully congealed—well, as beautifully as congealed duck blood can look—I took a break. I went out into the alley, fished my phone out of my pocket, and checked the missed calls. There was only one. Langston was the only person I knew in town. I doubted my parents would have been calling from the high seas of Indonesia. And I didn't think Beddingfield College was ready yet to give me a ring and beg me to return. It was Corinne. I called her back. She answered on the first buzz.

"Is this the Exotic Asian Babe Escort Service?" I asked.

"Sorry," she said. "This is the Exotic Oriental Babe Escort Service."

"My mistake."

"Happens all the time." Then she paused. I was trying to get something from the tone of her voice. If there was anything there, I couldn't hear it. While I was still thinking about that, she said, "While I've got you on the line, though, what would you think about an all-expenses paid trip to Buffalo?"

"Buffalo in March," I said. "Sounds attractive. I've been to Buffalo in January. How's it different?"

"The snow is a more charming shade of gray," she said. Then she paused. I waited. "I need a ride."

"Where to?"

"I heard there was some good Chinese food in St. Louis," she said. "I was thinking about coming there to try it."

I wanted to ask why she didn't get a flight. Or even buy a ticket on a bus. Or why she wanted to come to St. Louis. I wanted to ask. I didn't. It didn't seem like the right time for a long conversation. Especially after what she said next.

"I'm sorry," she said. "I don't have any right to ask you to come get me. You don't even know me. But I don't have anyone else I can ask."

Then I finally heard it. Tension in her voice. No panic. But there was some anxiety. I heard, in my head, the Warm-up Suit back in Buffalo. *You think she going to get away with this?*

There was another reason I didn't ask her any of the questions that were bouncing around in my head. There are times when you have to make your call quickly. Even a second's hesitation is deadly. That was definitely one of my rules. It's #4. When you shouldn't hesitate, don't. "Don't you think my girlfriend is outstandingly hot?" a guy asks you, and if you don't answer instantly, if you don't say without any hesitation, "Yeah, she's really good-looking," even if she has a face that could make a freight train take a dirt road, you are going to be immediately in a place in your friendship with that guy that's never going to be the same. This was one of those times. Either be gallant and step up or never hear from Corinne Chang ever again. My call to make. But it was going to have to be made *now*.

"Hey," I said. "You do have a right to ask me to come. Remember when I promised if you ever needed a big, sensitive, but manly American guy to rescue you, I'd be there?"

"I'm not at a rest stop, though," she said. Even through the phone, I could hear the relief in her voice.

"I can be flexible," I said.

"I know," she said. "I've seen you sleep in the front seat of a Toyota."

16

Rule #33: *When cooking pork in a wok, it's 80 percent done when the pink disappears.*

I asked for a few days off. I expected Mr. Leong to go through the roof. He took it well, though. A lot better than I thought he would. He didn't actually throw anything. It was some personal business, I told him. "No problem," he said. Which struck me as odd because in the time I'd been working there, Mr. Leong's perspective on what constituted a problem had a fairly wide latitude. A piece of pork fat that fell on the floor could send him into a fifteen-minute harangue about wasting good food through such carelessness—or as he put it, "You guys no care, you no pay for food. Food costs. You know? Food not free."

"Where you go?" he asked me when I told him I needed a few days away.

"I go get friend," I said.

"Friend boy? Friend girl?"

"Friend girl," I said. "But not girlfriend."

"No problem," he said again. "But you not come back, I find you cook someone else, I cut you into pieces." He held up a thumb and forefinger pinched closely together to demonstrate the size of the pieces he had in mind.

I promised I wouldn't cook anyone else.

"You come back," he said. "You, me, we have something to talk about."

"Okay." I didn't have any idea what he was talking about.

· · ·

"I'm taking off for a couple of days," I told Langston. The sun was out; even at midmorning, it was warm enough that I could feel dampness on the back of my T-shirt. We'd been pushing each other back and forth across the alley. We were changing up our rhythm spontaneously, stopping, speeding up, unexpectedly putting pauses in the movements to keep the sparring from becoming choreographed and routine. Except for Mrs. Trahn, who lived with her husband in an apartment on the first floor and who always came back from a walk this time of day, studiously ignoring us as she went past, we were alone.

We were both in much better shape than the first time we'd practiced together. We stopped now not because we were too winded but because we were both working the lunch shifts at our kitchens. We went back upstairs to the apartment.

"Why are you taking off work?" Langston asked. "You never take off work. The kitchen at the Eastern Palace is your Fortress of Solitude."

I told him about Corinne. I told him about the magical meeting Corinne and I had at that rest stop in New Hampshire. I told him about dropping her off at her friend's apartment in Buffalo. I didn't mention the part about punching out the Chinese punk who asked me if I was a friend of Wenqian's. Or the threats he made.

"What are you going to do with her when you get her here?" Langston asked.

"I haven't figured that one out yet," I admitted. "Might be that I don't have to do anything with her. Maybe she's just decided to relocate to St. Louis."

"Yeah," Langston said. "I can see that." He didn't say anything else. I was grateful. He changed the subject.

"Leong say something to you about anything out of the ordinary?"

"Said he'd cut me into pieces if I didn't come back," I said. "But that seems pretty ordinary for him."

"Anything else?"

"He said there was something he wanted to talk to me about when I did come back. You have any idea what that's all about?"

The side of Langston's mouth twitched up. "I'll let him tell you."

I would like to have thought that I hadn't given Corinne Chang a lot of my mental attention. That would have been less than accurate. I'd thought about her since I'd last seen her in Buffalo. I'd thought about the way she'd looked at me when we'd said goodbye. I'd thought about the four things I knew about her: (1) The puffy noises she made in her sleep. (2) The way she could listen. (3) The fact she was almost certainly lying when she said she was just taking some time off from her job. (4) The color of her underwear.

I also thought about the conversation I had with her jerk boyfriend on the phone. Or ex-boyfriend. I wasn't sure about that, either.

I had thought about it all. The only conclusion I'd reached was that the black bra and panties should definitely be higher on the list than in the place I'd put them.

17

Rule #41: *While there might not be any good reasons to go to Buffalo, there could conceivably be a reason to go back.*

Two days later, I picked up Corinne at a motel outside Buffalo.

The drive, from St. Louis across Illinois and Indiana, is not chock-a-block with scenic distractions. Which was good, because as I drove, I had enough distractions going on inside. I'd been busy since Corinne and I had parted. This was the first time I had a chance to be alone with my thoughts.

I wondered why I'd been so quick to agree to make this trip. I wondered if it had anything to do with the way Corinne had looked sleeping on the passenger's seat as we drove across New York. I thought it might. I made a list of the other people in my life for whom I would be out on the highway to Buffalo. That didn't take too long. I thought about guys I'd known, a few in high school, a few more in college, who had gotten involved with what Toby, my Beddingfield roommate, used to call "trouble drains."

Trouble drains were people—girls—who, while attractive and fun to be with, had a way of constantly being in crises or troubling situations. And what was worse, they had a way of sucking the people around them—especially boyfriends—right into the swirling vortex of that trouble. Get too close to a trouble drain, Toby insisted, and sooner or later you'd be caught in the swirl. It started slowly, he theorized. So slowly that you were just circling around imperceptibly until it was too late, and then you were spinning, spinning out of control and heading right down that drain.

I thought about the threatening call I'd intercepted on Corinne's cell phone when I was busy minding my own business. About the way her friend Ariadna had looked away when the subject of why Corinne was in Buffalo came up. I lost my train of thought, thinking about the black bra and panties, but I brought it back on track. The Bald Warm-up Suit. The sound of her voice when she'd called to ask me to come get her. I rapped on the steering wheel and watched Illinois, then Indiana, then Ohio go past, cold and gray. I wondered if I was scared and decided maybe just a little, although I preferred, I decided, the word "concern" instead. I wondered if I was thinking of Corinne in a way I had not previously thought about most girls I had known.

I had looked forward to being alone with my thoughts, but by the time I'd driven through Cleveland, still in northern Ohio, I realized that rather than being alone, the Toyota was actually getting pretty crowded with all those thoughts, and I was relieved when my phone buzzed and I pulled off onto an exit to answer it.

It was Corinne. I wondered why she wasn't still at her friend Ariadna's apartment. I was wondering about a lot of other things, though. That one would have to wait. I followed her directions to a motel.

On the way back to St. Louis, Corinne and I stopped at another motel, this one about sixty miles north of Columbus, right on the interstate. It was tricked out with gingerbread, made to look like someone had decided that what mid-Ohio really needed along the road was a Swiss chalet. The Toyota performed admirably. Its thirst for oil didn't appear too much worse. I kept a couple of plastic bottles under the front seat though, just in case it developed a sudden craving.

"This is the second date night you've taken me to a motel," Corinne said from the bathroom. She was combing her hair. I could see her reflection in the mirror. I was sprawled on the bed in a pair of sweatpants and a Boston College T-shirt. I was reading from a brochure I found on the nightstand about the local attractions in this part of Ohio. It turned out there weren't many.

"Actually," she said, leaning over and poking her head around the door so she could see me, "do you realize that every night we've been together since you picked me up, we've slept together?"

"We didn't sleep together at your friend's apartment," I said. "Or at my parents' house."

"We were under the same roof," she said, her voice coming from the other side of the bathroom. "That's close enough."

I let it go. I hadn't been around her all that much, but I'd already decided Corinne Chang had a strange sense of humor. Then, too, there were some other things I wanted to talk about more.

She came in and tugged down the covers on her bed. She had on a yellow T-shirt that came all the way to her thighs. I wasn't sure about the color of her panties. I was pretty sure the bra wasn't there at all.

She got in and reached over, clicked off the light between us, and we lay there. I had my arms folded back behind my head, looking at the ceiling. I tried to think a little less about her breasts and a little more about what we needed to talk about. I focused on the task. I did pretty well, especially considering the perkiness of the distraction. Distractions.

"Remember that afternoon we were driving across New York," I said, "and you said 'Okay, I give'? And then you asked me who I was?"

"Yep."

"And I told you?"

"Yep," she repeated. "You told me to some extent. I still don't know any of Tucker's Rules past the first three."

"Okay," I said. "Now it's my turn: I give. Who the hell are you, Wenqian?"

I rolled over and clicked on the lamp between our beds. She rolled over and looked at me, blinking in the sudden light. She'd left her hair down. Part of it fell over her left eye. I got up and sat in the chair over by the window. The heater in the room would have been humming if it had been working correctly. Instead, it was making a low, dull drone, like a jet taking off very far away. It was a little louder in the silence.

"How did you know my Chinese name?"

"There was a punk Chinese guy who came up to me when I was getting ready to leave your friend's apartment," I said. "He asked if I knew Wenqian. I didn't know who he was talking about. I thought he might just have been setting me up to hustle me or mug me. Just making up some name to distract me and give him a chance to get closer. If I had thought about it, it wouldn't have helped. I would have never figured there would be any way I'd just happen to run into someone from Buffalo who just happened to know that you were in town. He meant you, though, didn't he?"

Corinne nodded without looking at me. She'd pushed the covers down and was sitting with her back to the bedstead, her knees drawn up. She produced a red scrunchie-thing and pulled her dark hair back into a ponytail.

"You didn't tell him where I was?" she asked, still not looking at me.

"I told you," I said. "I didn't know what he was talking about."

"So what did you tell him?"

"I punched him," I said. She jerked her head in my direction. "I thought he was just talking, trying to get close enough to me to pull out a gun or a knife, to rob me."

"What happened then?"

"He went down," I said. "But then he started talking. He asked me if I thought 'she' was going to get away with it. If I thought 'they' were just going to give up. And he told me it didn't really matter much if somebody died in the process. So, yeah, I'm a little slow, but I've figured out who 'she' is. Want to tell me who 'they' are?"

She closed her eyes and was still for a minute, then she nodded. "Yes. But what happened after that?"

"Okay, so I'm staying with my friend in St. Louis," I went on. "Working at a restaurant. And you'll never guess who walks into the kitchen the other day to have a chat with me."

She looked up, and I saw a flicker of concern on her face. "The guy?"

"No, but that's a good guess," I said. I filed away her reaction. She knew Mr. Bald Warm-up Suit. She had some reason to be afraid of him. Or afraid for me. Which didn't make me feel any better. "It was an FBI agent," I said. "Wanna guess what she wanted to talk about?"

Corinne shook her head. She was staring straight ahead again. Her skin, in the light of the bedside lamp, was almost bronze, tight and smooth across her cheekbones.

"She wanted to know if I knew the whereabouts of a Miss Corinne Chang," I said.

Corinne didn't say anything. I let it hang in the air for a minute.

"Now we're at the part of the movie," I said after a while, "where I say, 'Whatever is going on with you—and now especially that I seem to be involved—we need to go to the cops,' and you tell me some good reason why we can't go to the cops."

Corinne folded her hands and put them under her chin, like she was praying, staring straight ahead. "I can't think of a good reason," she said. "But supposing we do. What am I supposed to tell them?"

"What do they want to know?" I asked.

Corinne shrugged.

"You don't have any idea?"

"I have lots of ideas."

For the next hour, while a cold wind in the cold dark outside rattled the motel windows, I sat in a chair near the window, my legs propped up on a table, while Corinne sat on the bed with hers crossed beneath her and told me some of them.

18

Rule #95: *When you're already lost and clueless, it's best not to clutter things with any more information that's as likely to be superfluous as not.*

We met with Ms. Masterson the morning after the Toyota got us to St. Louis, at a sandwich shop near the FBI's offices in Clayton, a suburb a few miles from downtown St. Louis. It was where lots of government offices and other businesses that preferred clean streets and safety over city squalor and random crime were located. Corinne ordered a sweet roll while we waited for her.

"You're not going to believe this," Corinne said. "But I've been craving a sweet roll ever since I saw you eat that one at the rest stop, back in New Hampshire."

"Can't expect this one to measure up," I said. "The cellophane wrapper imparts a plasticky undercurrent of flavor profile you just can't get anywhere else."

"Along with that special aging that takes place when they sit in that machine for a month or so."

I nodded.

Even so, she did some work on it. Corinne was halfway through the roll when Ms. Masterson came in. She was wearing a dark green skirt and jacket with a white blouse. She looked like any of the other office workers in the place getting a late breakfast, sitting at booths and tables, studying the laptops in front of them. I introduced Corinne. Ms. Masterson sat at our table, across from me and next to Corinne.

"Show her your badge," I said.

Ms. Masterson looked at Corinne. "You want to see my badge?"

"Pass," Corinne said.

"You should," I said. "It's pretty neat."

Both of them ignored me.

"You're Corinne Chang," Ms. Masterson said, pulling a small notebook from her purse, flipping it open and scanning it. Her hands looked strong. Her fingers were thick. Not fat. But powerful. I was willing to double down on my bet that she'd played field hockey in college.

"Born March fourteenth, nineteen eighty-eight?" she said, reading off the pad.

"Yes."

"And you have been living for the past five years in Montreal?"

"I have."

"You worked as a gem sorter for a diamond company there? Wing Sung Jewelry Importers?"

Corinne nodded. "It's not a retail company. We sold diamonds wholesale, along with a few other gems. We sold to larger jewelry stores all over Canada. Some parts of the U.S."

"Wing Sung?" I said. "Cantonese?" Corinne nodded. I did too, more slowly.

"What's that mean?" Ms. Masterson asked.

"Cantonese—they're mostly in southern China—and Mandarin speakers—they're dominant in the rest of the country—don't always get along so well." I didn't add that for many Mandarin-speaking Chinese in the northern part of China, Cantonese people, from the southern part of the country, are thought of the way a lot of New Yorkers would tend to think of Appalachian hillbillies, as slightly uncouth and unsophisticated country cousins. It was a snobbery that went back a long way in Chinese history.

"That's true," Corinne said. "But if you want to work in the diamond trade for Chinese, you'd better learn to get along with Cantonese."

"Which you did?" Ms. Masterson asked.

"Sure," Corinne answered. "I even managed to get along with him"—she tilted her head in my direction—"for four or five days."

"You cannot think of me as being worse than Cantonese," I said, feigning surprise. I didn't think Corinne had any prejudices against Cantonese. Most Chinese Americans of her generation wouldn't. I was working for a Cantonese guy, Mr. Leong, at the Eastern Palace, and I never heard much anti-Cantonese sentiment from the northern Chinese I worked with. I was just amusing myself. Corinne went along with it.

"At least they're Chinese," she said to me in Mandarin.

"Okay," Ms. Masterson went on, as if she hadn't heard our exchange, "so why did you leave Wing Sung?"

"The company went out of business," Corinne said.

"That's an understatement," Ms. Masterson said.

"It is."

I wondered what that was all about. I had begun, I realized, to think about Corinne Chang as something of a jigsaw puzzle that needed assembling. I had assembled a few pieces. Maybe some of the edges of the puzzle were done. Those were always the easy part. I was missing a lot more of the pieces in the middle of the puzzle, though. I didn't think this was a good time to try to put any new ones in place. I kept my mouth shut. Tucker's Rule #95: When you're already lost and clueless, it's best not to clutter things with any more information that's as likely to be superfluous as not.

"Do you have some idea why we want to talk to you?" Ms. Masterson asked Corinne.

Corinne nodded. I wondered if she needed a lawyer. I wondered if you're supposed to ask about getting a lawyer. I wondered if Corinne had the right to remain silent. I wished I'd watched more of those cop shows my roommate Toby was always watching back at Beddingfield. Former roommate. Mostly, though, I wondered where the hell all this was going. So I just sat and listened. Rule #95 was still in play.

"The FBI has been asked by the Canadian police to help out in an investigation of the Wing Sung company," Ms. Masterson said. "There's a strong possibility the case may cross, ah, jurisdictional boundaries."

Corinne took a deep breath, then let it out. Then she started telling the story. I'd heard it earlier, back in the motel in Ohio.

"I came to work one morning," she said. "It was a Friday. I'd been working at Wing Sung for almost five years. It was the same routine. Mr. Sung, the owner, was always there first. He opened up. The shop was on the third floor of the Mercantile Mart, in the Central Business District. Do you know that area, by any chance?"

"I've been there," Ms. Masterson said. I wondered why she'd have been to Montreal. I tried to work it into my theory about her having been a field hockey player in college. Maybe they had a big tournament in Montreal. Maybe there were some pieces in her puzzle that needed work. I decided I was too busy on the Corinne puzzle, though, to spend a lot of time on another one.

"So I get there, go up, and the door's locked," Corinne said. "And there's a sign in the window, saying that Wing Sung Jewelry Importers is no longer in business."

"That's it?" Ms. Masterson said. "No forwarding address on the sign, no telephone number? No nothing?"

"No nothing," Corinne said.

"What did you think?"

"I thought it was a joke," Corinne said. "I actually thought for a second or two that I was having a dream. It was like getting up in the morning and walking to your bathroom and finding it wasn't there anymore."

Corinne told Ms. Masterson what she'd told me that night back in Ohio. She used her key to get into the building. Everything was still in place, she said. Desks for Mr. Sung and two assistants? Check. Stacks of invoices in baskets on top? Check. Her forceps, viewing loupe, and notebooks, all in place on the counter in the back room where she worked, under a big skylight to let in the natural light? Check. The inventory, kept, she said, in a bedroom closet–size vault? Checked out. As in gone. Faded away. Departed the premises.

"Did you have the combination to the vault door?" Ms. Masterson asked. She was sitting with both hands on the table between us, listening carefully.

Corinne shook her head. "I didn't need it. The vault door was open when I got there."

"Do you know how much inventory had been in there?"

Corinne shrugged. "I didn't have much to do with that end of the business," she said. "So I'd be guessing. But if I had to do that—guess—I'd say we had about fifteen million dollars' worth of diamonds there, retail value."

"Would the other people working there know?"

"They could probably guess, like me," Corinne said. "But Mr. Sung kept track of inventory. And if you want an exact figure, you could probably call the police in Montreal. They could go in and check all our paperwork. It looked to me like it was all still there. Nothing seemed missing."

"Except the diamonds," Ms. Masterson said.

"Except them."

"Which is a pretty big exception," I said.

They both turned and looked at me like they'd forgotten I was there. *Tucker, you suave guy, you.* Ms. Masterson looked back at Corinne.

I was fairly sure the police had already done as Corinne suggested. It was a reasonable bet they'd been over every piece of paper in that office. They would have also interviewed everyone who worked there. Except for Corinne. Who was unavailable for an interview. Because she was, about that time, sitting at a highway rest stop outside a town that had originally been named for a cheese farm.

"Did you get in touch with either of the people who worked there?" Ms. Masterson asked.

"I called them," Corinne said. "They sounded as surprised as I was."

"Did you notice anything unusual in the time leading up to all of this?" Ms. Masterson sat back in her chair and lifted her hands, turning them over so her palms faced out. "Something out of the ordinary?" She leaned back in and put her elbows on the table. "You know what we're looking for. I mean, was it like things were just perfectly normal, nothing at all odd or unusual going on, and suddenly, completely out of the blue—bang!—your boss is gone, the other people in the office are gone, nothing? No clues beforehand?"

"Two things you ought to know," Corinne said. "One, about six months ago, Mr. Sung suddenly had a girlfriend. He was private about his life. He'd never talked about any relationships. Then one day a woman walks in and asks for him, and he comes hustling out the office, and it's obvious something's going on between them." Corinne paused, then added, "And it was a little weird."

"Weird how?"

"Mr. Sung is in his mid-fifties, I'd guess," Corinne said. "He was kind of a *lao touzi*—" She looked at me and raised her eyebrows.

"Nebbish," I translated. "What nerds become when they drift past middle age."

"And the girlfriend?" Ms. Masterson asked. "She didn't fit the—what'd you call it?—*lao touzo*—girlfriend image?"

"*Lao touzi*," Corinne corrected, and shook her head. "No. She was definitely a *gong-gong qi-che*," she said, and noticing Ms. Masterson's expression, she instantly translated. "Loose. *Gong-gong qi-che* is literally a 'public bus.'"

This time it was Ms. Masterson's eyebrows that lifted.

"Everybody can ride," I said. "Get it?"

"I do," Ms. Masterson said.

"Besides the girlfriend, there were also some guys who came around a few times," Corinne added. "They weren't the typical customers we got. They're what we'd call in Mandarin *huai dan*. A 'bad egg.' It's like a low-life type. Somebody who's shady, sleazy; somebody you wouldn't turn your back to."

Ms. Masterson sat back in her chair. She propped her elbows on the table again, folded her hands, and stuck her chin on top her knuckles. "They weren't the usual sorts of people who came into Wing Sung?"

Corinne shook her head. "The usual sorts of people who come into a wholesale diamond office are buyers or sellers. In the diamond business, it's a good idea to keep a low profile. Not many diamond buyers look like thugs."

"And so when you considered that these 'bad eggs' had started visiting the place, you thought that maybe something was going on, right?" Ms. Masterson said.

"Something was going on," Corinne said. "It wasn't business as usual. At first I just assumed it wasn't any of my concern. But then, walking in that morning and finding that whole bizarre situation, I was worried."

"Did you think it might be dangerous?"

"Yes," Corinne said simply. "And I thought whatever it was, it could be dangerous for anyone associated with Wing Sung."

"And that's why you left Montreal after you found the office deserted and apparently abandoned," Ms. Masterson said.

"I didn't know what was going on. I still don't. But I thought it was too much a coincidence that these guys had shown up a few times over the past few months, and all of the sudden, the place is closed and Mr. Sung is gone. That, and I didn't have any family or other connections in Montreal. It was a good first job in the field. But it wasn't going anywhere. I thought it was the right time to leave and try living somewhere else."

"Like Buffalo?" Ms. Masterson said, and Corinne nodded.

"So if you were going from Montreal to Buffalo," Ms. Masterson pressed, "how'd you end up in the wilds of New Hampshire meeting"—she tilted her head in my direction—"the world's only Chinese chef whose ancestors came over on the *Mayflower?*"

"Some friends were going skiing in New Hampshire," Corinne said, and I remembered the conversation she'd been having on the phone back at that rest stop. "I thought it was a good idea to get out of town as quickly as I could. They were going in that direction."

"So why are you here?" Ms. Masterson said, and then quickly added, "Not that you have to tell me. I'm just curious."

I interrupted. "It's been my familial experience that people in law enforcement aren't ever 'just curious.' They don't even ask you your favorite ice cream flavor without some reason."

"You're cynical for one so young," Ms. Masterson said. "The truth is I'm kind of a romantic."

"I don't doubt it," I said. "First thing I think of when I hear 'FBI agent' is 'romantic.' Maybe it's the gun thing."

"Give me a break," Ms. Masterson said. "You told me you met Corinne on the road. You take her to Buffalo, then she calls you to pick her up, and now here are the two of you, sitting together next to one another. Come on. Are you telling me this doesn't have all the makings for a love story?"

"I'm thinking of asking her to the prom."

"Would it be any less romantic if I told you somebody came to my friend's work and was asking about me?" Corinne said.

Ms. Masterson straightened. Her expression changed. Not dramatically. But we went from having a "just some new friends having a conversation" to "just the facts, ma'am." We went there in about a quarter second. Ms. Masterson, I decided, wasn't an amateur.

"Any idea how someone would have known you had gone to Buffalo?" she asked Corinne, who shook her head.

"Are you concerned about your safety now?" Ms. Masterson asked her.

"St. Louis is a long way from Buffalo—and even farther from Montreal. No one but Ariadna knows I'm here."

"So what're your plans now?"

"Stay in St. Louis for a while," Corinne said. "Maybe get a job waiting tables at the place where the Master Chef here is cooking." She looked at me.

"See," Ms. Masterson said, relaxing a little. "I told you. I'm a trained detective, and I'm telling you, all the clues are pointing to romance."

"I hope your crime-fighting skills are better than your detective work," I said.

Before she could answer, her phone buzzed. She took it from her purse and checked it, then excused herself. "I have an appointment," she said. "But let me know if you think of anything else that might be of use."

"She's a nice person," Corinne said, after Ms. Masterson had gone. She offered me the last bite of her cinnamon roll. I accepted. It wasn't bad. Not as good as the one in the rest stop. But not bad.

"She is," I said. "You should have asked to see her badge, though. It really does look pretty cool."

19

Rule #22: *No matter how bored you are in a situation, it could always be more boring sitting in the dress department of a clothing store.*

Over the next two days, we got Corinne moved into an apartment in a building one over from where Langston and I were living. A friend of Langston, one he had high hopes of eventually making more than just that, had an empty bedroom. Her name was Bao Yu. Around non-Chinese, she went by Jade. Which I kind of liked because unlike most Americanized versions of Chinese names that seemed to be picked completely at random for no reason except to sound as awkward or dated as possible, "jade" in Mandarin is *yu.* So it sort of made sense. Bao Yu — "Precious Jade" — was waitressing at the Eastern Palace.

The move didn't take long. Corinne's only possession seemed to be the bag that had been sitting at her feet when I met her. After I hauled it up to Bao Yu's apartment, I took Corinne to the Eastern Palace. I introduced her and pointedly explained to Mr. Leong and his wife that she was just a friend and not a girlfriend, and they immediately began referring to her as my girlfriend. Mr. Leong asked if she had any experience waiting tables. She did, she told them. She'd worked summers in a Chinese seafood restaurant in the International District in Seattle.

"What were you doing in Seattle?" I asked her.

"Growing up," she said. "I was born there."

"Wow," I said. "You're quite the woman of mystery."

"You bring girlfriend in here, you two be all time making love talk, making flirt talk," Mr. Leong said, interrupting us. "You not be working. You be wasting time. My time."

"You still have family there?" I asked.

She shook her head. "My parents died four years ago."

"I'm sorry."

"Car wreck," she said. Which was thoughtful. Not thoughtful that her parents died in a car crash. But thoughtful to tell me what it was. Sometimes somebody will reveal something, like "I'm going to die soon," and then not say anything else, and you wonder if you're supposed to pursue the conversation or if you're just supposed to say, "Okay," and let it go. It would have been gruesome and maybe too pushy for me to ask how her parents died. I appreciated her telling me. I also noted that she didn't break up or become emotional about it. She just gave me the information. Which meant she had come to terms with it. Or maybe she didn't want to show any of her feelings about it to me. I found myself hoping it was the former.

"I no have time pay for people to stand around making love talk," Mr. Leong said. "You want job making flirt talk, you go somewhere else."

We promised we would not utter so much as a syllable of love talk between us. Or flirt talk. I'm not sure if that assurance was what sold him. Still, he told Corinne to show up the next day to work lunch. We left the restaurant and walked out into the bright sun. It was chilly.

"You know when Mr. Leong said 'You got good dress, nice dress'?" Corinne asked me as we were walking down the alley to get back to the car.

"Yes," I said. "Mr. Leong's English is only slightly more successful than his comb-over, in case you hadn't noticed."

"Well," she said, "me no got good dress."

"No nice dress, either?" I asked.

"No nice dress."

"We go mall," I said. "You get good dress, get nice dress."

We then had to call a moratorium on speaking Leong-style pidgin because we couldn't stop laughing and I was trying to drive. While Corinne tried on some dresses at the mall, I sat outside the dressing room and, looking at the mannequins, tried to remember if I'd ever seen a real female with a neck anywhere near as long as these. I thought about Tucker's Rule #22: No matter how bored you are in a situation, it could always be more boring sitting in the dress department of a clothing store. I had made that one up as a child, when I'd had to go shopping with my mother. I'd always figured no matter how bored I was, I could be thankful I wasn't sitting in a women's apparel department. And now there I was. And I reflected that I had been right. Corinne came out of the dressing room and showed me the first one, a sleeveless black dress. It looked nice on her. Which is like saying it's cold in New Hampshire in the winter. It looked *really* nice.

"Jeez," I said. "You're a girl."

"That sounds suspiciously close to flirt talk," Corinne said. She turned away from me a second too late to hide her flushing face.

Ms. Masterson called me later that afternoon. I'd dropped Corinne and her new dresses at her apartment building. I went back to my own apartment and was thinking about dinner when Ms. Masterson called to ask how things were going. I told her. About Corinne's new job. And about going to the mall for dress shopping. I did not tell her how nice Corinne had looked in the dress. I didn't think full disclosure was necessary.

"Can I ask you something, a favor completely unrelated?" Ms. Masterson asked.

"Sure," I said.

"How would you feel about me coming by the restaurant during your slack times," she said, "and you giving me some cooking lessons?"

"FBI not paying enough?" I asked her. "You need to take a second job making shrimp fried rice?"

"I want to impress my boyfriend," she said. "He thinks I'm a lousy cook."

"Is he right?"

"Completely," she said. "Embarrassingly. Which would normally be okay. But he's kind of an amateur gourmet. If you can teach me some basics—like, say, that cucumber recipe you fed me the other day—I might be able to change his opinion."

We made plans for her to come in during the lull between lunch and dinner. I told Corinne about it the next afternoon when she was coming in to work the dinner shift.

"She's kind of driven, isn't she?" Corinne said. "She must have checked you out pretty thoroughly to know your ancestors came over on the *Mayflower*."

"You mean that crack she made about me being the only Chinese chef who isn't Chinese?" When she nodded, I answered, "First, there are lots of non-Chinese who can cook Chinese food, obviously."

"Just none as good as you are," she said.

"Also obvious."

"Or at least think you are."

"And second," I said, "My ancestors didn't come over on the *Mayflower*."

"They probably waited until the butler and the maids could go over first and get the house in order, right?"

"I come from a modest past," I said.

"Modesty must have worn off some time back," Corinne said.

I let that slide. "She *is* an interesting person. She's also worried about us."

"Why do you say that?" Corinne asked.

"She probably does have a gourmet boyfriend," I said. "And she does want to learn to cook some Chinese food. But if she's here at the restaurant learning to cook, that's also a reason for her to be around the restaurant where we're both working, to keep an eye on us in case there's any trouble."

Corinne pursed her lips. She had her hair pulled back and up into a loose bun. It made her look older. I saw Mr. and Mrs. Hsiang coming through the door. They'd already called ahead to plan a menu for a party of ten they'd invited.

"Then, too," I said, "you heard her theory on us. She might just want to hang around to see if we do have all the makings of a love story."

"Do we?" Corinne asked.

Before I had a chance to reply, she'd turned away to go greet the Hsiangs as they were seated. Which was just as well. Because I wasn't sure how I was supposed to answer that.

20

Rule #11: *Timing is everything.*

Snow sprinkled, drifting. Lazily. The flakes weren't coming down hard, like in a good snowstorm. Just kind of floating, working their way to the ground on their own good time. The dark air was so still that the flakes barely swayed at all as they came down, illuminated in a cone of light under the streetlight. I was thinking how much I enjoyed routine. I knew it wasn't supposed to be that way. Young guys, throwing off electric sparks of testosterone like a whip-cracking power line after a storm, are supposed to be jockish he-mannered dervishes of spontaneity. I considered myself as virile and adventurous as any other guy who might be ready to pose for a men's deodorant ad. I'd bounced out of New Hampshire and into this new place with what I thought of as fairly impressive aplomb. Devil-may-care spontaneity. I had to admit, though, I liked the ordinariness of a daily routine. Sleep late, get up, and practice *xing-i* in the alley with Langston. Then off to the Eastern Palace with Corinne, to cook and swear with Li and Jao-long until closing. Late dinner, usually eaten in the kitchen at the Eastern Palace or in the kitchen of one of the other places right around there. Then drive Corinne and myself back to our apartments, and off to bed to do the same thing all over again the next day. It was pleasant. Maybe a little boring if you thought about it too much. I didn't. I was happy.

Our apartments were close enough I'd park the Toyota on the street between the two. I went left, Corinne went right. We said goodbye. The front door to her building, inside an arched alcove, was so close that on a still night I could hear the metallic click when she pushed the key into the lock. It was a week after our conversation about Ms. Masterson and the matter of crushes, one night near the end of March, when we'd done just that, said good-bye after I drove us home from work. I walked toward my apartment next door. I didn't hear a click. I stopped, turned around, and started walking toward the entrance of her apartment building. Then I started to sprint.

One guy had Corinne pressed against the door. He was leaning against her. His forearm was pushed across her throat. Another guy was standing a couple of feet away. He was facing her with his back to the sidewalk. So neither of them noticed when I came up the walk behind them. I had on the running shoes I always wore in the kitchen. The treads were probably impregnated with enough grease to fry eggs in. It coated them, made them quiet. I'd already dropped my coat on the lawn. I could tell they were Chinese. It was dark; they weren't much more than silhouettes, outlined against the light from above the door to Corinne's building. There was something in the way they moved, though. The body language gave it away. It wasn't anything I could explain. Nothing obvious. A certain slackness in the shoulders, legs bent. There isn't some infallible sign for identifying Chinese people just by their outline from behind. Even so, I knew it.

Taking off my coat had been a gamble. It was the big, puffy insulated one I'd worn for three New Hampshire winters in school. The one I'd slept under that first night with Corinne in the Toyota. A heavy parka is a nice layer of protection between your flesh and a knife, if a villain happens to be carrying one. It can even be good padding against a punch, blunting the force. It would have slowed me down, though. Against two guys, I didn't want to be slow. By the time I was within range of the guy who wasn't holding Corinne, I could reach him with my outstretched hands. I did.

I grabbed both his shoulders from behind and dropped my own. I dropped them the way you would to close a car trunk lid that was almost shut but hadn't quite clicked closed. No power in my shoulders or arms, no windup. Just dropping, transferring my body weight through my relaxed arms. Not losing any power by tightening my muscles at all. Humans have a lot of balance to the front, with our feet spread out below. From behind, it's only the heels keeping us upright. And they roll back nicely when there's a pulling, jerking motion from behind. The guy went down. Hard.

I stepped past him even before he hit the ground. I heard his head snap back and make a dull *thwack* against the sidewalk. The other guy still had his left forearm pinning Corinne's throat, his right outstretched, his palm flat against the door. His weight was going forward, leaning against her. He was just turning at the sound of his colleague going down when I kicked in a hooking motion, raising my foot just far enough off the path to clear the ground. So the front of my ankle hit the front of his. His leg went out from under him. He was twisting and slipping, turning toward me, his arm coming off Corinne's neck as he tried to reach out to the ground that was coming up fast. I was close enough I didn't have to step at all. I brought my left hand up, palm open, like I was cradling a baby's head in it. Except I was hitting him with my open hand, right under the chin, at the top of his neck where it joined his head. A solid shot might have provided enough whiplash to mess up his vertebrae. Mine slipped off his jaw. Still, it hit with enough force that his head rocked back. His knees hit the ground. He pitched forward, onto his elbows. I punted into his midsection, aiming for the lowest part of his rib cage. He was wearing a jacket, a heavy one. Even so, the toes of my shoe made nice solid contact. I felt the impact. I heard him make a high-pitched squeal. I saw his face as he rolled away from me, expecting me to kick him again. I had been right. He was

Chinese. I looked at the other guy. He was trying to sit up. It was going slowly. His head had taken a hard smack. He was Chinese too.

Corinne's key was still in the lock. I turned it and pushed the door open and shoved her inside, then followed. It would have been satisfying to have gone back and confronted the bad guys. Put my hands on my hips and snarled, *Ready for some more?* It's a great way to get shot. Just because you've brought your hands to a fight doesn't mean the other guy hasn't brought a gun. Even if they hadn't, two against one is not good odds. The door clicked shut behind us. It was thick, heavy oak. Except for a small round window, it was solid. I'd never given much consideration to how comforting a thick door can be. Then I was pushing Corinne up the stairs toward her apartment.

"Don't stop," I said. She didn't. Neither did I.

I fished my phone out of my pants and called 911 as soon as we'd gotten into the apartment and I asked if she was okay. She nodded. "You sure?" I asked. She was. At least she said she was. She looked scared. Her eyes were wide and a little glazed. I could see her nostrils, still flaring in and out. She had all her color, though. I didn't think she was going to pass out. She was shaking. She jammed her hands into her coat pockets when she realized it.

Two patrol cars arrived, quickly. I went back downstairs to let the cops in when they rang the bell. The pulsing red lights from the cars at the curb had replaced the soft yellow streetlights. It was still snowing, a little harder. The flakes looked pinkish in the glare. The bad guys were gone.

"Whose coat?" one of them asked me, holding up mine, which he'd picked up off the lawn. I took it, and they came inside behind me. We all went up to Corinne's apartment.

I'd never been a victim of a violent crime before. In the strict sense, I guess, I still wasn't. Corinne was. For a victim, she was taking it well. The cops were helping. As soon as they met her, one of them got on his radio and said something in cop-ese, one of those sentences that have more numbers in it than words. Within a few minutes, while they were still taking down the initial information, a female officer showed up.

"Do you want to go someplace and talk alone?" she asked Corinne. Corinne shook her head. The officer had a soothing voice. She managed to sound solicitous and calm at the same time. Bao Yu was working that night and going to a party afterward. Langston had told me about it. He'd been invited too. (He still had what he called his "plan" for wooing Bao Yu. I thought "hope" might be a more accurate verb than "plan.") While Corinne sat with the female cop in the living room and gave her statement, I went into the kitchen to put a kettle on the burner. One of the other cops followed me in.

"Tea," I said. "It's sort of the universal lubricant for Chinese. When she gets finished talking with all of you, she's going to want some."

While the water started hissing its way to a boil, we sat at the table and I told him about the excitement from my angle. If he was impressed by my near-superhuman fighting skills, taking on two guys, he didn't mention it. I kind of wanted him to be awed, to ask where I'd developed such incredible powers so I could be modest about it. He didn't. He asked if I carried a cell phone, and when I told him I did, he said, "Might be a good idea to call us before you wade into a situation like that. It could have been dangerous for you."

"Think it would have been less dangerous for her if I'd called and waited for you?"

"No," he said. "I'm just required to say that. I'd have been just as happy if you'd beaten them both to an ugly pulp."

It took about an hour to fill out all the questionnaires and forms, for us to sign statements as to the particulars of the event, statements that we were offered medical help and didn't want it, and I think maybe a statement in there somewhere that we were not now nor had we ever been members of the Communist Party. I was tired and distracted. I had that lump in my stomach that comes from an adrenaline dump. I felt a little queasy. More than a little, actually. I wanted to go to the toilet in Corinne's apartment and see if something was going to come out from one end or the other. I didn't, though. It didn't seem like something the hero was supposed to be doing. And so far, I was giving myself some decent scores for heroics. I also knew the feeling would pass. Even so, that didn't make me feel too much better. After the cops finally left, Corinne and I sat on the couch and drank tea and held hands. After a while, when the tea had started to dissolve the lump inside me and the tiredness became almost overwhelming, I said, "I ought to leave so you can get some sleep."

Corinne nodded. We both stood and walked to the door, still holding hands. We stood there for a second. She finally let go of my hand and put her arms around me. I could smell her hair. She'd taken it down from the bun she'd worn it in at the restaurant. It looked like it did the night I'd met her. Without the stocking cap. That night at the rest stop in New Hampshire seemed like a very long time ago.

"Come on," she said. She took my hand. We went into her room and lay on her bed, still dressed. She let go of my hand to pull up the quilt that was folded at the bottom of the bed. She pulled it over us, then she lay back down beside me and rolled on her side. We wrapped our arms around one another.

"This is awkward, isn't it?" I said, after we'd both been quiet for a while.

"It is," Corinne said. "But not as much as I thought it would be."

"Had you given much thought to that?" I asked. "To what it would be like?"

"Wouldn't you like to know."

"I would."

"Well," she said, "here's what I'd like to know. I want to know which of your rules applies to this."

"This?"

"This. Right now. Right here."

"Let me think about it for a second," I said. I thought. Not about the rules, though. I thought about the fragrance of her hair, faint, but like the aroma of flowers that had been in a room recently, then taken away and were now just a perfumed memory. And the pulse I saw gently, steadily throbbing in the hollow of her throat. I thought about her hand, resting lightly on my stomach. I'd felt her fingers brush against me there. Twice. Then again. I thought about whether it was just a reflexive movement or if there was something deliberate about it. I thought about the whole length of her, stretched out beside me. I thought about my arm going to sleep under her head and about how much longer I could hold it there, and I decided I could probably hold it there a hell of a lot longer than I would have, until that moment, imagined. I thought about the pool of warmth around us that seemed like a space that was at the same time very, very small and simultaneously all the room I would ever need or want.

"Come up with anything?" she asked after a while, interrupting all those thoughts and a whole lot more.

Coming up with something, I thought, but didn't say. "In moments like this," I did say, "I apply Tucker's Rule Number Eleven: 'Timing is everything.'

"Timing," I said. "Not doing anything too soon, because it might ruin things."

"Timing can mean not waiting too long, though," Corinne said, "and having things get ruined that way too."

Oh, Corinne, don't I know it, I thought. But I didn't say it. And she didn't say anything else either. It was a long time before I heard her breathing deepen, and then she started making those soft puffy sounds I'd heard that first night in the Toyota, back in New Hampshire. I looked out the window. The yellow light of the streetlamp was back. The patrol cars and their rotating red lights were long gone. The snow was coming down, a little harder now. I watched it.

"So much for routine," I said very softly, to myself. So I wouldn't wake her.

Next morning, after I went back to my place, I showered and shaved and ate some leftover minced pork with chives that Langston had brought home a couple of nights before. Then I called Ms. Masterson and told her about the adventure.

"The cops said there's been a Vietnamese gang in the area," I said, after I told her what had happened. "The gangs are going after Chinese who live around here. They know a lot of them work in restaurants and get paid in cash and get home late at night. Convenient targets. So it could have been just a random try at a robbery."

"Were the guys Vietnamese?" she asked me.

"Nope," I said. "They were Chinese."

"Think it was a random robbery attempt?" she said.

"Nope."

"Me neither."

21

Rule #43: *You can put almost whatever you want in fried rice, but if the rice isn't cold when it goes into the wok, you won't be happy with it.*

I started picking Corinne up before work. She had been meeting me outside, on the street where I parked the Toyota. Ms. Masterson suggested we might want to exercise a little more caution. It was kind of nice. I'd buzz to be let in the outer door, where I'd had the stimulating encounter with Corinne's two muggers. Either Bao Yu or Corinne would buzz me in. Then I'd knock on their apartment door, and Bao Yu would yell loud enough so I could hear her, "Wenqian, your boyfriend's here!" Which I did not dispute in any way, since if I had, Bao Yu would have figured I was sensitive about it and would have teased me mercilessly about it. Or maybe I didn't dispute it for some other reason. I wasn't sure. I was sure I didn't want to think about it too much. And off we'd go, to work. Sometimes, if Bao Yu was working the same shift, it was the three of us.

Corinne and I joked about the mugging a little. I told her she'd probably invited the assault by walking up the sidewalk in such an obviously uppity manner.

"If you'd carried yourself in a more subservient way," I said, "they never would have picked on you. If you'd bound your feet like a proper Chinese woman, it never would have happened."

"For a master of mayhem, you sure took your time getting there," she said. "Were you waiting for them to exhaust themselves ravishing me before you jumped in?"

It wasn't very funny. It helped, though, to take the edge off the fear, the sick feeling we both had, I think, that things could have turned out much, much differently. What we didn't talk about at all was what had happened later that night. We hadn't held hands, hadn't touched at all, since then. I don't think either of us knew why. I sure didn't. I just knew it wasn't the right time. Not yet. I knew that part of the reason it wasn't the right time was that there was still something Corinne didn't want to talk about.

Once we were at the Eastern Palace, I got busy enough and so did Corinne, so we didn't talk much at all.

When everything is humming, when orders are coming in and going out, it's what's called in the slang of the Chinese kitchen "a busy anthill." If you look at an anthill from a human perspective, it looks like lots of random motion, chaos really. From the ants' point of view, though, every ant knows what it's supposed to be doing and is doing it. Especially at peak times during lunch and dinner, the action might have looked frantic from the view of a customer peeking into the kitchen. Corinne and Bao Yu and the other waitresses would come through the kitchen door at the Eastern Palace and give us the orders they'd just taken from diners. They just shouted them at us. In kitchens like ours, where everyone spoke Mandarin, the orders were in Mandarin. In places where there was a mix of Cantonese or other dialects, the fallback language was always English. The waitresses also wrote tickets for each order when they took them. These slips got stuck into metal clips fixed to a string that ran along an overhead pot rack. We never looked at them, though. We heard the orders; we knew who in the kitchen was working on which dishes on that particular night.

During lunch, when most of the customers were non-Chinese, mostly local office workers, it wasn't too tough. I helped Li and Jao-long with the simple stuff from the menu. Kung pao chicken. Broccoli and beef. Sweet and sour pork. Dishes that could be put together by combining basic ingredients and basic sauces. I could make some of these and still have time to prep for the evening when I was going to be cooking the more authentic dishes that were earning me my paycheck. We could all make on autopilot the food that the majority of our lunch crowd liked. In a Chinese restaurant, the expression we used for it was *shumu-zhu,* "cooking by the numbers."

Working in a Chinese kitchen, maybe working in any restaurant kitchen—I wouldn't know; I'd never worked in any of them that weren't Chinese—is sort of like dating had been for me during my recent, and abbreviated, college career. I'd go weekend after weekend without even the remote possibility of getting a date. Then, just when my romantic fortunes would begin to make the monastic life look like a debauched Roman orgy by comparison, there would be Amber Hershall. And her incredible blue eyes. Standing right next to me and smiling with those perfect teeth and saying, "So are you *ever* going to ask me out?" And a day later—one day later—during a commercial break in the show about kids growing up in a fifties I suspected never actually existed in the real fifties, my trusty roommate, Toby Ingersoll, would look up from the screen and say, "Hey, I keep forgetting to tell you. This girl in my trig class thinks you're really cute; she's asked me a couple of times to introduce her to you." And my dating life would go from the Dust Bowl to the glorious abundance of Happy Valley, just that quickly.

Business in a Chinese restaurant was something like that. Slow periods, when we'd stand around bored, then times when we'd be too busy to take a restroom break. Every day, though, tended to have its own reasonably predictable rhythms. There was the early dinner crowd, then a lull, then the later crowd that rolled in after going to the movies or to a concert. All of them tended toward the cooking-by-the-numbers dishes we served at lunch. Usually they hung around a long time too, keeping Corinne and the other waitresses busy. Later in the evening, the crowd would turn Chinese. That's when I did most of my work. Of course, just when it seemed like a dependable routine, Mr. Leong would stick his head into the kitchen and it would be, "Listen, listen! Mr. Chen coming in this evening! You know Mr. Chen? Oil-Splashed Duck Chen?"

Mr. Leong identified all his best customers by their favorite dishes. If Oil-Splashed Duck Chen was coming, we knew we'd have to get a duck into a stock pot quickly so we could boil it, then toss it into another pot of ice water so the skin would shrink and tighten. Then we'd pour ladles of hot, pepper-spiked oil over it after it was cut and laid out for a dramatic presentation. Mr. Chen would also want half a dozen other dishes; he always brought at least six guests with him, and we'd have to come up with a menu that worked well with the duck. When Oil-Splashed Duck Chen was coming unexpectedly, or Five Fragrances Phoenix Lin, or any of the other regular customers at the Eastern Palace who expected real Chinese food, it could go from a quiet night to a frantic one very quickly.

As it was, Ms. Masterson came in for her first lesson early in the afternoon, when the dining room was nearly empty. I'd only seen her in work suits. She came into the kitchen wearing jeans and an untucked purple T-shirt with a Northwestern University logo. When she turned around, I could see a bulge at her waist, under the shirt. She was carrying her gun. When I asked where she wanted to start, she asked me to show her how to make fried rice. It caught me off-guard. I forgot about the question I wanted to ask her, which was "Does Northwestern have a girl's field hockey team?"

"You're kidding?" I said instead.

"I thought fried rice was appropriate for a first lesson."

"Yeah," I said, "in the sense that going to the kitchen of a four-star restaurant in Paris for a cooking lesson and asking to learn how to make a peanut butter sandwich would be appropriate."

Ms. Masterson folded her arms. It caused her shirt to ride up just a bit so I could see the bottom of her gun's leather holster. "What are you going to start me out on, then?" she said. "Peking duck? What part of 'I don't know anything about cooking' didn't you understand?"

"I see your point," I said. "It's just that fried rice in Chinese cooking is a way to use up leftovers. You think of it more as something you throw together from the refrigerator, not a real meal."

We got started. I showed her how to get the ingredients ready. Most Chinese cooking, and all of it that depends on a wok, is about getting things done quickly and smoothly.

"In a French kitchen, it's called *mise en place*," I told her. "In Chinese, we call it 'waiting for the east wind.'" The expression came from some strategist back in the Tang Dynasty, whose army was fighting an enemy attacking with ships. A strategist advised his general to maneuver his own fleet in a way so the enemy's ships would be lined up side by side in front of him. Then the general waited for the wind to change, to the east, so he could set fire to the first enemy ship. He knew the breeze would carry the fire to all the rest. Get everything lined up and ready to go, and you only have to wait for the east wind to get it all done.

I took some rice from a tub in the cooler that we prepped every night. Most home cooks trying to make fried rice use fresh, warm rice. Rice fresh from the cooker, I explained to Ms. Masterson, will be too sticky, though, for good fried rice. After it's cooled overnight, the grains separate, so every grain can get a thin coating of peanut oil when it hits the pan. That's what gives *chao fan*— fried rice—its nutty flavor.

"And forget the soy sauce," I told her, as she used a spatula to shovel the rice, sizzling and crackling, around in the hot wok.

"That's strictly a takeout restaurant approach." Instead, I had her toss in a sprinkle of rough sea salt. Then we added the ingredients I'd assembled: cubes of Jinhua ham—"You can use Smithfield ham," I told her—along with peas and a scrambled egg and a sprinkle of green onions. When it was starting to get popping hot, with grains of rice starting to twitch and jump in the wok, I used my own spatula to scoop a couple servings into bowls. She manipulated her chopsticks with some enthusiasm and a lot less skill. (Someday I'm going to conduct research on why it's so difficult for some non-Asians to use chopsticks without looking like they're trying to remove an appendix while wearing mittens.)

"What do you think?" she asked me.

"Not too bad for your first time."

"You're right," she said. "It isn't. And I have to admit, it's a lot better than what I get in those little carry-out boxes."

We moved a couple of chairs from one corner of the kitchen over to the prep table and sat and ate.

"They're going to make another run at her," she said, in between bites.

"Who?" I asked, even though I knew the answer.

"The guys who jumped your girlfriend," Ms. Masterson said. "Do you have any idea what this might be about?"

I shook my head. "You know pretty much everything I know."

Ms. Masterson put down her chopsticks. It looked almost like she was relieved. She stretched her fingers and wriggled them like she was playing a piano. I thought about asking her if she'd like a fork. I thought it might hurt her feelings. I thought about correcting her on the "girlfriend" reference. Just like with Bao Yu, I wasn't sure why I let it go.

"And what we know is this," she said. "Corinne's boss is gone, along with, presumably, a rather substantial quantity of diamonds. Somebody thinks Corinne knows something about either the whereabouts of her missing boss or the missing diamonds, or both. Whoever it is does not appear to be disinclined to using threats and physical force to get some answers."

She picked up her chopsticks again and gently tapped them on the table. I didn't say anything. Rapping chopsticks on a table or plate like that, to even them out in one's grip, is very bad manners in Chinese etiquette. Westerners do it a lot. They don't understand that they shouldn't. I figured, though, that it was not my job to educate the Western world about the nuances of Chinese dining etiquette. I had enough problems of my own.

"And it is reasonable to conclude, as well," she went on, "that these people are going to try to get to her again and to you, as well, now that the two of you are connected."

I nodded. "Reasonable to conclude."

"So," she said, "what do you think?"

I looked at the bowl in front of me. There were about half a dozen grains of rice still sticking to its sides. Chinese mothers tell their children every grain of rice that's left in the bowl uneaten represents a tear the farmer will shed out of sorrow for the part of his crop going to waste.

"I think I've never heard anyone in the law enforcement community use the words 'whereabouts' and 'disinclined' in the same conversation."

"Well," Ms. Masterson said, "keep your eyes open and pay attention to what's going on and stick around. I have a feeling there are going to be some more new experiences for you coming down the road."

22

Rule #35: *Cultural stereotypes are invariably narrow-minded and unreliable, and don't ever be surprised when they turn out to be true.*

"You teach police lady make fried rice?" Mr. Leong asked me the next afternoon. There were only a few customers in the dining room, late lunches. The lull. I was using the time to prep for the dinner rush, slicing through the root stems of big heads of Chinese cabbage so I could separate the leaves. I'd pack the leaves into a pot in layers, putting baseball-size balls of ground pork in between them, pouring on some broth, then cooking it for the next few hours to make *shitzi tou*, "lion's head," a braised stew from eastern China. Mr. Shen had already made reservations for dinner that evening. I knew he'd want the lion's head on his table.

"Yep," I said. "I gave her a lesson. I think you might want to think about hiring her now. We could use another cook around here."

He ignored me. "You remember before you leave go get your girlfriend, I tell you something, I want to talk with you?"

I didn't. I'd forgotten all about it. I nodded anyway.

"You think maybe you best Chinese cook in city?" he asked.

"I don't know."

"You think anybody better?" he asked. "You think you friend Wu better?"

"He might be close," I said.

"You like chance? Chance prove it?" Mr. Leong said. "We have contest."

"Who we?" I asked.

"We," Mr. Leong said, vaguely annoyed. "Us." It never seemed to bother him when I answered him in his same pidgin. I'd been around Mr. Leong long enough to get away with ribbing him a bit by responding to his pidgin with some of my own. He was irritated because I didn't seem to be getting whatever the idea was.

"Lots of owners of Chinese places here in town. We decide to have contest, see who best Chinese chef St. Louis."

"Oh," I said. Being the best Chinese chef in St. Louis was, I thought, roughly like being the best downhill skier in Haiti.

"We make bet."

"*Ohhh.*"

It would be culturally insensitive to suggest that gambling is to a lot of adult Chinese males what heroin is to a junkie. Or that it is what a big, warm yard light is to moths on a June night. It would be racially stereotyping to note that historically Chinese gamblers have lost fortunes, houses, everything they own, betting on anything from card games to cricket fights. It would be an act of cultural insensitivity to note that much of the crime in Chinatowns all over the country, Chinatowns all over the world—as well as much of the socialization, parties, and get-togethers there—all revolve around gambling in one form or another. From old ladies playing mahjong to bigtime gangsters betting on horse races or on whether the next woman who walks by will be wearing yellow. I dislike stereotyping. And racist generalizations. And cultural insensitivity. That said, I was not completely floored when Mr. Leong mentioned that there was a bet involved in the proposed competition.

"I tell them you best," he said to me. "You prove me right, yeah?"

"I do, what I get?" I asked.

"You be famous," Mr. Leong said, breaking out into a broad grin. "You be most famous Chinese cook in St. Louis who not Chinese."

"Sad to think I've already peaked so young in life, isn't it?" I asked. He'd already walked out the kitchen though, leaving me to the cabbage leaves.

23

Rule #72: *Never depend upon luck, but don't ignore how really valuable it is.*

It wasn't quite spring yet, not in the "birds are singing and flowers are in blossom" sense of spring. Not yet. It was still chilly. Langston and I weren't talking. We didn't talk much when we were practicing together. We were going through a sequence, exchanging attacks and counters, sort of like sparring boxers. We knew them so well, we could do them on autopilot, letting our minds drift, the same way a pianist can cruise through a piece of music without focusing directly on it all the time. If we did that, if we did start mentally drifting, we weren't doing *xing-i* anymore, though. The second either or both of us lost focus, it just turned into dancing. We didn't dance. We concentrated on what we were doing.

In *xing-i*, the idea is to constantly move forward. Even if I stepped back, away from an attack, my hand or my foot was moving forward, striking or trapping Langston's arm, grabbing him, and pulling him in to me. Sometimes I stepped straight in to attack, sometimes I came forward at an angle, sometimes I swerved so I was coming at him in a curving kind of swoop, trying to catch him on a blind side, from an offbeat direction. But always I was driving forward until I completed the sequence, then I began moving back while he unleashed his side of the exercise.

"That's kind of not my personality," I once said to Langston's uncle when he was teaching us back in Andover. "I prefer to go around things when I get into trouble. I even have a rule about that."

"I know," he said. "That's why *xing-i* is good for you. Makes you confront something inside you that doesn't always come out."

I had a feeling even then that there were probably some things that really didn't need any coming out from inside me. Some things that were best left inside. I shut up, though, and kept training. I was doing the same thing now.

Since we were working out in our alley behind the apartment, there weren't many onlookers. Sometimes people stopped briefly to watch us as they walked to their cars in the stalls behind the apartment building. They usually didn't stay long. Mrs. Trahn continued to ignore us when she walked by on her way home from the market every day. There must have been a time when martial arts were exotic stuff in the United States. That was a long time ago, though. Everyone's seen them on TV, in movies. For most people, what Langston and I were doing was about as exotic as throwing a football around. But probably not as entertaining to watch. *Xing-i* isn't dramatic. Not a lot of jumping around or making gymnastic kicks or twirls in the air. It doesn't look like the stuff on the screen, that's for sure.

Half an hour passed. I was aware that someone had come up behind me and was a few yards away now. If it had been any kind of threat, Langston would have reacted to it. Since I didn't see anything in his face, I assumed it was just somebody hanging out. We finished the set. I turned around. It was Ms. Masterson. And a man. He was a little taller than her. Thin, wiry. Maybe military. More likely: cop. Or, given the company he was keeping: Fed.

Ms. Masterson was leaning against the railing of a back porch. The man stood beside her. I held up my palm to Langston. He stopped. We walked over to them.

"This is Joe Cataldi," Ms. Masterson said. "My partner." I introduced Langston.

"Joe's been on another assignment for a while," Ms. Masterson said. "He's going to be looking into the—uh—circumstances you and your girlfriend have somehow gotten yourselves into. So I thought it'd be a good idea to come by and introduce you."

"You guys look pretty good," Mr. Cataldi said. He gestured to where Langston and I had been practicing.

"For a member of the law enforcement community," I said, "you're not very observant."

Most cops, most people in law enforcement who actually have to deal with bad guys in a physical way, don't think much of Asian martial arts. With good reason. First, most of those arts, the way they're practiced in the West, are less about real fighting and more about posing or about winning competitions or about indulging in adolescent fantasies. People who get involved with them, especially guys, tend to think they're a lot tougher and a lot more skilled than they actually are. Most of the martial arts popular in this country don't ever require practitioners to actually hit one another or much of anything else in the way of hanging bags or pads. Punching and kicking the air all the time can give an exaggerated sense of skill and power. Very exaggerated. People who have to deal with physical situations on a regular basis—cops, the military—they tend to know a lot more about the realities of fighting than most martial arts "masters" or the guys who strut around with their belts and embroidered uniforms.

"It looked impressive," he said.

"Maybe, Mr. Cataldi," I said. "But that's probably about all it is."

"Come on," he said. "Masterson told me about the run-in you had out front here. Two guys against just you, and you seemed to handle them pretty well."

"No," I said. "I was lucky. It was dark. I came up on them from behind. I got just enough of a jump on them to stun them. Surprise them. We were lucky enough to have a quick escape, to be able to get through a door we could lock behind us."

"Maybe that was more than just luck," Ms. Masterson said. "A lot of being successful in situations like that is being prepared to take advantage of the circumstances. Didn't you tell me something about 'waiting for the east wind'?"

"If one of them had had a gun, that wind would have changed really quickly," I said. "I'd have gotten my ass burned. Fast. And Corinne would have probably been in even more danger than she already was. I was just lucky I didn't make things worse."

Mr. Cataldi nodded. "That can happen no matter how well you're trained, trust me." He asked me about techniques he could use when confronting someone he wanted to arrest. "We had some CQC at the Academy," he said, and he translated for me. "Close-quarter combat. But a lot of it was how to respond to an attack. Guy grabs for you or punches in your direction, tries to take away your gun, here's what you're supposed to do. Thing I always wanted to know more about was how to be the aggressor, how to approach someone who doesn't want to be subdued. Get him arrested and into handcuffs. It seems to me that martial arts, close-quarter stuff, all of it depends on *reacting* to aggression and not being proactive and initiating contact."

"Good point," I said. Then I shrugged. "I'm not really the person to ask. Cops, anybody in law enforcement, are going to have a different perspective than a regular person. If I punch out somebody, there will be a whole different outcome than if you do it. But I think what you want to do is make the bad guy start things, make him think he's being the aggressor, when really it's you who is starting the action and then taking advantage of his reaction."

"Show me," Mr. Cataldi said. He was still standing beside Ms.

Masterson, who was leaning against the porch railing. He took a couple of steps away so he was in front of me. His hands were dangling loosely by his sides.

"Oh boy," I said.

He wrinkled his brow.

"The old 'show me' thing," Langston said. He'd been standing beside me, taking it all in. Langston could be chatty as a grandma over tea. Or, like now, he could be so quiet you would forget he was there until he finally spoke. "Let me explain to you how 'show me' works in a situation like this," he said to Cataldi. "If Tucker tries to show you and you wipe his face with the ground, he looks stupid. If he shows you and he accidentally hurts you, he ends up looking like a bully, going around beating up untrained people."

Mr. Cataldi snorted and smiled. "Come on," he said, "I'm just curious about—"

While he was still talking, I shot my open hand toward his face, like I was stretching out my arm to stop a door from opening. He reacted automatically, raising his arms to just above his waist to intercept my push. I dropped my extended hand so it just touched his elbow. My father had showed me the way cops like to put an arm bar on someone they're trying to arrest, reaching in so their arm slides past the elbow of the suspect, then bending and wrapping around to grab the back of his upper arm, curling it around so the suspect's arm is bent behind his own back. Cataldi, by his initial reaction, was expecting that. As soon as I touched his elbow, I relaxed my hand and my arm. Becoming hard and tense is natural in a fight. It doesn't let you "listen" to an opponent's body when you're touching him, though. I relaxed and felt him start to squeeze his arm against his side. He was anticipating me trying to slide my arm in between him and his side, to make the arm bar. Instead, I let him draw the arm back. I followed, my hand still just touching his elbow, and went with the direction of his energy. At the same time, I stepped, putting my foot between his, and pushed him slightly in the direction he was already going as he tried to pull away from me. His foot caught on mine, he started to stumble, and as he did, he opened his arms again to try to regain his balance. I brushed my hand down, from his elbow to his wrist, then twisted, so his arm came up behind his back. With my free hand, I reached up and took his ear, gently, just grabbing hard enough to hold on. It wasn't going to hurt him unless he tried to pull away. He didn't. It is always surprising for a person to find out just how much it can hurt to have his ear grabbed and pulled.

"Ahhh," he said, "I get it, I get it, I get it." I was behind him, controlling one of his arms and controlling the rest of his body by pinching his ear.

"Got a pair of handcuffs I can borrow?" I asked Ms. Masterson. She was still leaning on the railing.

"That'd be a little too dramatic, don't you think?" she said.

I let go of Cataldi. When he turned, I saw he was still smiling. That was a good sign. Sometimes when you show up a man like that, make him look helpless, he doesn't take it all that well. A lot of guys, even if they've never been in a fight in their lives, secretly think they're fairly bad-ass when it comes to dangerous situations. A lot of other guys secretly think they aren't. They worry about not being tough. So you've got guys who think they're tough but aren't and guys who think they're wimps and probably are, and in either situation, when you make all that painfully obvious, they can react in some weird ways. Added to this was the presence of Ms. Masterson. Males getting shown up in front of females just adds another possible complication to the situation.

"You didn't exactly let me be the aggressor," he said. He was gingerly working his shoulder to make sure it was still functioning. "Don't tell me that was just luck."

"Trust me," Langston said. "It was just luck."

24

Rule #68: *Once the first body shows up, it all becomes a little more complicated.*

I was sitting in the window seat at Langston's apartment, which was now kind of my apartment too. I was looking for a crow I'd seen in the sycamore branches across the street. I didn't see him. Or her. I'm not sure how you tell a boy crow from a girl crow. Unless you are a crow, I suppose it isn't important to be able to do so. Looking for the crow made me realize I'd been here, living with Langston and working at the Eastern Palace and doing with Corinne whatever it was I was doing with her, for long enough I was expecting some reliable familiarity. I didn't see the crow, though. I did see some buds swelling out on the sycamore, little buttons of light, watered-down green. It had been slightly more than a week since Corinne had been mugged at the door of her apartment.

I went over the sequence of that night. I wondered if I could have done anything different. Corinne didn't get hurt. I didn't, either. So I figured all in all I'd done okay. I'd taken on two guys and put both on the ground. There weren't a lot of people who could do that. Even so, when I'd told Mr. Cataldi that luck had played some role in it, I was being honest. Then I thought about being with Corinne after the cops had left that evening. About being on her bed. About the aroma of her hair. Her hand resting on my stomach. It would have been easy. It would have been, I was willing to bet, thinking about it now, pretty great. I hadn't, and for the reason I'd given her. When I'd told her it was about timing, I was being honest with her. Somehow it just didn't seem right, not on the same night she'd been mugged. And maybe, I told myself, as much as I wanted it, there was something inside me that even more didn't want to be cliché. Doing what we'd both contemplated, right then? Too cliché.

I was still thinking about that when my phone rang. It was Ms. Masterson.

"Are you at work?" she asked.

"Nope."

"You know where Corinne is?"

"She's gone for a few days. To Seattle," I added because I knew if I didn't Ms. Masterson would ask.

I'd driven Corinne to the airport. She said she needed to see some family there.

"You still have family in Seattle?" I'd asked her.

"No," she said.

"Oh. Then . . ."

"I'll tell you about it later."

I hadn't pushed it past that. I was beginning to get a sense when Corinne wanted to talk about something and when she didn't. On the subject of Seattle, right at that moment, anyway, I got the distinct impression it was one that fit into the "Didn't Want to Talk About It" column.

"I'm going to come by to pick you up," Ms. Masterson said. In twenty minutes we were in her car, driving toward a complex of buildings that bordered part of the St. Louis Airport, where I'd recently delivered Corinne. This was the back side of the airport, though, away from the terminal. There were lots of rows of buildings, single story, that all looked like warehouses.

"Have you ever seen a body?" she asked.

"That seems a bit forward," I said. "I hardly know you."

"A dead body, Tucker," she said, still looking at the road. "Ever seen one?"

"Both my grandfathers'. At their funerals."

"This will be a little different," she told me. We pulled into the lot of the St. Louis County Medical Examiner's Office. It looked more like the front office for a business in an industrial park than a morgue. As we entered, Ms. Masterson introduced herself to a man in a lab coat. He nodded at me, and she explained, "He's here to assist in identification."

"Have you ever seen a body?" he asked me.

I didn't think my line would be as funny with him. I just told him I had. I was starting to wonder what the deal was. If I'd told Ms. Masterson or him that I hadn't, were they going to send me to a class on Viewing the Dead before they let me have a look at whoever this was supposed to be?

We followed him into the back, through doors that closed behind us tightly with a *whoosh*. It smelled like cleaning chemicals. The morgue looked about what I thought a morgue would look like, although I hadn't really given much thought as to what a morgue would look like, it occurred to me, until we were on the drive over. So my expectations weren't particularly specific.

He was definitely dead. His skin was the same color as chalk. Other than that, he looked like he was sleeping. Although I'd never seen anyone asleep whose chin was touching what looked like uncomfortably near his left shoulder blade. I assumed his neck was broken. Or that he'd been very, very flexible. I could see some bruises. One eye was puffy and swollen.

"Ever seen him before?" she asked.

I nodded. "I ran into him in Buffalo."

"Let's go talk," Ms. Masterson said. I followed her out of the room and into an open area in the lobby, where some plastic chairs looked like they'd been rescued from an airport lounge. I wondered why a morgue needed chairs. You came here, you saw the body, you left. Did a lot of people come here to sit and wait for something? I didn't see any magazines.

"Where is Ms. Chang?" she asked me.

"She went to Seattle for a couple of days," I said. "I told you."

"You're sure that's where she is?"

"I'm sure I took her to the airport and stood beside her while she checked in for a nonstop flight to Seattle, and I'm sure I walked with her to the security line, and I'm sure she went through the line and turned around and waved to me before she went down the concourse."

"So you're pretty sure," Ms. Masterson said.

"Pretty sure," I said. "Why are you asking?"

"I just want to be certain she's all right."

"I can call her and check."

I thought about her cryptic explanation for going. Going to Seattle to see family, although telling me she didn't have any family there. I decided not to mention it to Ms. Masterson.

"Maybe later," Ms. Masterson said. "Right now I want you to tell me about your contact with the late person we just saw."

I told her about my encounter with the guy, that he'd asked me about Corinne but had used her Chinese name, which I hadn't known at the time, and that he'd taken off when I said I didn't know anyone by that name, and that, coincidentally, he seemed not to want to be around when a cop car started down the street. Ms. Masterson didn't ask if I'd punched him. I didn't say I had. I figured I was already in deep enough.

"But this isn't one of the guys who attacked Corinne?" she asked.

I shook my head, then nodded when she asked if I was sure.

"So here in St. Louis, we have a dead Chinese male with whom you had a previous encounter, in Buffalo, New York. A male who shows up dead, who looks like he got that way after being beaten into it. We'll have to wait for the coroner's report, but it's a fair chance that he didn't expire from a heart attack, I think."

I bit my lip. It didn't seem appropriate to grin. I guessed being flippant was Ms. Masterson's way of dealing with these sorts of situations. I could understand that.

"But this dead Chinese male is not one of the Chinese males with whom you had an encounter just last week, right here in St. Louis."

"No," I said.

Ms. Masterson crossed her arms. She sat back in the plastic chair and stretched her legs out in front, examining her shoes. They were black, with low heels. Sensible shoes.

"So there may be no connection."

"Possible," I said. "But unlikely."

"Now it gets a little more complicated," Ms. Masterson said.

"I bet."

25

Rule #54: *Being honest is vastly overrated.*

When I wasn't looking at corpses or wondering what Corinne was doing in Seattle, I was thinking about which dish I was going to present in the "Best Chinese Chef in St. Louis" contest. I thought, too, about my reaction when Mr. Leong told me about the contest. Excited? That would be a little much. Worried? Not really. When he'd asked me about entering the contest—or, to be more exact, telling me that he had entered me—more than anything else I thought it would be fun. Fun in the same way it was fun to be close to Chinese conversations, particularly when the conversations were about stuff they probably didn't particularly want to be overheard. And overhearing them and letting them go on and on, and then casually breaking in to offer some comment. The looks of surprise—incredulity sometimes—that brought on were fun. In a similar way, it was going to be fun to get into this contest.

It was fair to say there wouldn't exactly be a lot of contenders for St. Louis's best Chinese chef. On the other hand, there were a lot of Chinese restaurants in town. Most had Chinese cooks in the kitchen. There was a good-size Chinese and Chinese American population in St. Louis. The fact that I had a job working in the kitchen of a Chinese restaurant and turning out dishes that appealed to Chinese diners who knew what good Chinese food was meant something. I had my doubts that being named the best Chinese chef in the city was going to be the highlight of my cooking career. Still, it was more than jack squat. I had to admit to myself, too, that I kind of liked the idea of being a non-Chinese guy who was at least in the running for the best Chinese chef in the city. So I gave my dish some consideration. Langston and I had talked about it, every morning, at breakfast ever since Mr. Leong had told me about the contest a week before.

"The secret to winning any contest like this is knowing who's judging it," Langston said. He'd been told that the judging panel would consist of some business people in the Chinese American community in St. Louis. "There aren't going to be a lot of *mei-shijia* there. No gourmets who really know Chinese food. We're going to have to cater to their tastes. You could make something spectacular, something that would have a true *meishijia* sobbing tears of happiness, and it might not impress these judges. That makes it tough."

I agreed. There are some classics of Chinese cooking. What-ever Langston was planning for his own entry, he wasn't saying. We were friends. We trusted one another well enough to punch and kick within fractions of an inch the places where we could re-ally do some damage. Langston had told me about his first crush, Mindy Collingswood, way back when we were in fifth grade. He knew about my mother's youngest brother, who got caught try-ing to pass bad checks in Laramie, Wyoming, and spent some time in prison there. For guys barely out of our teens, we had a lot of history. A lot of shared secrets. But for chefs, even chefs who are good friends, there's still some ego involved when it comes to cooking. He didn't tell me what he was planning; I didn't ask. He'd done the same. Which wouldn't have made much difference for me because I still didn't have any idea.

I was standing in the kitchen waiting for the kettle to boil for tea and mulling it over a day after Langston and I had our talk about the contest when there was a knock on the door of the apartment. Corinne was on the other side. She was wearing jeans and a dark red sweater that fit very nicely. She'd returned from

Seattle a couple of days earlier. She gave me a call from the airport when she got back; I drove over and picked her up. I told her about the body and how it had once belonged to the guy who was looking for her in Buffalo. I tried to glance at her face when I gave her the news. It was already evening, though, and dark. I couldn't see any reaction.

"How bad was it to look at the guy?" she asked.

"Better for me than for him," I said.

"You're being flippant," she said. "You're trying to sound casual to hide the fact it must have been pretty gross."

"Partially. It wouldn't look good for me to break into racking sobs in front of you. I'm supposed to be tough and stoic."

"Says who?"

"It was in the *Boys' Manual* we all got issued at birth."

She made a snorting sound and said *"Chee,"* drawing it out, a sound that from a Mandarin speaker meant she thought I was full of crap.

"What kind of reaction do you want me to show?" I said. "Would it help if I became hysterical?"

"You could just be honest," she said, "tell me what you are really feeling."

"Being honest is vastly overrated."

"Which rule is that?"

"Rule Number Fifty-Four." Then I added, "I was scared to go into that morgue. I was worried I'd get sick and heave all over the floor at the sight of a body that got that way by being beaten to death. I didn't," I said. "Just for the record. And, yeah, it looked pretty bad," I went on. "And I wonder if somehow I'm not in some way responsible, indirectly, for that happening to the guy. I don't know how. I do know I'm not going to spend a lot of time fretting over it. Still, I run into the guy a couple of months ago, I punch him—and now he's followed us to St. Louis and somebody beat him to death. It's reasonable to think we're connected in some way."

"So why couldn't you just have said that?" she asked.

"One," I said, "because it's obvious. No need to. Two, because getting all caught up in my feelings might make me less objective and less able to figure out what the hell's going on."

"And three?"

"And three," I said. "Because tough guys have an image of being stoical and it must be maintained at all times."

"Rule number?"

"That's number twenty-six."

She didn't say anything on the ride back to the apartment. We hadn't mentioned it since.

Now, I opened the door and she came in. The sweater, I noted again—and this time more in detail now that she was inside—fit very nicely. I noticed too, as she walked into the kitchen to take the kettle off the stove now that it was at full, steamy whistle, that the jeans fit every bit as well.

"So where are we going again?" she asked over her shoulder.

"Across the river," I said.

"Which one?" she asked. "The Mississippi and the Missouri; they're both right here. I can't keep them straight."

"Mississippi," I said. "It separates Missouri from Illinois. Didn't you have geography in school?"

"Yes," she said. "But appearing not to know as much as a man makes a woman more appealing."

"Says who?"

She opened the cupboard and took out two teacups.

"It was in the *Girls' Manual* we all got issued at birth."

We both had the day off. I hadn't left town since I'd gone to Buffalo, and I wanted to give the Toyota some exercise. And I'd heard about some fish markets over in Illinois that were worth investigating. We set out, the two of us.

The Mississippi carved the border between Illinois and Missouri a few million years ago. As it did, the current left behind bluffs on the Illinois side. Giant ones. Some of them are more than twenty stories tall, towering over the river. The highway Corinne and I took was called the Great River Road. And it was. Pretty great. The bluffs were limestone. They reared up like chalky white palisades, with just enough room at their base for the road, the river flowing right along directly on the other side. Eagles soared and wheeled overhead. The sun was dancing on the rippling, chocolate brown water. It was nice to be driving again like this, out on a highway instead of in town. The Toyota was humming. I'd added about a quart of oil the night before to keep it that way.

In a little riverside town, we stopped at a small café where the booths were situated beside aquariums. Sitting down, diners could look right into them. A snapping turtle the size of a car tire sat on the bottom, slowly rotating his giant dinosaur head and looking dully at us, staring, unblinking. He was alive, I thought, probably before my grandfather was born. A silvery school of catfish glided past. Outside on the lawn where we'd parked, there were long, tubular wire-mesh fish traps that had probably caught some of them. I looked at the catfish while Corinne studied the menu.

"Fried catfish," she read. "Fried crappie. Fried buffalo—buffalo?"

"It's a kind of fish, not the mammal," I said. A solitary catfish nosed over and looked me over through the aquarium glass that separated us. It was almost big enough to consider me on its own menu.

"Fried frog legs, fried turtle." She stopped. "Do you think the salads are fried as well?"

We both had the catfish, and Corinne ordered a bowl of turtle soup. Neither of us took a chance on salad. She dipped her spoon in the soup bowl when it came and took a bite, looking over at the glass wall of the aquarium beside us. The same snapping turtle was still sitting there, staring off at something in the distance I couldn't see. I could have fit both my fists into its mouth with room for a few extra fingers.

"Your brother is delicious," Corinne said to the turtle, speaking Mandarin.

When I turned to look at her, she was holding the spoon out for me, giving me a taste. Her eyes were dark and big. I opened my mouth, and she put the spoon in. Then she went back to her bowl for more. Although I wasn't sure it was the best turtle soup I'd ever tasted, I was reasonably sure it was a spoonful of soup I would remember for a while.

Lunch done, we took the road a little farther north, toward a sign marked FERRY LANDING and pointing toward the river. As we pulled into the gravel lot, we watched a deckhand on the ferry toss a hawser cable back to shore. We'd driven across the Alton Bridge; I thought it would be fun to go back to St. Louis the other way, on the ferry.

"They'll be back in twenty minutes," said a tall man. He had ambled around the side of a squat blue concrete block building beside the gravel drive that led to the ferry dock. He was wearing a woolen knit cap that, given its color, was probably designed to distinguish him from a deer. He yanked at the building's door, giving it a swift jerk when it stuck. From the outside, the place looked like it could have withstood a direct bomb blast. The lettering above the door was faded and had begun to flake. TERRY'S BOAT SUPPLIES & FRESH FISH. When I opened the door with the same jerk he'd applied to shake it loose from the frame, the aroma came out to meet us: it smelled like the bottom of a fishing boat. Inside there were fish everywhere. Catfish, big-headed buffalo, slim little perch, crappie, some others I didn't recognize. They were all lined up on metal trays, glistening on snowbanks of ice. There were a couple of dozen carp, all longer than my arm span. With their thick, horny-looking scales, they looked like they were wearing armor.

"I didn't think Americans ate carp," Corinne said softly. We were walking around looking at the catch.

"Some do," I said. "It's popular in some parts of the South. Some urban blacks eat it. It's kind of a specialty dish."

"Weird."

It was. In Chinese cuisine, carp is prepared in hundreds of different ways. To the Chinese, not eating carp would be like not eating chicken to Americans. The carps' eyes were still shiny wet and bulging. They'd been caught that morning, probably, and were still fresh. The scales were green at the edges, with a delicate pink tinge inside. I gently poked the flank of one. Firm. Meaty. We wandered up and down the rows of tables, looking at the catch for a while. A woman was leaning against the counter at the front, watching a small TV.

"You see anythin' you like, you let me know," she said without looking at us. The man in the flaming orange cap disappeared through another door behind the counter, carrying a length of hose he'd lugged off a shelf.

"You want to get on the next ferry," he said, suddenly coming back out again. "It's almost here." We did, and it was.

We drove the Toyota up on the dock and onto the ferry, nosing it into a space near the bow. I obeyed the sign to be sure it was in PARK. Along with a couple pickup trucks, we crossed back over the Mississippi. Corinne and I stood at the railing and watched the roiling, cloudy brown water that frothed and chopped around the ferry's hull slicing through the current, and landed on the Missouri side, at the edge of what looked like miles and miles of open, rolling farmland. Most of the fields were bare, the colors umber and tan. It was the earth in the last couple of seasonal seconds before spring. I could see some fields that had already been turned over for seeding. The freshly tilled dirt was rich, deep black. Before we docked, I asked one of the dock-hands for directions back to St. Louis, and once landed, we were off.

Even though we were less than twenty miles from St. Louis, this was farmland, rural, open, the fields rolling, separated by rows of dark, squat trees. There weren't many houses. We glimpsed a few, off in the distance.

"What happens when the river floods?" Corinne asked. "Aren't all these farms underwater?"

I pointed to a house on stilts, off the highway and almost concealed in a thicket of trees. "The people in those, I guess, just sit it out and wait for the water to go down. But the others?" I shrugged. "I guess they get wet."

We drove on another mile without saying anything until Corinne spoke again.

"Can I ask you something?"

"Fire away."

"Have you ever been in love?"

"No," I said. For some reason, that spoonful of soup she'd offered me and ladled into my mouth came to mind. Along with the memory of her eyes looking at me as she did.

"That was fast," she said. "You didn't have to think about it."

"I have some rules to determine if I'm in love," I said. I felt a quick, hot flush and the sudden desire to be out of my jacket. I glanced at the heater dial in the Toyota. It was set where it had been all day, on low. It just suddenly seemed to be working a lot harder.

"Some rules," she said. "Imagine that."

"And I've yet to be in a situation where the necessary criteria were established."

"You're kind of a starry-eyed romantic, aren't you?" Corinne said.

We kept driving. The sun was still above the horizon. It had fleshed out some streaky clouds, turning them pink. The light was soft, almost creamy. After a while, she said, "Can I ask you another question?"

"Absolutely."

"One completely unrelated to the previous one?"

"Go," I said.

"Are you even in the slightest attracted to me?"

I was fortunate. The stretch of road we were on was straight. I wasn't sure I could have navigated any bends or turns at that moment. The heater again suddenly seemed to have cranked up all on its own.

"What are you talking about?" I said. "Of course I am attracted to you."

"Are you attracted to me as much as Langston is attracted to Bao Yu?" she asked.

"Steel isn't attracted to a magnet as much as Langston is attracted to Bao Yu."

"Didn't answer the question."

"You would be surprised how attracted to you I am," I said. "And I, being a cool and distant sort, very much into my image of — we talked about this whole thing before — being completely in control, I would be embarrassed and uncomfortable if you did know how attracted I am."

"Interesting," Corinne said.

"It is," I said. "However . . ."

"However?"

"Yes," I said. "However. There is often a 'however' in life."

"One of Tucker's Rules?"

"Number fifty-seven: 'There is often a "however" in life.'"

We drove awhile, neither of us saying anything. Both of us

thinking lots of things. At least, I was. Some of them I'd thought about before, in vague ways. Others, like the thoughts I'd had that night on Corinne's bed lying next to her, were pretty well defined.

"So," she said, "what's the 'however'?"

"However," I said. "I get the feeling there's something you're not telling me."

From the corner of my eye, I saw her shrug. "Lots of things I haven't told you," she said. "Lots of things you haven't told me about you. I don't even know how many rules you have."

"That's not what I'm talking about," I said.

"Look," she said. "Didn't you have to watch the videos in junior high school, the ones about dating and stuff?" She changed her voice, suddenly sounding like those silky-smooth counselor types who narrate the kind of videos probably every kid in the country has had to suffer through. "You're growing up and you're starting to interact with each other in more 'grown-up' ways. Pretty soon, you'll start thinking about spending more time with friends of the opposite sex, time alone together. It's a way of learning to relate to one another, to learn about each other. It's an important time in your life, and it can be fun as well, if you remember to be careful and keep your clothes on at all times."

I had a sudden urge to stop the car, pull off the road, and start asking questions. I was already making a list of them. I wanted to start with the reason she left, once her job—and her boss— disappeared like they did, and how she ended up at a rest stop in New Hampshire. I wanted to know what she was doing in Seattle. Then I'd work my way down to just who the hell that body was I'd looked at the other day and what kind of connection she had with it. Him. There were questions I had a feeling she had answers for, some she might share with me and others I was afraid she wouldn't. Maybe that was why I kept driving and kept my mouth shut.

She was quiet after that, all the way until we made it to the interstate that would take us back into St. Louis.

"It takes time, Tucker," she finally said.

"I guess," I said. Because I didn't know what else to say.

It was almost dark when we got home. I didn't have any answers. Still, the day hadn't been a total loss. I had tasted that soup off her spoon. And I had a dish for the contest.

26

Rule #15: *A rub of fresh ginger on a wok heated until it smokes will sanitize it; few other problems in life are so easily solved.*

"His name was Bobby Chu," Ms. Masterson said. "He was a member of a gang called the Flying Ghosts."

We were sitting at a table at the Eastern Palace, Ms. Masterson, Corinne, and me. The restaurant didn't open for lunch for another half-hour. Ms. Masterson came to the kitchen door, and Tuan, a new dishwasher we'd hired, heard her knock and let her in. She wasn't dressed for a cooking lesson. We didn't have one scheduled anyway. I took her into the dining area where Corinne and Bao Yu were both folding napkins. Bao excused herself. Ms. Masterson and I sat down.

"You ever hear of the Flying Ghosts?" Ms. Masterson asked.

I shook my head, but Corinne nodded. "Sure. They're kind of small, but they're in Montreal and other cities in Canada. Probably in this country too."

"Ever run into them?"

"How much do you know about Chinese gangs?" Corinne asked her.

"A little," Ms. Masterson said. "Not a whole lot."

Corinne pushed a stack of napkins to the side and folded her hands on the table. "There are Chinese gangs in every big city in the United States and Canada."

"They're like the Mafia," Ms. Masterson said. "They run gambling, drug smuggling—and people smuggling—and prostitution, right?"

"And they offer 'protection' for businesses," Corinne said. "Pay them a monthly percentage of your profits, and nothing bad happens to your shop or your business. No mysterious fires or vandalism."

"They're called tongs, right?" Ms. Masterson said.

"That word is Cantonese," Corinne said. "It literally means a 'hall.' But that's not exactly it. It's more like a meeting place, clubhouse, something like that. In the early days, when the Chinese were immigrating to this country, they became essentially slave labor to build the railroads—" She glanced at me as if I were personally responsible for this.

"And we appreciate it," I said, "every time we have to stop for thirty minutes at a railroad crossing to let a train crawl through."

"They formed associations for protection and for socializing," Corinne went on. "And sometimes to organize crime. 'Tong' isn't a word we use in Mandarin. We call gangs like that the 'shadow societies.'"

"Shadow societies?" I said. "Do they have secret handshakes and stuff?" They both ignored me.

"It doesn't sound quite so dramatic in Mandarin," Corinne said.

"Did you know any shadow society people in Montreal?" Ms. Masterson asked.

"I knew *about* them," Corinne said. "Everybody in the Chinese community in every big city knows about them. But I didn't know any shadow society people personally. Most Chinese don't. Just like most Italian Americans don't personally know anyone in the Mafia."

"Do you think it's possible that the men who showed up at the Wing Sung company could have been members of a gang?" Ms. Masterson asked. "Think it's possible that the late Mr. Chu was also affiliated?"

Corinne straightened up in her chair and seemed to be considering it. "Possibly," she said. "It's probable, in fact. When it comes to Chinese here in the West, most crime is connected in one way or another to gangs."

Ms. Masterson nodded slowly. "So let's assume, the three of us, that the Flying Ghosts or some other gang has some interest in what happened at Wing Sung."

"A financial investment?" I said. "Maybe Mr. Sung was on the hook for gambling debts, or they were leaning on him to pay them protection; something like that."

"Something like that," Ms. Masterson said. "I just stopped by to let you know we'd identified Chu."

"Will there be a big memorial service?" I asked.

"I doubt it," Ms. Masterson said. "Chu did not seem to be an imposing figure. The information we got on him from the cops in Montreal is that he was a small-timer. Pretty low in the organization."

"A *wu ming shao zu,*" Corinne said. "A little soldier with no name."

"Chinese gangs have lots of those kinds of people in them?" Ms. Masterson asked.

"Sure," Corinne said. "That's who does all the work. Lots of times they're in the country illegally. They're usually not very well educated. They might not even speak English. They get used by the gang. They're dispensable."

"Rough life," Ms. Masterson said. "Same way back in the old days for Italian immigrants, Irish."

Corinne shrugged, then nodded. "It's not like the choices for them are joining a gang or going to med school. It's a chance to make money, to feel like you're important, like you're part of a group. That's pretty attractive compared to the other stuff they could end up doing."

"Like working in a Chinese restaurant, for example," I said.

"Good point," Corinne said. "But at least we're not found beaten to death."

So far, I was tempted to say.

"What were you doing in Seattle earlier this month?" Ms. Masterson asked, suddenly. It was a police technique. Quickly change the topic when you're questioning someone, and it's more likely something will slip out. Assuming Corinne was hiding something that might slip.

"Qingming," Corinne said.

"Oh," I said. That was at least one question answered.

"Oh?" Ms. Masterson said.

"I wondered," I said. "Makes sense."

"Not to me."

"Qingming is a Chinese festival," I said. "It's when you go to your ancestors' graves and clean them up, sweep up leaves or whatever, and leave offerings."

"I went to my parents' graves," Corinne said.

"Like Memorial Day?" Ms. Masterson asked.

I nodded. "Only not many people on Memorial Day decorate their ancestors' graves with bottles of liquor, roast chicken, rice dumplings, stuff like that."

"Chinese ancestors like to eat well," Corinne said.

"Speaking of eating well," Ms. Masterson said, "am I ready for the second lesson?"

"We've just been talking about a dead guy, a dead guy we both went to look at, and you're thinking about food?"

"Life goes on," Ms. Masterson said.

"Are you sure you're not Chinese?" Corinne asked.

27

Rule #44: *When it's interesting, you may as well stick around to see how it comes out.*

These carp, unlike the ones Corinne and I had seen a few days earlier at the fish market, were still alive. Like the catfish back at the riverside lunch place where we'd eaten, they were swirling lazily in the tanks of the market, looking me over with their big, expressionless eyes, moving on after considering me as a possible food source. I wasn't. But they were. The day wasn't going to end well for one of us.

I'd parked the Toyota behind the Eastern Palace and walked down to Seafood City, a few blocks away. It wasn't even nine o'clock in the morning yet, but the place was already busy. Cooks, amateur and professional, in lots of cultures make a big deal of going shopping first thing in the morning. Chinese, in particular, seem to think that food tastes best if it's purchased not long after the sun comes up. Or maybe they think that's when all the good buys are. I've never known why. Now, though—while the chill of the night still hadn't lifted outside, making me zip up my jacket on my walk there—the place was filled. I liked to listen to the bickering and arguing between the guys behind the counter and the customers, mostly older women, on the other side. I could pick out several dialects of Chinese as some of the women chattered among themselves. Other customers added Vietnamese, Laotian, and Cambodian. Behind the counter, it was all Spanish. The two sides came together in broken English marked by accusations and protestations and lots of intercultural exclamation points.

"You charging that much for those shrimp? How old those shrimp!"

"Those shrimp fresh!"

"Fresh, yahh! Mebbe they fresh las' week!"

"Why you bussing me ovah dis? You tink I own dis place? You tink I getting rich here?"

It went on and on. It was good-natured. Neither side expected the price to change. It seemed like it was enjoyable for all of them to bicker. It was kind of like the UN.

I waited my turn, pointed to the fish I wanted, then waited again while a fishmonger hauled it out of the tank in a dip net. He tossed it, thrashing in the air, to another, who heaved the fish onto a wide flat stainless steel table beside a sink. The carp still thrashing, the fishmonger whacked it hard, then hard again on its head with a short, nasty-looking club.

"You want cleaned?"

I didn't. I took the fish after he'd bagged it and paid at the counter, then walked back toward the Eastern Palace. The sun was up enough now to cast long shadows. Mine stretched out in front of me, holding a plastic sack of fish.

Five willow fish is one of those Chinese dishes—there are literally dozens and dozens of them in China's culinary lore—that has at least a couple of stories behind its creation. Like most dishes with those kinds of stories about how they were created or developed, few of the tales are really all that credible. But they are interesting. The best one concerning five willow fish explains how a hermit living in a lakeside hut created the recipe's particular method of cooking fish. The story might be legend, but the hermit, Tao Yuanming, was real. He was a middle management office worker during the Eastern Jin Dynasty, in the fifth century. When he got tired of the bureaucracy, he chucked it all to go off and live in a hut on the shore of a lake. He became one of those semi-crazy eccentrics who lived in isolation, writing poetry and thinking deep thoughts.

I explained all this to Ms. Masterson, who had been waiting for me at the rear door of the Eastern Palace that morning when I got back with my carp. She was there for her next lesson, the one I'd promised after our conversation with Corinne about Chinese gangs the day before.

"Was that a popular job in China back then?" she asked. "Being a hermit?"

"China back then was lousy with 'em," I said. "The Chinese have a thing for the eccentric, the iconoclast, the person who goes off and lives by himself, lives a life of contemplation and doing artistic stuff."

"Kind of like guys who take off from their home and their college and go out to master Chinese cooking?"

"Kind of," I said. "But I don't drink enough wine to qualify as a real Chinese eccentric."

I had the carp stretched out on a cutting board in front of me.

"You want to learn to cook Chinese food," I told her, "you need to be able to dismember animals. A carp's a good place to start."

"So how come the knife's in your hand?"

"Because it's a cleaver, not a knife. And because I'm going to show you a way of cleaning a fish that takes a lot of practice. You might want to watch it first."

"A gracious way of saying I'd be in over my head," she said.

"I'm the soul of graciousness."

I used the Jiangsu method of cleaning a fish, taking out the entrails through the gill slits so the fish remains whole. It's harder than it looks. It makes for a nice presentation of the fish when you're done, if you do a good job. Using my cleaver, I sliced slash marks across its flank. Then I flipped it and did the same on the other side. I cut deep enough to go well into the flesh. My cuts opened wide pink gashes in the meat. I put the fish in a bamboo steamer and covered it, then put the steamer on a wok that was already boiling water.

"That's it for now," I said.

"You pinched the fish," Ms. Masterson said. "Then you held your two fingers against your other middle finger. Is that some kind of ancient Chinese cooking ritual?"

"You're observant," I said. "You'd make a good cop. Actually, it's an old trick to measure the cooking time of a whole fish. You hold the fish at the thickest part of its body between your thumb and forefinger. Then you measure that space on your other middle finger. For every joint of that finger between your thumb and forefinger, you can assume you'll need to steam the fish about fifteen minutes."

"How did you learn that?"

"Results of a youth wasted in the kitchen of many a Chinese restaurant," I said. I started putting together the ingredients I was going to use in today's lesson with her.

"Are you worried?" Ms. Masterson asked me.

"Not really. There's no way a *laowai* is going to be named the best Chinese chef in town."

"I'm not talking about the contest," she said. "I mean are you worried that someone—some people who seem organized, probably some people who are involved in the kind of gang activity that often features a lot of violence—have made two runs at you? Are you worried about the fact that they are obviously after something and they are just as obviously not going to stop until they get it?"

"About that?" I said. "Oh yeah. Worried like you can't believe. Didn't you have to study psychology as part of your training?"

She tilted her head in acknowledgment.

"Then can't you recognize anxiety in my behavior?" First

Corinne, now Ms. Masterson. I was getting kind of tired of having to explain my fragile psyche.

"You don't show a lot."

"Part of my charm."

"You have a nice job here, I understand," she said slowly. "But you're not really tied down here." She raised her eyebrows.

"What am I going to do? Run? Where?"

When she didn't say anything, I took the other carp from the bag and put it on the cutting board, handed her my cleaver, and began talking her through what I'd just showed her. She did a reasonably good job. When I began to assemble the ingredients we needed for the rest of the dish, she leaned against the counter.

"You're staying because of Corinne."

"Corinne has even less reason to stay here than I do," I said. "At least I have a friend here."

"And she has you, who brought her here," Ms. Masterson said.

"More like she didn't really have any other place to go," I said.

When they were done, we ate the fish. I was happy with it. Ms. Masterson ate but not with her usual gusto.

"It's excellent, really," she said, when I asked her about it. "It's just that steamed carp isn't my usual breakfast."

"Most important meal of the day," I said. "Didn't your mother teach you that you should start off with something substantial?"

"If my mother knew I was eating steamed carp for breakfast," Ms. Masterson said, "she wouldn't think my becoming an FBI agent was the weirdest thing I've ever done anymore."

When Ms. Masterson left, I cleaned up the dishes we'd dirtied, then started peeling and chopping broccoli. Chinese cooking—the real thing—doesn't use Western broccoli. They even had to come up with a name to describe it when they first saw it. But it's expected in lots of Chinese American dishes; we always had plenty on hand, and while the task really should have gone to one of the dishwashers who served as prep cooks, I liked doing it. It scored me points with the dishwashers, and it was so mindless it gave me time to think.

I thought about what Ms. Masterson had said, about my hanging around just because of Corinne. That wasn't exactly true. Not *exactly.* I had a good job. Friends. No place else in particular to go. *Would I still be here,* I asked myself, *if Corinne wasn't here too? And was it worth it?*

I scooped up the broccoli with my cleaver and tossed them into a stainless steel bowl. And it hit me. The same way leaving Beddingfield to come to St. Louis had hit me. All at once. Like it had been forming in my subconscious, and all of a sudden, standing there chopping broccoli in the kitchen that morning in the Eastern Palace, it all came out. Clear and obvious.

Was Corinne playing me? The whole thing: the weird phone call I'd intercepted back at my parents' house; the trip to Buffalo; Bobby Chu; the phone call from her to come pick her up; the trip *back* to Buffalo; the mugging—all of it. I wondered if that night lying on her bed and the conversation we'd had driving back after the afternoon in Illinois, if the whole thing wasn't some trouble a very unusual woman was in—and was dragging me in as well. If maybe Corinne was one of Toby's "trouble drains"—a supersize version of it. And whether she was or wasn't, there was still the big question: How was all this supposed to end?

I picked up another head of broccoli. There was no shortage of Chinese restaurants. There were a limited number of chefs who could cook like me to fill the kitchens of those restaurants. I could get a job anywhere. I sliced the stem from the broccoli and began peeling it. My cleaver was so sharp it separated the tough outer skin into paper-thin shreds. That crow I'd seen back in the sycamore outside the apartment: I never had seen him again. Maybe he'd left town. Maybe that was a sign.

I finished the broccoli and rapped the side of my cleaver against the cutting board, the steel pinging a sharp rhythm. I was so lost in thought, I hadn't noticed someone had come in to the kitchen behind me when I said aloud, to myself, "Nope." And I let out a long exhalation. "Gotta remember Rule Number Forty-Four. When it's interesting, you may as well stick around to see how it comes out."

"How what comes out?" Thuy asked me.

"Good question."

28

Rule #45: *Never pass up the opportunity to have dumplings.*

The contest was simultaneously simple and elaborate. Typically Chinese. It would have been easy just to invite all the contestants to some place, have them all present their meals, and be done with it. That wouldn't have had all the razzle-dazzle, though, that would bring a lot of publicity to the event. It wouldn't have had the grand air of importance and formality that were essential for the restaurant owners to present their image to the public. Then, too, some of those owners could have argued that their chefs were working under unfair conditions if the contest was held away from the kitchens where they were accustomed to cooking. I knew the chefs; I'd eaten in their kitchens in the months I'd been in St. Louis. I didn't think any of them would have a problem. I figured the real reason the owners wanted their chefs in their own kitchens for the judging had to do with the attention it was going to draw. And the business it would mean.

Five restaurants had put their reputations on the line by nominating their chefs for the contest. Over the course of five nights, the five chefs were presenting their best, one each night. A panel of judges would go to each of the five restaurants in turn, bringing their appetites with them, and sit for a sampling of the dish. As soon as the story of the upcoming contest was published in the *St. Louis Chinese News* and then in the *St. Louis Chinese-American Journal,* reservation requests started coming in for every restaurant participating. The local St. Louis paper got wind of it and gave it a story too. Within a couple of days, all five restaurants, including the Eastern Palace, were booked solid. We were booked for every night that week, in fact, even on those nights when I wasn't going to be presenting my dish. I'd never seen Mr. Leong so happy since he'd discovered a styling gel that kept his comb-over in place.

The five owners got together at Wei Hong's, a little café that sold Chinese pastries and tea and was kind of a gathering spot for restaurant workers. They each put their business cards into a box, and Mingyu Sun, the girl who worked at the counter, reached in and pulled them out, one by one. That's how the contest schedule was decided. We'd get a visit from the judges, Mr. Leong told me after he came back from Wei Hong's, on Thursday.

"Not too bad," he said. He had already developed a complex theory as to why this seeding was bound to work in our favor. "The judges have three nights before, only one after. They forget what the food tasted like on Monday and Tuesday," he told me. "They remember Wednesday. Then they eat your dinner Thursday, it be most fresh when they thinking. They still thinking about it when they eat on Friday. Friday guy no gotta chance. They been eating this kind of good food all week. They sick of it."

It took Mr. Leong about five minutes to lay out his fascinating theory on why Thursday was so absolutely perfect for me that the contest was already more or less in the bag and I may as well consider it accomplished.

"What are the other chefs preparing?" I asked. "Do we know yet?"

"Yeah, yeah," Mr. Leong said, shuffling his hand into his pants pocket. "I write it."

We sat down and looked at his list. At China Gate, the head chef, Jiangguo Wen, was making *mapo* tofu. It was a good choice. A Szechuan classic. A braise of finely chopped pork, mixed with chili paste, little nubbins of black beans, and crumbles of soft, custardy tofu. *Mapo* tofu got its name, "pockmarked tofu," supposedly because it was the invention of an old lady—*po* in Mandarin—who was disfigured, or "pockmarked" (*mazi*) by smallpox. I knew Wen's version of the dish at China Gate. He made his own Szechuan chili sauce to go into it, instead of the prepared stuff from a jar. He had an advantage. Wen was from Chengdu, a city in Szechuan Province. He had relatives there who sent him a steady supply of Szechuan chilies. Chinese chefs make a distinction between *huajiao,* "flower peppers," and *shanjiao,* or "mountain peppers." Most of us had to settle for the former, which were more common. Wen, through his relatives, had access to some of the mountain peppers. These were a pure strain, much more fiery than what we could get, with a smoky, snappy flavor that upped the taste of the dish noticeably. In fact, we had a small jar of oil infused with Wen's special peppers in the kitchen at the Eastern Palace, a gift from Wen. We'd ground the carmine dried peppers into powder, then added them to a couple of cups of hot peanut oil. We used just a few drops of the oil on pot stickers, to give them an unmistakable piquancy. There was no way I could make an infused oil taste the same. Not without those dried peppers. It made Wen's *mapo* tofu unique. There were certain to be some judges who had a thing for Szechuan spiciness. Wen would have their votes.

Parker Huang, who was manning the first wok station at the Din Ho Restaurant, was going with a soup called Buddha Jumps Over the Wall. I was surprised. It was probably the most famous dish from Fujian Province—and certainly one of the most complicated meals of any style of Chinese cuisine. Even a basic recipe called for more than two dozen ingredients. Dried scallops. Boiled pigeon eggs. The leg tendons of pork, duck stomach, chicken, bamboo shoots. It was extravagant. The rest of us would be plinking out "Twinkle, Twinkle, Little Star," while Parker was performing all four of Vivaldi's *Seasons.* The dish was supposed to be so delicious that the aroma alone would have the Buddha leaving his meditation cushion and hopping over the monastery walls for a taste. Popping the lid off a pot of that soup was going to be impressive. I wondered, though, how many of the judges would really be able to appreciate a gourmet delicacy like that.

Langston and I had both been right about Hung I-mien, the head chef at the Red Dragon. He was going with soy sauce chicken. *Chicken,* I thought. *It was too safe. Jiang su ji* was one of those dishes, from Canton, that Chinese and Westerners both liked. It wasn't exotic. A whole chicken braised in soy sauce, with anise, rock sugar, and some other stuff, then hacked into pieces and arranged on a platter. It was sold in a dozen good Chinese restaurants all over town. Even some of the cheaper take-out joints had it on their menus. *Jiang su ji* was good, even in the cheap joints. And it would please the judges, a taste of familiarity. It lacked the flair, the exoticism, though, that I was guessing the judges would want in a winning entry. If Parker was going overboard with his Buddha Jumps Over the Wall soup, Hung was being too conservative with soy sauce chicken.

And Langston?

"He is making steamed shredded three meats," Mr. Leong said. He looked at me.

I cocked my head and pursed my lips. Which I tend to do when I don't want anyone to know what I'm thinking. As with my initial meeting with Ms. Masterson, I lack the ability to conceal my thoughts with a blank face. Sometimes, like with her, I go for looking up and raising my eyebrows. Or I do the head cock and pursed lips instead, which is another one of my ways of trying to be a blank slate. To add to the effect now, I crossed my arms and sat back in my chair.

Langston's the one to beat, I thought. His choice was a good one. An excellent one. It was a Shanghai-style classic. Three meats: lean pork, ham, and chicken were all steamed, along with slivers of bamboo shoots, then sliced finely into long, skinny needles. The shreds went into a bowl, laid along the side vertically, alternated with the shredded bamboo shoots until they filled the bowl. Put a plate on top the bowl, flip it over, and pull it off and you have a perfect mound of the meats sitting beautifully on the platter in three colors, drizzled with a light chicken stock–based sauce. It was a very "Chinese" Chinese dish, with lots of eye appeal. It was also just right for putting in the middle of the table for diners to sit around, picking it apart slowly with their chopsticks, nibbling and talking, and talking and nibbling, for a couple of hours, sipping tea all the while. The problems of the world could be solved over a mound of three steamed meats and bamboo. It was too subtle and at the same time too plain—steamed meat wasn't really all that exotic—for a lot of non-Chinese diners. Chances were good, though, that the judges would eat it up—literally.

"You worry?" Mr. Leong asked me.

"No worry," I said. I unfolded my arms and stood up.

It was a little past eleven when we finished cleaning the kitchen that evening. A party of twelve had come in at nine. I was fairly sure they were college students. From their ages, I was guessing grad school. About half of them were Westerners; the others were Chinese. I peeked out through the swinging door when Corinne delivered their order. I knew the Chinese students had done the ordering. Boiled dumplings. A soup of ham and winter melon. Orange peel chicken. Dry sautéed green beans. Crispy garlic shrimp.

"They specified boiled, not steamed dumplings?" I asked Corinne when she came into the kitchen to deliver the order.

"*Shui jiao,*" Corinne repeated. "Don't you speak English?"

Tuan, who'd just finished up a load of dishes and was leaning with his back against the rim of the sink, snorted. He was picking up enough of the language to start to get some jokes.

The boiled dumplings were consistent with the rest of the

order; it was a pretty typical Szechuan dinner menu. I assumed the Chinese in the group were showing their Western colleagues some of the basics of Szechuan cuisine. The three of us went to work; it didn't take long. By the time the grad students filed out of the Eastern Palace, telling a beaming Mr. Leong who was standing at the front counter that they were delighted to be having "real" Chinese cooking for a change, the dining room was completely empty. We relaxed in the kitchen.

Li took a generous helping of dumplings from the freezer and tossed them into a heated wok, where they instantly began to crackle and hiss. At the Eastern Palace, we all preferred dumplings fried on the side of the wok—"pot stickers"—to the steamed or boiled versions. Well, actually Thuy and Tuan, our dishwashers, liked them better steamed. But dishwashers were too low in restaurant hierarchy to have a full vote on stuff like that. So they were learning to eat them the way the rest of us liked.

Eleven o'clock is late for most people to eat. And usually none of us who worked in the kitchen or in the dining room wanted a big meal at that time of night. We weren't really hungry. We'd been nibbling, sampling, all night long. We needed more to decompress from the dinner shift than to sit down to a full meal. For some restaurant crews, that means a trip to a local bar. We had a ceramic jug of fiery Chinese liquor we broke out occasionally. Mostly, though, we just wanted to sit around for an hour or so, snacking, drinking tea, talking. The first restaurants in China were probably doing business back in the Song Dynasty, starting in the tenth century, catering to travelers. They specialized in the same sort of light snacks and tea. A thousand years before, cooks at those Chinese restaurants sat down after their places closed, eating and drinking more or less exactly what we were eating and drinking.

Corinne came in after the last customers had finally ambled out; we'd just sat down. Langston banged twice on the door, then paused, then banged again once. It was the system all the restaurants used, the code that let you know there was a cook from another restaurant, or a waiter or waitress, who was coming by to sit around and talk and eat.

Thuy got up to let him in. Langston nodded at him, walked over to a rack of dishes, and picked up a small plate. Then he pulled a chair up to the table.

"You see the list?" he asked. He sat down. I passed him the little jar of hot chili pepper oil.

"I did."

"Five willow fish," he said.

"Steamed three meats," I said.

"Both classic dishes," Langston said. He spooned just a couple of drops of the orange-red oil onto the plate, then used a pair of chopsticks to swirl the dumpling around in it.

"By a couple of classic guys."

"You think anyone's in the running but us?" Langston asked.

"I was ruminating on just that," I said. "Parker's soup is a good choice if the weather's cold. But I think it'll be a little warm this time of year for it to have the full effect."

Corinne found her own spot at the table and helped herself to the platter of dumplings. She picked up the ceramic teapot and poured a cup for Langston, peered over into mine and saw it was still full, then poured for herself.

"Hung's soy sauce chicken?" Langston said, after he'd swallowed a bite of the dumpling.

We both shook our heads at that one. "And *mapo* tofu?" I said.

"A sentimental favorite," Langston said. "But the judges are going to want to go with something that's a little more exotic."

"Chinese-y," I said, "but not too far-out."

"Yep," Langston said. "You know them. They're thinking of what kind of publicity they can get out of this. They'll hope for a write-up in the paper. It's great publicity for all the Chinese restaurants."

"But it would sort of defeat the purpose if the winning dish is something like hot and sour cat," Corinne said. "It's got to be Chinese. Just not too Chinese."

"Right," I said. "That would not bring in lots of business."

The homey sounds of eating temporarily suspended conversation: slurping tea, sucking air to cool off the hot dumplings, the clack of chopsticks.

"You know, I've heard that all my life," Langston said, after he swallowed a dumpling. He reached for another. "But do you think there's some place in China where they really do eat cat?"

Corinne shook her head. "Maybe the Cantonese. You know the saying about Cantonese. If its back is to the sun, eat it."

"Never heard of any Cantonese dishes that have cat in them," Langston said. "I don't think anybody, unless he was starving, would eat cat. Especially not a Chinese."

I turned to Thuy. "Vietnamese do, though, right, Thuy?"

"Shut up, *fan tong*," Thuy said. It was the first time I'd heard him speak Chinese. He called me a rice bucket. It meant I wasn't good for much. As Mandarin insults go, it was mild. He'd heard one of us say it in the kitchen, I was guessing, and added it to his repertoire. Now he was trying it out for the first time.

"You're starting to fit in just fine around here," Langston said.

"Eat shit," Thuy said to him, reaching for a dumpling.

29

Rule #23: *Never be predictable.*

I lost.

By three seconds. It had been the mile run we made in sixth grade PE. And I lost, to a guy named Ry Grant, running back for the North Andover Middle School Eagles. Which ruined, with those three seconds, the plan I had to impress Addie McDaniel with my speed, so much so that she would want to go out with me over the upcoming summer. And two days later, Doug Armand told Langston and me he'd seen Ry and Addie eating pizza together in Papa Gino's at Shawsheen Plaza.

"Pepperoni or just cheese?" Langston had asked.

Pepperoni or cheese? I had a ball in my throat that tasted like I'd been trying to swallow clay. A summer I'd already had planned with Addie was dissolving right there as I walked along Lowell Street. I didn't feel like crying—and I'd have rather had my arm cut off than have cried in front of Langston and Doug—but I felt that maybe life was going to be a little tougher than I had ever considered it. In the face of that kind of realization, crying wasn't going to help. By the sixth grade, I already knew that. The thought of Ry and Addie sharing slices didn't make the realization any easier. I was, though, completely confident in one thing: I wasn't about to show I was bothered by it.

"Pepperoni or cheese?" I said, as nonchalantly as I could. "What difference does that make?"

"I'm hungry," Langston said. "Helps me visualize the scene better."

I'd never said a word to Langston about my crush on Addie McDaniel. And a lot of times Langston seemed like he wasn't really dialed in to much that was going on around him anyway. So I figured it was my secret, and I intended to keep it. At other times, though, it was hard to tell just how much Langston knew. Because a while later, after Doug had peeled away from us to head for his house, right out of nowhere, Langston said, "Hard to figure what some people see in other people."

"What do you mean?" I asked.

He shrugged. "You know, Addie McDaniel, for instance. Hard to figure how she'd be interested in a guy like Ry Grant. Guy's a jerk."

Nine years later, it was me shrugging, standing over a wok sizzling with chunks of pork and little, dark green trees of Chinese broccoli. It was Monday, the first night of the competition.

"Take a break," Mr. Leong said to me. "We no busy now. Go down to Din Ho watch."

"Pass," I said.

"Go," Li said. "We're covered here. Every table booked all night. So, busy but no surprises for us."

I knew Li was being optimistic. Everyone in the kitchen *had* gone over the reservation book; we knew most of the names, had a good idea of what they'd be ordering. I knew, too, that Li was willing to take the risk of the "anthill" getting too busy, the Eastern Palace getting swamped with some unexpected orders, if it allowed me to go watch the competition. Which that night was at Din Ho, where Parker Huang was leading off in the batting order of the contest, preparing his Buddha Jumps Over the Wall soup.

"No thanks," I told them both. I said the same thing the next night, when Jiangguo Wen made his *mapo* tofu. After that, they stopped asking.

The week went by slowly. Waitresses were talking about the contest, scoring it according to their own evaluations, most of which seemed about as reliable as Mr. Leong's strategy. The other cooks mentioned it, those in our kitchen and those who dropped by after work. We didn't talk as much about it, though. It was part of our image, as cooks, not to seem too eager or too invested in the contest. On Thursday I was up. I cleaned two big carp and carved deep slashes in their silvery flanks. I put each in a bamboo steamer, stacked the steamers, then balanced them over a wok bubbling with boiling water. I could smell the sweet, meaty aroma of the fish and the delicate woody scent of the bamboo as they began cooking. I shredded carrots, black mushrooms, and big, dark green leaves of pickled Chinese cabbage and fresh slices of bamboo shoots that had just appeared at the Chinese market where I bought the carp. I slivered a couple of thumb-size knobs of ginger. I'd had the stock going since about noon—made from chicken bones, slow simmered until it was glossy and thick. I added a blob of rendered chicken fat for richness. Once the stock was just hot enough to send some bubbles floating slowly to the surface, I added the carrots, mushrooms, pickled cabbage, bamboo shoots, and ginger. That's the tough part, really. If the stock is too hot, bubbling, the individual vegetables get their flavors all mixed together as they cook. They need to be separate. They were.

I plated the carp, then added the five ingredients in neat clumps along the flanks of the fish. I thickened the stock, not with the cornstarch or arrowroot starch that most Chinese chefs use. Instead, I did it with water chestnut flour, which gives the thickened sauce just the right texture, not too gloppy, not too thin. I ladled the sauce just lightly over the fish. Ready to go.

I delivered the fish, their heads in opposite directions on the platter, like they were swimming around in a circle, and presented them to the six judges. I recognized most of the panel. Eric Tsang was president of the Chinese-American Association. He was big, with a wide, smooth, and florid face. Tsang was a major booster for the Chinese community, leaning on local businesses to sponsor lion dances at New Year's and regular street fairs, and the Chinese Language School. Mrs. Zhao, sitting beside Mr. Tsang, was the director of the Language School. Her hair was done up in an elaborate swoop, with strands of gray showing. She had the very high, pronounced cheekbones that a lot of Chinese associate with the far Western regions of China. Dr. Luo was on her other side. He ran a medical clinic where all the older Chinese women in the area went because they were comfortable only with a Chinese doctor. The others I didn't know by name. I recognized their faces; knew who they were. A couple of young hotshot lawyers and the wife of a guy who owned a Lexus dealership.

I stood by the table while they looked over my presentation, murmuring "ummmh" and "ahhh" and "hmmm." Dr. Luo peered at me though thick glasses and said, "You steamed it instead of frying it." It was an implied question.

"*Yu-er-pu-ni,*" I said. "The taste of fat without being oily. If I'd fried it, the flavor of the fish would have been lost. You couldn't taste all the vegetables with it."

"People like five willow fish fried nowadays," Dr. Luo said.

I didn't say anything. Which I thought was elegant.

Eric Tsang reached over and slowly spun the heavy glass lazy Susan so the fish platter stopped in from of Mrs. Zhao. As the Language School's director, her status as an educator made her the senior-most of the group. She had the first serving. She used her chopsticks to lift some of the meat from the flank of the carp, up near its head. Bad luck to eat a fish from the back to the front. The first bite should come from the head. In fact, the first bite should have come from the cheek of the carp. I was guessing Mrs. Zhao was being humble, not taking the choicest bite. The lazy Susan rotated; each of them took some of the fish, lifting it in their chopsticks, looking it over, then tasting it.

I stood and watched while they ate the fish. Mrs. Zhao looked up as she made delicate little chewing motions. Mr. Tsang looked down, I noticed, as he chewed. Nobody was making eye contact. Each seemed lost in his or her own thoughts, evaluating the fish. I could tell, for the lawyers, it was the first time they'd ever tasted five willow fish. They ate, tentatively at first, as if they wondered whether they'd like it. It was encouraging to see them go for second helpings, digging in with more enthusiasm.

"I must say it is amazing that you would know this dish," Dr. Luo said, when the fish had been reduced to its skeleton and tail. "Where did you learn to make *wuliu* fish?"

"Old family recipe," I said.

Two days later, Saturday, Corinne and I were both working through the lunch and dinner shift. Li had taken a couple of days off to visit his sister. Jao-long and I worked both shifts. Early on, just before we got busy, Mr. Leong pushed open the swinging door into the kitchen and held it there while he stuck his head through.

"Sorry, Tucker," he said. "Bad news is you don't win. Good news is you friend Wu? He win."

"By three seconds?" I asked him. He cocked his head and looked at me like I'd said something strange. "Never mind."

Corinne, later that night, echoed Mr. Leong's sentiments.

"I'm sorry you didn't win."

We were standing in the hallway outside her apartment. The whole building had a faint aroma like fresh ginger, lemongrass, and five-spice powder had all been put into an aerosol and sprayed. The building where Langston and I lived had its own particular aroma. There was a little less ginger in ours.

"Me too," I said. I leaned against the wall.

"But you're not that sorry."

"Well, I'm not racked with heaving sobs," I said. It was warm enough that she hadn't worn a jacket or a sweater when we left the restaurant. The black dress she was wearing, the same one we'd bought at the mall a few months before, was cut low enough that I could see the creamy brown half-moon of her chest. Just a hint of cleavage, nothing more. It was enough.

"I'm a *laowai*," I said. "My Mandarin is probably so perfect you forget that."

"So what does not being Chinese have to do with it?"

"Not everything," I said. "But a lot. I'm cooking in a Chinese restaurant. Cooking real Chinese food. I'm playing in their ballpark, playing by their rules."

"Which are not your rules," Corinne said. "Which must be tough for you."

"Sometimes those rules don't seem to make much sense. Sometimes they really *don't* make much sense. They're unfair. They're stacked against you."

"But you still play there?"

"Yes," I said. "And that's where the fun is. It's hard to explain." It was. I had thought a lot about it. I still couldn't explain it. Even to myself.

"I like being able to play in that ballpark," I said. "I take a lot of pride in it. There aren't a lot of people who aren't Chinese who can play there. In fact, even most Chinese can't play in the ballpark of a Chinese restaurant kitchen. So sure, it would have been nice to have won. But in a way, for me at least, just being able to play the game is a kind of winning."

Corinne nodded. She looked past me like she was thinking about something else. Neither of us said anything for a while. Then, all the sudden, she reached out and took my hand.

"We could," she said. She looked up at me.

"Oh yeah, we could," I said. "Easily." I knew what she was talking about.

"Just as easily as we could have that night after those guys jumped me," she said.

"More easily."

"More?"

"Yes," I said. "This time the evening didn't begin with you getting mugged."

"That wouldn't have been the most romantic start of things, would it?"

I agreed with her.

She kept looking at me. "But we won't this time either, will we? Even though I didn't get mugged."

"No, we won't" I said. "Although I wouldn't say 'won't' in the sense of 'entirely, never-a-ghost-of-a-chance won't.'"

"Just not tonight," she said. "Not now?"

I nodded.

"It isn't because you're depressed about not winning, is it?"

"No."

"Is it because you're still thinking about becoming a Shaker?"

"I was never thinking about becoming a Shaker," I said. "I thought I made that clear a long time ago."

"It's because we aren't ready?"

"It's because it'd be too obvious. And worse, it'd be too predictable."

"And you do not like being predictable, do you?" she said. "It's one of the rules, isn't it?"

"Rule Number Twenty-Three."

"So you'd be willing to give up a night of"—she widened her eyes a couple of times in rapid succession—"you know, just to avoid being predictable?"

"I didn't say anything about 'giving up'; I just said not right now."

I kept looking at her. I realized it was one of the few times I'd looked at her square on. Almost all our conversations had taken place driving somewhere or while we were working, with our attention divided. We hadn't had many face-to-face conversations. It felt a little weird. Not bad. But different.

"I feel concerned about this," she said.

"How so?" I asked.

"We promised Mr. Leong we wouldn't engage in flirt talk," Corinne said. "And I think this definitely qualifies as flirt talk."

"Nope," I said. "This is well beyond flirt talk."

We held hands and didn't say anything for a while. After she closed the door, I walked over to my place. For the first time since I'd lost the mile race back in the sixth grade, I thought about Addie McDaniel without feeling regret over those three seconds.

Rule #18: *When things seem to be going too well, there's usually something that's going to change things.*

Langston came home a couple of hours after I did that night. I could tell he felt self-conscious about having won. I could tell mainly because he didn't mention it. Langston would complain about having lost at something for at least a couple of years. He still occasionally brought up the Monopoly game we'd played, one that went on most of a summer just before our freshman year at Andover High. He still insisted I'd won only because of a string of dice rolls that put him on Park Place, which I owned, three consecutive times around the board. When he won at something, though, he never wanted to talk about it. Normally, I'd go along with it. He might be uncomfortable losing. He was squirming, though, at winning. I felt sorry for him. I couldn't let this one go, though.

"So," I said, after he'd come in and slouched into the big chair he'd rescued from an eviction down the street and which he insisted was real leather. "The best Chinese chef in St. Louis. Sitting right here in my presence."

"Yeah," he said dismissively, "I'm great. But get this—" He grinned. "So we're having a celebration at the restaurant afterward, and Bao Yu comes because I'd invited her, and I say, 'Okay, so now that I'm officially the best Chinese chef in St. Louis, is there any chance you'd be willing to go out with me?'"

"You actually asked her out?" I said. "After months of pining for her from afar?"

"Oh yeah," Langston said. He ran his hand through his hair. It stood up at the crazy angles it always did unless he combed it into submission. "Not only did I actually ask her out," he said. "I did it in front of Janet Shen, that waitress at Din Ho, who was standing there with her."

"So what'd Bao Yu say?"

"Nothing."

"Nothing?"

He shook his head. "Not a word." His smile—I didn't think it was possible—got bigger. "But Janet, standing right there, says, 'Of course she'll go out with you. She'd have gone out with you six months ago, you dumbass, if you'd asked her.'"

We sat and talked for a while, and then I went to bed. I lay there and stared up at the ceiling, hands behind my back. I could still feel the warm skin of Corinne's hand. I felt happy for Langston. I thought that, all things considered, things were going not that bad.

Tucker's Rule #18: When things seem to be going too well, there's usually something that's going to change things.

31

Rule #74: *No matter how bad your day, it can always get worse if someone points a gun at you.*

Corinne told me about the threatening phone calls the night the guy came by in a car and pointed a gun at me.

Yes. Rule #18: When it's going too good, something's coming along to change things. When you're strolling down a sidewalk and someone pulls up in a car and sticks a gun in your face, that's very certainly in the realm of Rule #18.

Almost a week after the end of the contest, I was walking from the Asian grocery store back to the restaurant. The same walk I'd taken to get the carp for the judges. The same path I'd been on when I got the first carp to make the dish for Ms. Masterson. I was a regular on that route. I went by Dr. Luo's clinic. I veered off to my right to open the door for an old Chinese lady who was struggling with it. Without stopping, I looked in the window of a tiny shop that made and sold fresh tofu, from scratch, every day. A couple of women stood at the counter, buying bricks of smooth tofu made earlier in the morning. I heard the car approaching from behind, slowing, and pulling over to the curb. I kept walking. The car came up so the front passenger window was even with me. It was rolled down. A guy stuck his head out, holding a gun, an automatic of some kind. He'd turned the automatic on its side, like they do in movies about modern-day gangsters who don't know how to shoot.

He spoke in Mandarin. It was badly accented with the flavor

of a low-class Hong Kong upbringing—mixed with what he must have thought made him sound like a ghetto gang member.

"*Woei, ji bai!*" he said.

I concentrated on him, on what he was saying, instead of on the gun. I really badly wanted to concentrate on the gun. The insults weren't going to do too much damage. That gun, on the other hand . . . But I tried to ignore it. If he was going to shoot me, he'd have done it and moved on. Or maybe he just wanted to see me sweat. Maybe he wanted me to beg, and then he'd kill me. Either way, it was better to think about what he was saying and to watch his facial expressions and not to focus on that small, efficient-looking black hole of the barrel. He had thick, full eyebrows, like a couple of hairy black caterpillars were resting on his forehead.

"Hongkie," I said.

"What?" He said.

"You're a Hongkie," I said. "You said *'woei, ji bai'* instead of *'wei, ji bai,'* like most mainland Chinese would have. You're from Hong Kong."

"Yeah, you think you're pretty fucking smart," the driver said in English. He leaned forward over the steering wheel so he could see me. His hair was so slick with some kind of oil that there was a luster to it. It was almost blue-black. It looked dyed. A curl hung down on his forehead, as if it had just fallen there. It had probably taken him ten minutes in the mirror with a comb to get it that way. He moved his head slowly, as if he didn't want to disturb the whole effect.

I kept looking at his partner, Eyebrows. Eyebrows with the gun. I was fairly sure these were the same two who'd jumped Corinne outside her door that night. They looked younger now that I was seeing them in daylight. Since I'd come up on them from behind at her door, I'd seen them mostly from the back.

They were thin to the point of being skinny. Eyebrows was wearing a short-sleeved polo shirt, and I could see the ropy veins in
his forearms. They both had poufy pompadour hair, like Chinese
gang members. They both looked jittery. I wondered if they were
using crack or something else to keep them wired. Chinese gangs
like selling heroin; it was, for the moment at least, their preferred
stock in trade. But gang members used other drugs, meth or
crack. If this pair was wired with meth, that was just one more
fun factor in the equation. Someone's pointing a gun at you *and*
he's just crispy enough to make him a little unbalanced. Or a lot.
Nice.

"I'm not too fucking smart," I said. "I'm the one standing here
with a bag of *longan* fruits, and you guys are the ones with the
gun."

Eyebrows said something to the Curl that I didn't catch. Then
he spoke to me again.

"You wonder why we don't *tiu* that slut?" "*Tiu*" was young-
tough-guy slang for "screw." In this case, he meant it as something more felonious. The other word he used was "*jian huo,*"
another Hokkien street slang expression. He was still holding the
gun sideways. He was still pointing it at me.

Common sense said Eyebrows wasn't going to shoot me.
Then again, common sense didn't have all its vital organs about
four feet from the barrel of that gun. I tried to keep my breathing
steady. I focused on the exhalations. All I knew about guns was
stuff I'd heard my father say, usually when he was making fun of
the way they were used in crime shows on TV. Even so, I knew
that at this range, even if he was stupid and nervous, or jittery on
crack, he'd have to work hard to miss me.

"You're smart enough to know why we aren't rubbing her," he
said. The Curl leaned over, again to speak across the inside of the
car to me, again turning his head slowly so his 'do wasn't threatened.

"She gonna tell us where they are," he said. "Yeah."

Eyebrows smiled. His mouth smiled, at least. His eyes didn't. They looked like snake eyes. Cold. Reptilian.

"Probably not," I said.

The smile broke. His forehead crinkled, just a little.

"Probably," I said, "you'll do something stupid. You're scared, both of you, because you haven't gotten whatever it is you're supposed to get already. And if you screw up much more, you're going to get squeezed by your White Fan" — I used the Mandarin expression for their boss — "and so you'll panic. Do something stupid. And either get caught or . . ."

Eyebrows was trying to take it all in. He didn't look like he assimilated information quickly.

"Or?" he said.

"Or you'll mess up again," I said. "Like you did that night outside the apartment."

The look on his face, which he tried too late to hide, told me it had been him. Them.

"Shheeet," he drawled out. "You talkin' trash."

I couldn't tell if it was his accent or if he was trying to sound like a gangbanger. I just stood there, looking at him. The weight of the gun had pulled his hand down. The weight of having to think probably distracted him a little too. The weapon was pointing to about my knees now. He looked straight ahead, then back at me, trying for a contemptuous sneer. He couldn't pull it off. He jerked the gun up and pulled it back inside the car.

"Let's go," he muttered. The Curl slammed the gearshift out of neutral and managed to squeal the tires as they pulled away — then the car abruptly swerved, just missing a produce delivery truck that had pulled into the center lane in front of them.

I looked around. Cars kept going by. One of them, a candy-apple red Honda, slowed and turned into the parking lot behind me, which Dr. Luo shared with the tofu shop. The driver, a young

Chinese woman, looked briefly at me, wondering, I guess, what I was doing just standing there, a plastic bag hanging from my fist, looking around stupidly in the middle of the morning. The little bell on Dr. Luo's office door jangled. An old Chinese woman, different from the one who'd gone in, came out and looked up at me and smiled. A cloud passed over the sun, still low in the sky. Life went on. I could taste something warm and metallic in my mouth. I felt like someone had reached inside me, grabbed my stomach with both hands, and twisted. I wondered what the right thing to do was after having been threatened with a gun. I didn't know if there was an appropriate response. But I did the only thing I could have right at that moment. Stiff-legged, I walked into the narrow alley between Dr. Luo's clinic and the next building. I sat down. If anyone had been watching, they would probably have said I was not so much sitting as I was falling. The brick wall of the clinic was at my back. I was grateful for it; if it hadn't been there, I would have probably been lying on the ground instead of sitting. My hands shook. I put them in my lap, which didn't help. I put them on the ground on either side of me, pressing my palms hard enough into the rough, gritty concrete to make them sting.

There was a feeling of unreality about it all. *A gun? I'd actually had a gun stuck in my face?* I looked around. The morning was still bright. Cars kept going by on the street. It was the same normal day it had been ten minutes ago. Except someone had threatened me with a gun.

I slapped my palms together and rubbed them to get off the grit, then rubbed my face, my elbows resting on my bent knees. *Two choices,* I thought. *Sit here and quiver awhile and feel the tides of fear that are washing over me in sickening waves. Or get up and walk back to the restaurant. Screw it,* I thought, staring between my knees. *It's a good day to sit and feel sorry for myself.*

"Young man!" The voice cut into my thoughts. I looked up. It was a Chinese face looking back, from a couple of yards away. A woman. Old enough that her hair was past gray and more white. She was well dressed, in a skirt and blouse, with a thick yellow sweater on, and a necklace with a teardrop piece of jade hanging from it.

"You cannot be sitting around in an alley like that! This is a decent neighborhood," she said briskly. "We do not tolerate this sort of behavior."

It put things in perspective. "Yes," I said, then picked up my bag of *longan* fruits and pushed off the wall and stood. "But you know what happens."

"What happens when?" she said. She was perfectly straight, her posture erect. She'd turned herself so her right hand, holding her purse, was turned away from me.

"What happens when you allow *laowai* to start moving into the neighborhood," I said. "Place just goes to hell."

I walked around her, staying far enough away so she wouldn't feel threatened, and went to work.

"Will you come in for a minute?" Corinne asked.

I did. She put a kettle on the stove and got out a teapot and a couple of cups. It was close to midnight. It had been busy at the Palace. It felt good to sit. A chef's working career isn't much longer than a professional athlete's. The long hours standing, bending over or squatting to get pots or food stored on low shelves, the hours, the heat of the kitchen—they begin to add up. I was a long way from having to think about that. Even so, I could feel the muscles in my lower back slowly start to unclench as I relaxed in Corinne and Bao Yu's apartment kitchen.

"I've been getting some calls," she said. "Threatening ones." She sat down opposite, poured both cups full, then pushed one across the table to me.

"Funny you should mention that," I said.

"You've gotten some calls too?"

I shook my head. "They were a little more direct." I told her about the two in the car. And the gun.

"Were you scared?"

"You've done my laundry before, remember?" I asked her.

"What does that have to do with anything?"

"Well," I said, "Trust me. I don't think you'd have wanted to have washed my underwear after that."

She told me about the calls she'd been getting on her cell phone. A voice she didn't recognize told her that she needed to be careful, that people were watching her, that something bad could happen to her in the near future.

"They think I have the inventory. The diamonds."

"But you don't?"

"Sure I do," Corinne said. "That's why I'm working ten-hour shifts as a waitress, listening to wrinkly old Chinese businessmen proposition me. And that's how I'm able to afford these upscale digs." She fanned her hands over the tiny kitchen.

"The question was rhetorical."

She looked at me and didn't say anything.

"We need to tell Agent Masterson," I said. "About the encounter I had this morning and about the phone calls."

She took a sip of tea and continued to look at me over the cup. "Has it occurred to you that our relationship is built largely on someone trying to hurt me?"

"We have a relationship?"

"If you'll recall," she said, "I asked you pretty much the same question not that long ago. Your answer was not exactly forthcoming."

"No, no," I said. "You asked if I was attracted to you. I answered straight up. Being attracted to someone isn't the same as having a relationship. If it were, Langston and Bao Yu would already be the Hottest Couple of the Year instead of just now going out together for the first time."

Corinne tilted her head. A thick strand of her hair dropped down. It lay along her neck just for a second, and I could see it coil, with an inky shimmer, in the kitchen light.

"You're an interesting person," she said.

I picked up my teacup. It was so hot, I had to hold it with my fingertips. I didn't say anything because, really, what can you say when someone says you're interesting? Agree and you sound like a pompous jerk. Disagree and it sounds like you're just trying to get them to talk more, to tell you more about why they think you're interesting. And that comes with its own potential for pompous jerkiness. Better just to shut up.

"Are you scared now?" she asked.

"A little bit." I took a sip of the tea, sucking in just a little with a lot of air to cool it. Chinese drink tea so hot it can blister paint. It was just short of boiling. I sat back in the chair, rubbed my face, and realized I was tired. Part of it was the adrenaline dump from the morning. I'd had someone point a gun at me and threaten me. It was a new experience. It wasn't one I thought I could ever get used to.

"Mostly, though," I said, "I'm getting pissed. I don't like being scared. So after I'm scared for a while, being scared turns to being angry."

"I haven't ever seen you angry," she said.

I put my cup of tea back on the table. "You will," I said. "Probably. And then maybe you'll think I'm really interesting."

32

Rule #51: *If you can't be tough or smart, at least try to be interesting.*

I called Ms. Masterson the next morning, Friday, after Langston, Corinne, and Bao Yu all piled into the Toyota with me and drove to Forest Park.

"Where are you?" she asked. I told her.

"I'll be there in half an hour," she said.

She was. We were easy to find. Forest Park is one of the largest urban parks in the United States, bigger, in fact, than Central Park. I was told this the third day I was in St. Louis. St. Louisans are proud of the place. It's a sprawling big square of green, very close to the center of the city. Ballparks, open meadows, and acres of woods there have stayed like they were two centuries ago, while the city grew up all around it. Spacious as it is, there still aren't that many places where several dozen Chinese and Chinese Americans can hide. Even if they tried. Which this crew didn't. They, along with a few *laowai* like me, swarmed all over the grassy, shaded lawn to the south of the Art Museum. The Park Board workers had already put up the tents, arranged in a wide, open rectangle. Some park workers were unloading a pickup truck full of plywood sheets and metal support poles; the plan was to turn it into a portable stage for all the performances for the festivities that were about to unfold.

"What's going on?" Ms. Masterson asked. I'd seen her park

her car in the Art Museum lot, in a space with a sign reading RE-
SERVED FOR MUSEUM BOARD MEMBERS.

"Chinese Festival," I said. "All weekend. Folk dancing, food, ac-
robatics, drumming, food; there's a calligraphy booth where you
can have your name written in Chinese, a big parade with the lion
dancers. Did I mention the food?"

"How's the food?"

I shrugged. "About what you'd expect. Has to be pretty Americanized to sell well. Egg rolls, fried rice — stuff like that."

"So if it isn't all that great, how come you're talking about it?"

"Sometimes I like Americanized Chinese food," I said. "That
gloppy sweet sauce, everything fried, way too salty. Gotta have it
now and then."

"Can't saying something like that get you thrown out of the
Traditional Chinese Chefs Union?"

"Probably. I'm behind in my dues, anyway."

"Where's Corinne?" she asked.

I tilted my head toward the parking lot. "She just went to
get some of the rope they're using to hang up the lanterns and
streamers," I said. "She's with Langston. She'll be right back."

"Got time to have a little talk?"

"I think I can work you in. I'm really just here as a token anyway."

We walked right across the street from where the setup was
going on, to a low concrete wall that served as a bench. Off to
our left was a three-times larger-than-life statue of Louis IX, who
gave the city its name despite the fact he'd been dead for about
five hundred years before the first settlers came here. We looked
down a steep, long hill and out over the whole eastern half of Forest Park and off further in the distance, over the downtown part
of the city. The view was grand, a landscape unfolding out that
reached to the end of the park, nearly half a mile away.

"I told them they were probably already in trouble with their White Fan." I'd given Ms. Masterson a play-by-play of the street-side encounter with Eyebrows and the Curl the day before. "And I said it'd cause them to do something stupid and get caught."

"Did they know what you were talking about?"

I shrugged. "I'm not really up on Hong Kong street slang or Chinese gang slang. 'White Fan' is a title, sort of like an under-boss. He'd be the person those two would report to. If they screw up, he'll be the one who comes down on them. But the word might be dated. Maybe there's a new term for it."

"They got the picture, though," Ms. Masterson said. "You pro-voked them." She shook her head. "They were pointing a gun at you, and you stood there and provoked them."

"I'm impetuous."

"Really?"

"No," I said. "I was being sarcastic. I'm not impetuous at all." I thought, just for a second, about picking up Corinne at that rest stop. Well, except for that. Or for listening to the call left on her cell phone. Or for driving all the way back to Buffalo to pick her up when I could have just sent her the money for a plane ticket. But mostly I wasn't impetuous. Honest.

"I'm just getting tired of having these people threatening me, threatening Corinne. It's distracting. It sucks up energy, worrying about it."

"This is kind of serious, Tucker," Ms. Masterson said. She was sitting beside me. It was clear, the sky bright, deep blue. I could see the Arch way off on the horizon.

"Kind of?"

"Very serious, actually," she said. "I just know you have a pen-chant for understatement, and I wanted to cater to it. It's also a good policy when explaining to civilians about the potential for danger that they not be unduly alarmed."

"How can you tell if they're unduly alarmed?" I asked.

"In your case," she said, "I guess you might get so excitable that you'd actually fold your arms across your chest or something theatrical like that. You're an interesting case, Tucker."

I thought it might be a little precious for me to observe aloud that she was the second woman in less than twenty-four hours who had made that observation. So I kept it to myself. Because again, how do you reply? I did, though, allow myself a moment to enjoy it. Being "interesting" isn't maybe quite as rewarding as if she'd called me "mysterious." Or "enigmatic." Then again, Corinne hadn't called me anything like that, either. I'd settle for "interesting." I was still mulling over the possibilities of other adjectives I might like to be called when she spoke again.

"Think about how tough this is for me," she said.

"Yeah, I've been ruminating on that," I said. "Keeps me awake nights."

She sighed. "I want to cause you enough worry to be concerned, but not so much I cause you a lot of undue anxiety."

"Exactly how much anxiety is due in situations like this," I asked her, "before it becomes undue?" I told her what I'd told Corinne the night before.

"So," she said. "At the risk of sounding like your counselor, what are you feeling about all this?"

"I'm scared," I said. "I don't like being scared. I can handle it for so long before getting scared turns into getting angry."

"I have that feeling about you," she said. "You seem like the kind of person who's easygoing, doesn't get too upset about much. But when you get pushed, find yourself being driven into a corner, then you get angry."

I didn't know what to say to that. There was only so much me-talk I could take.

I'd turned sideways on the concrete wall to face Ms. Masterson and so I could also see across the street to find Corinne. I spotted her at the same time she saw me. She came over and sat down beside me.

"Anything you can tell me about the two with the gun?" Ms. Masterson asked.

"They're from Hong Kong, probably originally from Hokkien," I said.

"How do you know?"

"The guy asked me if I wondered why they didn't *tiu* Corinne," I said. "He stuck the word in there; it came out like he didn't mean it. I think he was nervous, trying to sound tough. So he automatically went back to the Hokkien dialect."

"What's '*tiu*'?"

"Literally it means to screw," I said. "But in that context, he was using it as a term of aggression, asking me if I understood why they hadn't killed her."

"So we're looking for people from Hong Kong but with roots in—where was it?"

"Hokkien," I said.

"That should narrow it down," Corinne said.

Ms. Masterson looked at her.

"There are several hundred million Chinese who speak Hokkien," Corinne said. "It's the native dialect in Fujian, a big part of southern China. It'd be like looking for a killer and trying to narrow it down to only those Americans who speak with a southern accent."

"Here's the part I don't get," Ms. Masterson said. "Why would these guys be trying to scare you?" she asked.

"I'm not really an authority on Chinese gang mentality," I said. "But at least partly it's a macho thing, I'd guess. They started it by making a run at me. The guy back in Buffalo."

"Rest his soul," Ms. Masterson said.

"You were in the wrong place at the wrong time," Corinne said.

Which would again be a good way to define our relationship, I thought about saying, but I knew Ms. Masterson wouldn't know what I was talking about, so I kept it to myself and kept going.

"If — what was his name?"

"Bobby Chu," Ms. Masterson said.

"If I hadn't happened to be outside there on the sidewalk that morning," I said, "and if young Mr. Chu had gotten to Corinne first, they probably wouldn't have had any interest in messing with me."

"You're not the primary target here," Ms. Masterson agreed. "But now they have to include you because otherwise they feel like you're going to be between them and Corinne?"

"Right," I said. "And if they had gotten to her first, Ms. Chang here, being a shy and fragile Oriental flower, would have wilted and told Chu whatever he wanted to know."

"Uh, yeah," Ms. Masterson said. "Funny you mention that." She shifted around on the ledge so she faced Corinne.

"What exactly did he want to know?" she asked. "What did the two men at your apartment door want to know, the same two who are now pointing guns at your beloved here and who are, we can safely presume, calling to chat you up with threatening messages?"

"You've asked me that before," Corinne said.

"I have," Ms. Masterson replied. "And you still haven't given me an answer that's going to help me out."

Corinne looked out at the skyline. "You can figure it out," she said. "They think somehow I have the inventory — or I know where it is."

Ms. Masterson shifted back. She didn't say anything. She just looked at Corinne. I wondered who was going to crack first. Either Ms. Masterson was going to say, *And do you have it or know where it is?* Or Corinne was going to say, *I don't*, without Ms. Masterson asking. It was a good matchup. FBI agent toughness versus about three thousand years of Chinese stoicism.

Ms. Masterson broke. I'd have bet on that. "So, is there anything you can tell me concerning the whereabouts of those diamonds that might be useful in, you know, saving your life? Do you have them, by any chance?"

"Sure," Corinne said. "I already explained this to Tucker. I've got them. I'm worth millions. I just enjoy working in a Chinese restaurant in St. Louis, living in a tenement, and hanging out with the White Devil here."

"Wait a minute," I said. "I take exception to that."

"You do?"

"Sure," I said. "That's a perfectly lovely apartment you're in."

From the grassy area where the festival was being set up, someone started banging a hammer against a metal pole, making a clanging, tinny noise. Ms. Masterson stood up and straightened her dress.

"Well," she said. "I'm going to give your description of the two in the car to the police in University City and to the police in St. Louis as well. They'll be on the alert for the car and these two. That's about all I can do right now."

She continued, "This is going to be an exciting story to tell your children one day. All about how you met and fell in love and had to dodge Chinese gang members and try to solve the mystery of missing Montreal diamonds. But . . ." She paused. I looked up at her. "But try to be as careful as possible, so you can survive long enough to actually have those kids."

33

Rule #55: *Sometimes being tough isn't anything more than knowing when and where to run.*

The world smells different in the spring. It also smells different in St. Louis than where I had always smelled spring before. Maybe it was just that in St. Louis there was a longer time to experience it. I was used to the short and icy springs of New England. Spring, back in Andover and up in New Hampshire during my stay at Beddingfield, was a hiccup between winter and summer. Springtime in New England was a one-night stand. Here, in the Midwest, spring had kept promising and flirting and an infatuation developed. In the end, though, spring delivered here. The world was green and fresh, the air cottony soft, warm, with the aroma of what seemed like a whole botanical garden of new flowers on it.

Now, a day after our conversation with Ms. Masterson, the earthy smells of spring were mixed with the sweet, oily aroma of sizzling egg rolls. And smoky fried rice. The sharp, meaty fragrance of pork being seared, glistening in its own succulent fat. That unmistakable perfume of soy sauce hitting a hot griddle that could make my mouth start to water even if I was completely full. Langston and I stood at the edge of it all. Corinne was somewhere in the crowd. She had volunteered to work an afternoon shift at a booth sponsored by the Chinese Business Association that was handing out information for new immigrants. How to re-up their visa status, get medical care, sign up for English classes.

The day before, the same grassy lawn by the Art Museum had been filled with volunteers decorating tents and hooking up propane tanks to fuel wok rings set into portable tabletops. Now it teemed with festival-goers. They were lined up a dozen deep and more at the food booths. On the stage, a troupe of Chinese drummers pounded out a vibrating, bassy concert we could hear even though we were only on the edge of the festival grounds. On the stone ledge where Corinne, Ms. Masterson, and I had been sitting yesterday, a family was arranged, a mother and father balancing paper plates of glistening brown fried noodles on their laps, feeding three young kids, who, in between slippery bites of the noodles, were gnawing on skewers of grilled chicken.

"All kinds of ethnic fun," Langston said.

"Oh yeah," I said. "One happy family."

Everybody's got ethnic festivals. Street fairs to celebrate Cinco de Mayo, church parking lots that turn into weekend celebrations of Polish sausage and polka, Italian American days. The Chinese have them too. One difference is that at Chinese festivals, there's often a certain electricity. It's an undercurrent that buzzes and hums, unnoticed unless you're sensitive to the vibrations. That happens, I guess, when you bring together a bunch of people who are ethnically and genetically pretty close to being exactly the same, but who are simultaneously separated by ideologies as different as Hong Kong brashness and Taiwanese nationalism. Toss in some political conflicts between groups, some of which go back to the time when people were carving their thoughts on bone, and it gets even more interesting. The Taiwanese keep immigrants from mainland China at a cool distance. Han Chinese, the biggest ethnic group from the mainland, have a tendency to look down on Chinese minorities like the Hakka. There are subtle slights, rivalries, the echoes of long-ago disputes. All of it is invisible to the average non-Chinese attending one of these festivals.

I knew about some of it. It was something that revealed itself slowly in Chinese restaurant kitchens. Most of it meant more to Langston than it did me. Langston's great-grandfather had been a bigtime silk merchant in Shanghai back in the thirties. His warehouses were looted when the Japanese invaded in 1937; the Wu family barely made it out of the city. They left China, went first to Malaysia, which turned out not to be such a great step because the Imperial Japanese Army was heading in the same direction. The Wu family spent the rest of war as prisoners of the Japanese. Langston's grandfather went to Taiwan after the war, and later his father came to the United States to go to college. He never went back to Asia. Langston and his two sisters were both ABCs—American-born Chinese.

"Yeah, one big happy family," he said. "Just slightly dysfunctional."

"Slightly?"

We wandered around. Under a stand of pines, there was a demonstration of *taiji*. It was average. The demonstrators knew the movements. They didn't have any *jing* in them, though, none of the crackling energy that elevates *taiji* from a form of gentle exercise into a fighting art. *Taiji* was a kind of moving meditation for them, a pleasant exercise. They "pushed hands," facing off and rolling, deflecting, and pushing in, arms interlocked, like graceful dancers. But they didn't have the soft, concealed, explosive power of real *taiji* experts. A troupe of lion dancers paraded by, twisting, turning, crouching under the long silk trail of the "lion," its gaudy red and gold head snapping its jaws and jerking to and fro to the sound of drums and cymbals from dancers gathered around it.

"Have we had about all the fun we can stand?" Langston asked after we'd been there and looked around for a while. We'd left the crowd and were sitting side by side at one of the rows of metal picnic tables that had been assembled under a dining tent. I had nearly finished a paper boat of fried rice in front of me. It was okay. It wasn't as good as what I could have made. It wasn't even as good as Ms. Masterson's first efforts.

"Agreed," I said. I tossed the last couple of bites of the rice into a trash can at the end of the table. "We just have to find Corinne."

"Found," Corinne answered. She'd come up from behind us and slid onto the bench beside me.

"I assume I am easy to spot in this crowd," I said to her.

"Not really," she said. "Look around. There are more of your kind around here than there are of mine."

"My kind?"

"*Laowai.*"

"I meant that I must be easy to find because of my rugged good looks and suave demeanor."

"Oh yeah," she said. "That's what I meant by 'your kind.' The rugged-good-looks, suave-demeanor kind."

"There is no 'kind' of that," I said. "I am unique."

"Listen," Langston said. "Love to hang around here all afternoon eating pork fried rice and listening to your witty repartee, but, instead, how about we head home?" He'd gone out the night before with Bao Yu. I hadn't gone to bed until after two in the morning, and he still wasn't home yet. I assumed things were going at least okay between the two of them.

"Fine," I said.

"It isn't repartee," Corinne said. "It's flirt talk."

I saw a head and shoulder duck back behind the flap of the Chinese Students Association tent. Maybe twenty yards away from us. It was the movement that caught my eye. It was too quick, too jerky. It didn't fit the rhythm of the rest of the festival. Nobody moves that way in a big crowd. I stared at the place where it disappeared. The head didn't reappear.

"Let's go," I said. I'd parked down the hill from the festival.

The tents, the music, the crowds, were all between us and the Toyota. The easy thing to do would have been to turn to the left and follow the sidewalk down the slope, then cut back across at the foot of the hill, along the street where I'd parked. Instead, I went straight, with Corinne and Langston beside me, into the festival, aiming for the tent where I'd seen the head and shoulders duck back out of sight.

I was fairly sure I recognized the head. It was time to find out if I was right.

The three of us plunged right into the heart of the festival.

Langston had known me a long time. So maybe he could sense something in the way I was walking. Maybe he just knew something was up. It was hard to tell with Langston. He and Corinne were following me. I could feel him move over to my left side.

"*Shenme shi qing?*" he asked, very quietly, staying close to me so Corinne didn't hear. "What's up?"

"Not sure," I said, "but it will be interesting to find out."

Corinne took a couple of quick strides and caught up with me on my right. Without looking, I reached for her hand. She didn't say anything. She hadn't known me all that long. Three months or so. Maybe, though, she knew, too, that something was up. She didn't ask questions. She just kept walking with me, kept beside me.

I kept the pace slow, leisurely. Like the three of us were just wandering through the festival, enjoying ourselves. We stopped and looked at the booths displaying Chinese crafts, intricate paper cutouts, calligraphy, cheap ceramic tea sets. Trying to look as casual as I could, I stepped away from Langston and Corinne and fished my phone from my pocket and hit Ms. Masterson's number.

"Remember where we were at Forest Park yesterday?" I said when she answered. She did.

"We're there now. So are the two guys who pulled the gun on me."

"You're sure?"

"No," I said, "but I'm going to find out."

"Just stay where you are," she said. "I'm just passing the Parkway entrance to the park; I'm on my way. Stay on the phone."

I kept the phone in one hand, took Corinne's hand with the other, and angled the three of us toward the tent where I'd seen the head pop around then jerk back. When we reached the tent, I went past it, looking straight. I didn't bother to look around for anyone. Whoever it was I'd seen—or thought I'd seen—I didn't think they'd still be there. I was looking for somebody else. It didn't take too long to find him. Benjamin Ma was the cook at the Hunan Wok. He was walking toward us with his girlfriend beside him, a busty redhead who was almost half a foot taller. I lifted my chin without breaking stride.

"Hey, Ben," I said, "how's it going?"

"Not bad," he said, continuing to walk in the other direction. I turned my head as they both walked by, trying to make the movement as natural as I could.

"You going to be at the Palace after work tomorrow?" I said to Ben's back. He pivoted, still walking, and stuck his thumb up. I looked past him. I saw the Curl and Eyebrows. Hanging back, trying to stay in the crowd. But it was them. It was the Curl's head I'd seen from around the corner of the tent. They were following us. I tried just to glance, to keep my head turned to Ben so it wasn't obvious I was looking at them. I wasn't sure it had worked. Eyebrows was wearing a tan hoodie, big and bulky, and a pair of jeans with sneakers. The Curl had on the same jeans and sneakers, with a T-shirt and a red-striped cotton dress shirt over it, unbuttoned. It didn't look like there was any way the Curl could be concealing a gun. That hoodie, though, I thought, was a perfect way to cover one in Eyebrows' waistband.

I slowed my pace enough so Langston could come up beside me.

"Just keep walking," I said, loud enough so they could both hear me. "And don't look back. There are a couple of guys following us."

Langston didn't say anything.

Corinne said, "Okay."

"They're the same guys who jumped you outside your apartment," I said to Corinne. "The same guys who stopped their car and pushed a gun in my direction."

Langston made a "hmm" sound. And didn't say anything else. Neither did Corinne. She squeezed my hand. When I glanced over at her, I saw her lips pressed together tightly. She looked straight ahead. I liked that. She didn't say *What're we going to do?* or get panicky. She just kept walking. I'd expected Langston's reaction. His "hmm" was to let me know he heard, he understood, and he was thinking about our options. I was thinking about them too.

I looked around as we walked. I didn't see any cops. If I had, I realized, it wasn't going to help. What was I going to do? Ms. Masterson had told us she would give the police the description of the two. But they'd threatened me in one of the suburbs of St. Louis City. City and suburb police departments don't always communicate. I didn't have any guarantee that city cops I might find would have any idea of what I was talking about. And by the time I explained it, the two would be gone. They could disappear into the crowd, keep an eye on us, then make their move when we finally did leave. I didn't like the option. It wasn't good. It was the best one I could think of, though. And, I admitted to myself, I was tired of this. I didn't have to push it now. And maybe it wasn't fair to Corinne and Langston that I would. Even so, I'd had enough. I lifted my phone.

"Still there?" I asked.

"Yep," she said.

"My car's parked at the bottom of the hill west of the Art Museum, on Valley Drive," I said. "We're going there now."

"Stay where you are."

"Nope," I said. "It's too crowded. Somebody's going to get hurt."

"Tucker—" I heard her say. And then my phone was back in my pocket.

We were at the outer edges of the festival, still walking. I was still holding Corinne's hand. There were enough people around I didn't think the two would do anything too extreme. At least for the moment. There weren't nearly enough people for us to blend into the crowd, though. And, with every step we took, the crowd was thinning. If we stopped moving now, we would be obvious. If we kept walking, we were soon going to be on our way down the hill, heading toward the street where the car was parked, right out in the open. I thought of that gun Eyebrows had stuck in my face. I'd already made a choice, though.

"Car's down there," I said. "We need to get there as fast as we can."

"Okay," Langston said. I looked over at Corinne. She nodded. We ran.

34

Rule #57: *There's often a "however" in life.*

The Art Museum was built on the highest hill in Forest Park. It looks out east to the long slope of Art Hill, with its statue of Louis IX on a horse, his sword lifted high. In the winter, there could be a couple of hundred sledders on the hill in front of the museum. On the south side of the museum, the shoulder of the hill slopes away from the museum buildings and the big, open space where the festival was still going on. We were at the top of the shoulder. When we started to run, we went down its grassy flank. There were some big trees. Their branches already had leaves, so it was shady under them, with dapples of sunlight in places. The ground was steep enough for us to move fast. I kept my strides short, though. I wanted to sprint but didn't. I didn't want to start running full tilt and risk stumbling. The ground was too uneven to go all out. Langston and Corinne were taking the same strategy. Running with quick, short strides, all of us abreast, all of us watching the uneven ground as we went over it.

I hadn't heard a lot of gunfire before. I went a couple of times with my father when he had to qualify, for his job, at the state police range over in Concord. It was exciting for a few minutes. The reality was that after the first few dozen rounds were fired, it got kind of boring. It wasn't boring now. Also, the sound was a lot sharper and louder than it had been at the range with my father, where I'd had on ear protectors. The first shot rang sharp, crisp. The air was clear, low enough in humidity that the crack carried. I involuntarily hunched when I heard the shot. I felt a sharp tug between my shoulder blades where the muscles in my back gave a quick spasm. Like stiffening my back muscles was going to stop a bullet. I tried to shrug my shoulders to loosen things. It's hard to do when you're running. I looked right, then left. Langston and Corinne were both still upright, still running. I took those as good signs.

In about thirty seconds, we were most of the way down the hill, into the woods near the bottom of the slope. The trees got thicker there. The ground cover was dense, overgrown. There wasn't any way a park mower could have gotten into the tangle here. There wasn't any grass to mow. Long ropes of grapevines twisted around on the ground, and the only other cover was a heavy mat of dark leaves, damp. I could smell the dirt and wet mulch where we kicked them up as we ran. Corinne was a couple of strides ahead of me. She tripped on a vine, went down to one knee, but before I could reach her, she was back up and getting her stride. It was impossible to get into the kind of flat-out, loping stride that would have given us much distance. On the other hand, all the trees made us harder targets. And if we were slowed down trying to get through it, so were the two coming after us. At least I hoped so. I fought the urge to turn and look back. I didn't want to risk falling if I did. And if they were behind us, there wasn't much I could do about it anyway.

Off to the left was a rock the color of concrete, about the size of the kitchen table in our apartment. It was rounded, with a silhouette that reminded me of a crouching bear. Or maybe a tiger coiled to spring. I was considering it as I ran and listened for the sound of another shot. Multitasking. I didn't think I was doing a very good job of any of it. Even so, I was distracted by the rock. I wanted to ask Corinne about it. *Hey,* I wanted to say, *that rock over there. Think it looks more like a bear or a tiger?* I didn't.

And then we were all three past the rock, and I heard a second shot and then a dull, clunking sound like someone had dropped a golf ball on a sidewalk. I heard Langston make a *huuhh* sound. He was a couple of paces behind me.

"You okay?" I yelled. I twisted around to see where he was. Hearing that noise from Langston, I felt my face flush. I suddenly wanted to throw up the fried rice I'd been eating only ten minutes ago but what seemed like about six months ago.

"Branch clipped me," Langston said. "I'm okay." He huffed. His face was pink. But he wasn't struggling. I glanced again at Corinne. She looked the same. She'd tied her hair back earlier in the day. She looked grim, determined. She was staring at some finish line up ahead, I thought. I wondered where it was. The Toyota had been a dependable machine, taking me all the way from New Hampshire out here, including a trip back to Buffalo to pick up Corinne. It was sucking a lot of oil, true. It was still a good car. It wasn't bulletproof, though. I didn't have a plan for what would happen after we got to it. I thought about how this seemed to be becoming a habit for me, making impulsive decisions and hoping that once made, something would open up for me. Then I thought that I was perhaps being just a little too introspective for a guy running down a hill through the woods with a couple of low-level Chinese gang thugs shooting at him.

I felt a quick flash of relief. I could see the road lined with parked cars. Another car was pulling up and stopping, double-parking, blocking off the street. Both doors opened, and I saw Mr. Cataldi jump out and take a squatting position, pointing his gun directly at the three of us. Behind him, on the other side of the car, I could see Ms. Masterson's head and shoulders over the hood. She had a gun pointed at us as well.

"Get! Down!" she shouted. We did. All three of us. Corinne was close enough to me I could reach out and push her. I put my hand between her shoulder blades and shoved, and since she was already leaning over, scouting for a place to land, she went down fast. It sounded like all the air in her lungs came out at once. I

dived. Corinne's elbow clipped my cheek as we went down. The
carpet of dead, wet leaves was thick, sloppy. I went face first into
it. My shoulders were hunched. My right arm hugged Corinne;
she had her left arm around my neck. I heard Langston hit the
ground, along with a squishy sound as he plowed into dank
mulch. I tensed, waiting for the shots. Wasn't much I could do
about it, short of burrowing into the clammy, matted leaves.
I gave it some consideration. Instead of the shots I expected, I
heard Mr. Cataldi.

"Stop! That's all! FBI!" Mr. Cataldi shouted, then it was Ms.
Masterson again. "Put the gun down! Put the gun down now!"

Corinne was trying to suck air in through her mouth in short
staccato bursts. I could feel my pulse in my temples. I realized
there was a rock digging into my left knee. Then I heard the wail
of sirens, way off in the distance, drawing closer. I lifted my head
just high enough to turn and glance at Langston. He stared back,
a big smear of dirt covering most of one cheek. There was a dried
leaf, ragged and torn, hanging from his hair, right in front of his
face. He didn't pull it off. He just left it there, keeping his face as
close to the ground as he could.

"Wow," he said.

Mr. Cataldi and Ms. Masterson were both trotting toward us.
As they got closer, Ms. Masterson said, "Are you all okay?" They
both had their guns out, both pointed up the hill past us. Ms. Masterson stopped where we were. Mr. Cataldi kept going, up the hill
toward the two who'd been chasing us.

"Okay," I said. I pulled my knee off the rock and got my leg
beneath me and sat up.

"*All* of you!" she said again. "Tell me if you are okay?"

"Okay here," Langston said. He pushed up with his hands and
sat on his knees.

Corinne rolled over. The front of her jeans and shirt were
streaked with mud. "Okay," she said. She sat up.

Ms. Masterson ran past us, following Mr. Cataldi up the hill. Below, the road was thick with police cars, lights churning. Cops were coming up toward us, at least a dozen of them. I looked over my shoulder. The Curl and Eyebrows were both face-down farther back up the hill, arms behind their backs. Mr. Cataldi was putting handcuffs on the Curl.

Corinne sat with her legs out in front of her.

"That was an experience," I said. I realized I was shaking a little.

"First for me," Langston said.

"Me too," Corinne said. "And that was enough."

The three of us stayed where we were, sitting on the damp, mulchy ground, which wasn't all that comfortable but which seemed, at least for the moment, at least for me, far preferable to doing anything so strenuous as actually trying to stand up. I had a feeling, given the way I was still shaking, that effort was going to take a while.

"Come on," I said. "Brisk run in the park. Who feels like jogging home?"

They both shot me expressions that told me they didn't appreciate my humor.

"You two are the reason our generation's in such poor shape," I said. But like them, I stayed right where I was.

35

Rule #97: *When you get tired of having things happen to you, start making things happen yourself.*

Five minutes later, when I did try to stand, I made it okay, but my knees were still wobbling. The last time they'd felt that way, I thought, was when the same two guys had pointed a gun at me. My knees didn't feel any weaker or wobblier now than they had then, I didn't think. Overall, I decided, though, that between having a gun pointed at me and having one shot in my direction, the latter was worse.

Langston was on his feet too, bent over, arms straight, hands on his knees, trying to get his breath. We were surrounded by cops. All of them talking at once, their radios chirping and crackling. One of them was giving directions to somebody. Ms. Masterson had come back to where we three were. The Curl and Eyebrows were being taken down the hill by four cops who were not being entirely solicitous in the way they pushed the two along. I glanced back at Langston. He straightened as I watched, then I saw him flinch. He rubbed his hand on his butt, pulled it away, and looked at it. He looked up at me, then showed me his palm. There was a dark blotch on it. I thought it was dirt.

"What the hell?" he said. He seemed perplexed. He twisted around to stare at his butt, and when he did, he swiveled in my direction. I could see a dark stain over one of his pants pockets. He touched it, more gingerly this time, and pulled his hand up to look at it again, as if he wanted to be sure.

"I got shot," he said. "In the ass. Can you believe it?"

Corinne was standing beside me now, gently yanking a twig from her hair. The front of her jeans was damp and dark from her knees all the way up to her waist. It looked like she'd tried to slide into third on a muddy baseball diamond.

I looked at Langston. "Are you going to live?"

"Do you think it could have hit any vital organs?" Langston asked back.

"In your ass?" Corinne asked.

Langston was trying to walk in small circles now, hopping and flinching with each step.

"There's some pretty important stuff in that immediate vicinity," he said.

Then one of the cops noticed Langston's limp and said, "Whoa, there." He took Langston by the shoulder. "We're going to need you to stand still here for just a minute."

"What's taking so long?" Ms. Masterson said.

"Park's jammed," another cop said. "Some big Chinese festival going on."

"Better be on the lookout for some opium dealing," I said. "Any time those people get together . . ."

"He's just been shot at," Ms. Masterson said to the cop when he cocked his head at me. "He's a little wired right now. It's the adrenaline talking."

"No," Langston said. "He talks like that all the time."

"He has some deep-seated issues with Asians," Corinne said.

"All three of them," Ms. Masterson told the cop, "are a little odd. But basically harmless."

The cop shrugged. "We're trying to get the ambulance through on a service road, and they're lost. Should be here in a second."

It took a little longer than that. The EMTs, when they got there, lowered the gurney so Langston could slide onto it. He did, favoring his left side. When one of the EMTs told him to lie flat on his back, he said "Are you serious?" He lay on his right side.

We told him we'd follow him to the hospital. He said he hoped he would still be alive by then. The EMT said that in his professional opinion that was a pretty good possibility.

Corinne and I sat in the waiting room at the ER. We'd ridden over with Ms. Masterson about half an hour after we'd watched Langston loaded into the ambulance. We'd stood around at the park for a while first. Now we were sitting around in the ER. It was less fun than it sounded. We were both still wet. We looked like we'd spent the afternoon crawling through the woods. Ms. Masterson had stayed with us the whole time and had asked us both about a dozen times if we were sure we were okay. My cheek was a little puffy where Corinne had clipped it when I dived beside her. Other than that, we told her, we were both okay. She asked me why I hadn't followed her orders and stayed where we were. I considered some clever responses. But I was still too wired to come up with anything good.

"Maybe I just got tired of waiting for something to happen to me—to us—" I jerked my head in Corinne's direction. "Maybe it was time for something to happen to them instead," I said.

She gave me a long look but said nothing other than to excuse herself and go off to do whatever FBI agents had to do after they've drawn their weapons. I assume it involved at least as much excitement as we were having. Finally, Langston came through the swinging doors and into the waiting room. He walked slowly and stiffly. A nurse was walking beside him.

"Aren't you supposed to be in a wheelchair?" I asked.

"Sitting down is not a priority for me," Langston said. "I've just had a bullet taken out of my ass."

"You did not," the nurse said. She was blond and had large breasts. I tried to read her nametag, just because I like to try to remember people's names. I did not get past her breasts, though.

They really were large. "The bullet grazed his cheek," she said. "Barely."

"And thank you for the compliment you gave to me on my ass back there," Langston said.

She flushed. I glanced at Corinne. She looked back at me. Very softly, she said, "Does that sound like flirt talk to you?"

"Possibly."

A cop came down the hall. I recognized him from the park.

"How you feeling?" he asked.

"Fine," Langston said, "for someone who's just survived a gunshot."

"Looked at the doctor's report," he said. "'Gunshot' might be exaggerating a bit. Doctor said he wiped the wound with some hydrogen peroxide and put a little dressing on it."

"Was a gun shot at me?" Langston asked.

The cop nodded.

"Bullet connect with me?"

"Can't argue with that," the cop said.

"Then I've survived a gunshot."

"He's a little theatrical," the nurse said.

"I might be weak from blood loss," Langston said.

"We had a guy in here the other night who gashed his finger opening a can of tomato sauce," the nurse said. "He bled more than you did."

"So can I go home to recuperate and try to rebuild what's left of my life?" Langston asked.

The cop smiled. "Are you kidding?" he said. "You said it yourself. You're the victim of a gunshot wound. Do you have any idea how much paperwork we're going to be doing on you?" He pulled a clipboard from under his arm, thick with a sheaf of paper clipped on it. "We might as well get started." Then he looked at Corinne and me.

"The hospital cafeteria has some of the best blueberry croissants in town," he said. "You'll have time for them, trust me. Why don't you go get something to eat while we interview the wounded warrior here?"

"Do you think these are the best blueberry croissants in town?" Corinne asked me after she'd torn off another piece to contemplate it a moment before popping it into her mouth. I swallowed the last of my own.

"Not sure," I said. "I do not have the broad spectrum of experience necessary to make that call."

"Do you think it might be worthwhile for us to explore that subject further?"

"If the other blueberry croissants in town taste anything at all like this," I said, "I think that'd be an excellent idea."

Mr. Cataldi came through the entrance to the cafeteria and looked around. We weren't hard to find. On a Saturday evening, there were some people in scrubs sitting around drinking coffee and a couple of families eating. Otherwise, the cafeteria was empty. He sat down after filling a cup of coffee at the counter. He asked about Langston. Then he told us that Eyebrows and the Curl were in custody. They'd asked for a lawyer, he said.

"They say anything else?" I asked.

"They claim they were just trying to scare you."

"Langston's ass says otherwise," I said.

"They say that was an accident," he said. "The one with the gun says he wasn't aiming at you. Their story is they were shooting to try to get you to stop. They think the bullet might have hit something and ricocheted into your friend."

I thought about the tiger-shaped rock. Or bear-shaped rock. That sound I'd heard. It could have been a bullet ricocheting off a rock. It didn't sound like the way bullets ricochet on TV. As with the blueberry croissant situation in St. Louis, I had to admit it wasn't an area on which I had a lot of authority.

"Did they say why they were trying to scare us?" I asked.

"They said they would prefer to, ah, delay further inquiries until the arrival of counsel."

"They really said that?" Corinne asked.

"I'm paraphrasing."

"What are they going to be charged with?" I asked him.

"I don't know yet," Mr. Cataldi said. "Technically, they're under the jurisdiction of the city of St. Louis. It'll be up to the prosecuting attorney. My guess is attempted murder."

"Really?" Corinne asked, surprised.

"Cops in St. Louis take a dim view of thugs shooting at people in Forest Park," Mr. Cataldi said. "It's bad for the city's image."

"Not all that great an experience for those being shot at, either," I said.

"How're you both doing?" Mr. Cataldi asked.

"Blueberry croissants are helping," Corinne said. She picked up the last piece, the end of the flaky, crusty crescent, and appraised it before eating it.

He looked at me. "Ever been shot at?"

"Eric Fletcher got me in the arm with a BB gun when I was thirteen," I said.

"Was it as serious a wound as your friend's?" he asked.

"Little more."

Mr. Cataldi nodded. He took a sip of his coffee.

"One more thing," Mr. Cataldi said. "According to their driver's licenses, neither of them are U.S. citizens. They both list Montreal as their residences."

"O Canada," I said.

36

Rule #27: *Never be afraid to get someone's complete attention if the situation warrants it.*

Two days after Eyebrows and the Curl made a run at us, they were still in custody. Ms. Masterson had called the day after the excitement to update me. A lawyer had appeared by the next morning, requesting bail for them. A prosecuting attorney for the city objected. The two were not citizens; if they were released on bond, there wasn't much to keep them in the country. Her argument was apparently persuasive. Both had been denied bail. Both were awaiting a hearing.

Corinne and I were back at the Eastern Palace, working the dinner shift. I was caught up with orders. I'd just plated stir-fried shrimp sprinkled with Dragon's Well tea. My guess was that Mr. Wen was dining with us. He was from Shanghai originally, had gone to college here. Now he was a local real estate baron in St. Louis. He liked the standards of Shanghai cuisine. He brought in clients at least once a week and ordered something from Shanghai. Like the shrimp. It was an easy dish to make, the shrimp stir-fried with just a light coating of egg whites and cornstarch, then tossed with fresh Dragon's Well tea leaves. I'd dribbled a little of the tea itself onto the shrimp, to accentuate the flavor, then tossed a sprinkle of the wet fresh-brewed leaves on top.

"You need any help, Jao-long?" I asked.

"Beef with broccoli," he said. *"Da-bao."* For "takeout." We didn't need to look into the dining area, to the counter where the orders were placed. We both knew the customers wouldn't be

Chinese. If the order had been for some real Chinese food, Jao-long would have never accepted my offer for help. The ants on the hill would have had to have been frantically crawling around, going completely crazy, before a chef would accept help from a colleague. We weren't nearly that busy. At any rate, accepting help to turn out an Americanized dish like beef and broccoli wasn't an admission that a chef was too busy. More likely it was a matter of sharing the boredom.

"Got it," I'd said to Jao-long. And I'd started to go to the locker where we had cubes of beef ready.

"Guy out back looking for Corinne," Thuy told me. He held a white plastic bucket, empty now. He'd been outside, dumping the limp, soggy leftovers from the stockpots into the dumpster. "Kind of weird. Why didn't he just come to the front?"

"Don't got it," I said to Jao-long. I put down a long-handled spatula that in Mandarin is just called a *shao,* or spoon, but in kitchen slang is a *gui-tou,* literally a "turtle's head" (which is slang itself for a penis with a big head).

I went through the kitchen door, into the dining room, then to the lobby, where Angela Li, the hostess that evening, was talking to a couple who were standing there, probably waiting for their order of beef and broccoli. They'd have to wait. I passed them, went out the front door of the Palace. I circled around to the alley. I tried to steady my breathing. I was angry. Deep-down-inside angry. I'd been angry ever since the Curl and Eyebrows had tried to jump Corinne. Maybe even before then. I wasn't sure. I *was* sure I had a target for all that anger. I stepped around the corner of the building quickly to find it. Him. It was less than twenty steps to the back door now. The more of those steps I was able to make before he knew I was coming, the better it would be for me. I could see his head and shoulders over the dumpster between us. He had his back to me. I stayed as close to the wall as I could. As I came around the edge of the dumpster nearest to me, he pivoted around quickly. He was skinny. Wearing a beige, short-sleeved polo shirt and black slacks. His black hair and thin mustache were both salted with white. I figured he must be in his late forties. His small eyes darted around like he was searching for an escape route. At the same time, he looked like he was afraid to move at all.

"Where's Wenqian?" I asked him. Confusion showed on his face. I liked that. That was the tactic Bobby Chu had used on me back in Buffalo. I only hoped I'd be more successful than Chu had been. In a few more steps, I was right on top of the man. With the natural swing of my arms in stride, I brought my right arm forward and up. He saw it coming and reached out to push it away, but I twisted my forearm at the same time, creating enough torque to intercept his arm and go around it. I grabbed his throat. With my left hand, I got a grip on his crotch. Under the material of his pants, I could feel a soft, warm package. Males have a natural disinclination to grab another guy's crotch. There isn't anything natural about grabbing someone there, at least not for most guys. I felt a little queasy, just for a second, but my anger was stronger than any squeamishness. A lot. I grabbed and squeezed. Not too much. Enough to get his attention. In case my hand around his throat wasn't doing the trick. I heard him make a high-pitched squeal. For a second, I thought he might wet his pants. While I was able to overcome my reluctance to grope a man's crotch to inflict some damage or at least some serious intimidation, I wasn't sure I'd be able to do so if he peed into it.

"Where's Wenqian?" I asked him again. I'd used it before to confuse him and get an advantage. Now I was repeating it just because I didn't know what else to say. I squeezed tighter on his throat, surprised at how good it felt. I thought I might just keep doing this, just keep going. I felt hot, flushed, like someone had jabbed me with a needle full of adrenaline. What would it be like to just keep squeezing? I could imagine this feeling just getting better and better. Still holding him, I pivoted. He pivoted with me, up on his toes, prancing as quickly as he could. We looked like we were waltzing and he was really, really eager to follow my lead. I shoved him hard against the brick wall. His head went back, and I heard it crack dully. I was still seeing things through a red haze.

"How about instead of telling me about Wenqian, you and I do a little talking?" I said to him in a voice that didn't sound like mine.

He kept squealing. I really didn't want to have any long conversations with him anyway. What I very much wanted to do was just to keep squeezing, keep my grip on his throat and his crotch, and keep squeezing and watch his eyes start to bulge. Then I was aware that someone was holding my shoulder.

"Tucker!" It was Corinne. "Tucker! Back off." She said this in Mandarin. She'd come out the back door. She was standing beside me, her hand gripping my shoulder tightly. Not as tightly as I was doing to the guy's throat and sack.

"You know him?" I asked her. But I kept looking at him.

"Let him go, Tucker," she said. "Please."

I released his crotch. It was still dry. All three of us stood there.

"Tucker," Corinne said quietly. "Meet Mr. Sung. My ex-boss."

37

Rule #5: *When someone has a grip on your crotch, they deserve all your attention.*

There are a lot of advantages in speaking another language. Any high school guidance counselor will be delighted to explain them. When those counselors are urging kids to sign up for freshman French, though, there's at least one advantage they probably don't mention. Even though it's a nice one. It's the one where you can understand what's being said in front of you without those doing the talking knowing that you understand it. Like I said before, I never got tired of that. Native French speakers or Spanish speakers might be a little careful in front of a stranger. They might figure their conversations with others can be overheard and understood. I'd never had any Mandarin-speaking Chinese I didn't know pay the slightest attention to me when they were speaking to one another in my presence. They saw a Caucasian face and assumed I thought they were speaking some exotic language no non-Chinese could possibly understand.

In Asian markets sometimes, I'd be standing beside a couple of old Chinese women. They would be muttering to one another about why those big hairy foreigners were coming into a place like this when they didn't know the first thing about cooking anything that was for sale there. I'd let it go on for a while, and then I'd speak up and say, "Yeah, I know what you mean. And they smell funny too."

Learning Mandarin was a long, slow process. I still made plenty of mistakes in grammar, and my pronunciation got corrected from time to time. But moments like that made it all worthwhile.

Mr. Sung switched to Mandarin pretty quickly after I let him go. Not long after I'd eased my grip on his throat and his crotch and he'd stopped squealing. He stayed up against the wall where I'd shoved him, touching his throat gently with his fingertips and shifting around, stepping on one foot, then slowly shifting to the other. He seemed to be testing to see if everything was still in place.

Corinne stood in front of him. She was wearing the black dress we'd bought at the mall. It was one of the first spring nights that could be called warm. Even so, with the sun dropping, so was the temperature. There was just enough cool in the air to raise bumps on her bare arms. She didn't seem to notice.

"What?" she said to Mr. Sung in Mandarin. Her shoulders were stiff. Her hands balled into fists. I wondered for a second if she was going to take a swing at Mr. Sung. I considered stepping a little closer to be able to stop her if she did. But then I figured what the hell, and I stayed where I was. Mr. Sung looked around. He glanced at me as if I might step in. When you're depending on a guy who's just hoisted you up by your throat and crotch to come to your rescue, you're in some trouble. He kept himself pressed up against the wall like he was trapped.

"What?" she said again. It was, I thought, the first time I'd seen Corinne at a loss for words. Her eyes were open wide. Her fists released into open palms that she turned over, her thumbs pointing out. Finally, she said, "Care to explain any of this? *Any* of it? Anything at all?"

"Wenqian," Mr. Sung said. He was trying to sound soothing. It wasn't working all that well. Maybe it was the tremble in his voice. I couldn't catch any accent.

"Yes," he said. "I can explain all of it. I don't think the time to do that is standing out here in an alley by a dumpster in the dark, in front of this *laowai*."

I kept my face a blank as much as I could. I still wasn't any good at it, even though I'd had some practice recently. I just kept looking at Corinne. I didn't see any advantage in letting him know I understood what he was saying.

"Oh, really? Where exactly would be a good place for you to explain it? Wait a minute," she added, without giving him a chance to answer. "I can think of a place. How about the office back in Montreal? You know, the one where I worked for you for all that time? The one where I walked in one morning and found it empty? That would have been a good place for you to explain it. I don't remember seeing you around that morning, though."

Now I watched Sung. He'd determined, apparently, that Corinne wasn't going to hit him. He straightened his shoulders, took a step away from the wall, then caught himself. He moved gingerly again, testing to see just how much it was going to hurt to walk. From his posture, I thought he might need a few minutes, at least.

"I certainly didn't do anything to cause you any trouble," he said. "You or any other of the employees."

"Aside from leaving us high and dry."

"I did what I thought was best for the company," he said. "That company was founded by my father. I have responsibilities for it you couldn't—"

"*Aiya!*" Corinne cut him off. "What responsibilities? *You. Took. Off!*" she said, slowly, emphasizing each word.

"I have your paycheck," he said. "I can explain. But I need to see you someplace where we can sit down and talk in a civilized way."

I was beginning to get the idea that Sung was a bullshitter. Now that neither Corinne nor I seemed to be a further threat, at least not an immediate one, he adjusted his shirt collar and

smoothed back his hair. He was trying to look like the successful diamond merchant, a man of means, a force in the business
world. He wasn't doing a great job.

"I have a phone number you can call," he said to Corinne. He
reached behind him, pulled out a slim wallet, and took out a card
that had been folded over. He handed it to her.

"Give me a call, and we'll meet and straighten out all this
mess," he said. By now his voice was almost haughty, like he was
transforming himself from a skinny guy in cheap clothes to a dignified businessman.

"Good evening to you," he said to Corinne. He pointedly
didn't look at me. He walked away, still trying to look dignified. It
wasn't easy. He was waddling a bit, his legs spread wide. Corinne
and I watched him go. He disappeared around the corner of the
restaurant. It was nearly dark. The air had gotten even cooler.
Corinne rubbed one bare arm, holding the folded paper in the
other.

"So that's what it's like when you're angry," she said.

38

Rule #61: *Trying times call for expensive tea.*

"You didn't mention the FBI to Sung," I said to Corinne.

We were sitting at the kitchen table back at the apartment. Langston was gone. He hadn't been home — he'd have left a note if he had been. Which meant he was off hanging out with Bao Yu and some of the guys from his restaurant's kitchen or somebody else in the Chinese restaurant business, eating pot stickers or dried watermelon seeds, and drinking tea or fiery Chinese liquor. I sort of wished I were with him. Ms. Masterson was sitting in the third chair, pretending to like Longjing tea. When I poured her cup, I explained its history.

"Supposedly the grandson of one of China's emperors went to the Hu Gong Temple, in Zhejiang Province," I said. "He tried the local tea and was so impressed that he took some of the leaves back to the emperor. The emperor named the eighteen tea bushes in front of the temple imperial property. They're still there; still producing tea."

"Is that where this came from?" Ms. Masterson asked. She peered into the cup at the limpid green liquid still sending up tendrils of hot steam.

"The tea from those bushes sells for more per ounce than gold," I said. "This likely came from right around the area, though. It's a variety called *que shi.*"

"Bird's tongue," Corinne translated.

Ms. Masterson nodded and took a short, breathy sip.

"How is it?" I asked.

"Hot." She put down the cup. "So," she said, turning to Corinne, "How come you didn't say anything to Mr. Sung about the FBI?"

"Or the guys who jumped you outside your apartment?" I added. "The same guys who shot at us in the park?"

"I don't trust him," Corinne said. "The less information he has, the better off we'll be." She glanced at me. "Isn't that one of Tucker's Rules?"

"Matter of fact, it is," I said. "Number sixty-three. When you're confronting an ex-boss who's being investigated by the FBI and who knows what other law enforcement agencies, it's best to be stingy with information you give him about the situation."

"Good rule," Corinne said, then turned to Ms. Masterson. "What do we do now?"

"We do some thinking about why the suddenly corporeal Mr. Sung has come here," Ms. Masterson said.

"To see me," Corinne said. "To explain what went on back at the shop in Montreal."

"And to give you your back pay," I said. "Remember? He told you he had what he owed you."

"You believe that?" Ms. Masterson asked, looking at Corinne.

"No," Corinne said. "It makes no sense."

Ms. Masterson turned to me. "You believe that?"

"I try to be optimistic," I said. "You think it's possible he may have come all the way here for some reason other than to explain to one of his ex-employees why he skipped out on his own business and to give her a handsome severance package?"

"It's possible. It is also possible I may get used to your incessant smart-assedness," she added. "But I doubt it."

"I thought for sure I was growing on you," I said. "Doesn't matter right now." I looked at Corinne. "For right now, it seems the better question is this: How did Sung know you were in St. Louis?"

Ms. Masterson tilted her head and shot her finger at me. "Precisely."

Corinne picked up her teacup and looked inside. "He didn't know Ariadna," she said. "Other than her, the only people outside of here who could have any way of knowing I'm here would be those Flying Ghosts who were in his office."

"Are we to assume Mr. Sung just might be in cahoots with the Flying Ghosts?" Ms. Masterson asked.

"You know what 'cahoots' means?" I asked Corinne.

"I do," Corinne said. "I have been speaking English for quite a while now."

"Just checking," I said. She rolled her eyes.

"I think we might assume that Mr. Sung and the Flying Ghosts are in cahoots," she said.

"I would venture to guess, speaking as a professional investigator," Ms. Masterson said, "that Mr. Sung became involved in some sort of scheme with the Flying Ghosts. Probably some sort of financial deal. Diamonds would be an excellent commodity to use to launder money."

"How does that work?" Corinne asked.

"I'm speculating here a little," Ms. Masterson said. "The Flying Ghosts, like a lot of organized crime groups, have a lot of money that is hard to account for when filing income tax forms."

"Chinese gangs pay taxes?" Corinne asked.

"No," Ms. Masterson said. "But they have to have some explanation for all that money they've got. If they put it into banks, they have to answer questions about where it came from. If they try to invest it in something like, say, real estate, they have to have an explanation for it."

"They can't just leave it sitting around somewhere," I offered.

"No, for some obvious reasons and some not so obvious. Obviously, if they have stacks of money sitting around in their homes or offices, it can be stolen. Not so obviously, if they have lots of money and don't do anything with it, they can't grow. They can't get wealthier unless they invest it some way."

"And diamonds are a good investment for them?"

"Very good, especially for a smaller gang like the Flying Ghosts. Diamonds are conveniently sized; they're perfect to be easily put into a safe or safe-deposit box. They can also be resold fairly easily, in most parts of the world, without any questions asked."

"So Mr. Sung was selling diamonds to the Ghosts?" Corinne asked. "Who bought them with money they've collected from drug dealing, prostitution, or any of their other enterprises?"

"Sung gets the dirty money and gives them the diamonds," I said. "Then he uses that money to purchase more diamonds, adding to his inventory. He's the middleman, in effect."

"He only has to report the sales," Ms. Masterson said. "He doesn't have to account for where the money for those sales came from."

"So he got into these transactions with the Flying Ghosts," Corinne said. "And he got in over his head."

"Way over," Ms. Masterson said. "And he did what a lot of people do when they are not career criminals but find themselves involved somehow in criminal activity. He went into a panic. He took the inventory and ran off."

"But technically, at least part of that inventory belongs to the Ghosts," Corinne said. "Especially if they've given him money and he hasn't given them diamonds. He's planning to what? Disappear? Start a new life in Tahiti or somewhere?"

"What are the odds something like that's going to work out in the long run?" I asked.

"Long run?" Ms. Masterson said. "Not good. There are people who have the skills and the personality to take off, disappear, create a whole new identity and life for themselves somewhere else."

"Mr. Sung probably isn't one of them," Corinne said, looking down into her tea again. I wondered how much of this she'd put together already.

"Nope," Ms. Masterson said. "Unless he had a lot of cash—even if he had a fortune in diamonds—it'd be difficult for him to live for any length of time."

"Can't go to a dealership and buy a car with a handful of diamonds?"

Ms. Masterson shook her head. "He had a substantial amount of wealth, but no easy way to turn it into fungible assets."

"So he ran, didn't think about any long-term plans," I said. "And now he's having a shortage of funds."

"He's got probably a million in diamonds," Corinne said. "But he can't buy a taco."

"How would he turn those diamonds into taco-purchasable cash?" Ms. Masterson asked.

"That would be tough for him," Corinne said.

"I get the impression Sung doesn't do 'tough' very well," I said.

"Umm," Ms. Masterson murmured, while taking a tentative sip of the tea. "What would he do in a difficult situation like that?"

Corinne held her teacup in both hands and looked into it, thinking.

"Mr. Sung isn't a bad person," she said slowly, still looking into her tea. "It's more like he's a weak person. He worries a lot about appearances. He wants people to think he's successful, that he's important. I don't think he ever cared much about that younger girlfriend. I think he just liked having people see her with him, think that he was successful or whatever, that he could attract a woman like her."

I took a sip of my tea. It occurred to me that bird's tongue tea tastes the way a freshly cut lawn smells. Grassy, herby, like spring. It was expensive, and I could make a can of it last for months by drinking it only every once in a while. On the other hand, my funds were not tied up in hard-to-negotiate diamonds. I took another sip. Corinne went on.

"When the gang people started showing up," she said, "that's when I first noticed it about Mr. Sung. He should have been scared. And I think, in some ways, he was. But they didn't come in and threaten him the way they do with a lot of business owners. They came in and treated him like he was an important person. They spoke to him with lots of respect."

"They sucked up to him," I said.

"Exactly. They made him feel like he was doing them a favor. He enjoyed that. By the time he would have realized they were using him, I'm guessing it would have been too late."

"So he runs," Ms. Masterson said. "But that still doesn't answer the question of what he would do when he became desperate for money."

"Probably," Corinne said, "he would have contacted them."

"The gang?" Ms. Masterson asked.

Corinne nodded. "Sooner or later."

"Even though by that time, they would have been looking for him, looking for whatever he would have owed them."

"They're his only chance of getting any money," Corinne said.

"What's his play there?" I asked. "Are Chinese crime gangs noted for their tendency to forgive and forget?"

Ms. Masterson smiled and tried another sip of tea. It had cooled enough that she was able to get some down without flinching. "This kind of grows on you," she said.

"Don't get used to it," I said. "It's expensive. I only break it out for special occasions."

"Like crime solving?" Ms. Masterson asked.

"Yep," I said, "so solve. Sung has to turn the diamonds over to the Ghosts; otherwise he's right back where he started."

"Unless he's got some leverage," Ms. Masterson said. "Unless he has an angle he can work."

"Like what?"

"Like me," Corinne said. She put her cup down. "He's told the Flying Ghosts that I took the diamonds."

"How would he explain his disappearance?" I asked.

"A good lie always has some element of truth to it," Ms. Masterson said. I sensed she and Corinne were on the same wavelength.

"He would tell the Flying Ghosts that he panicked," Corinne said. "Which is true. Now that he's in trouble, he's gone back to them and told them when he took off it was partly because he was scared, partly because he was off looking for me."

"And now he's found you," I said. "Probably with their help. Sung and the Ghosts are now working together, and if he's convinced them you have the diamonds, it takes the heat off him; if you can't produce the diamonds, they can focus their anger on you.

"They'll believe Sung?" I asked Ms. Masterson.

"For the time being," Ms. Masterson said. "And it'll give Sung a believable story. Now that he's found you and they know it, he can always say he talked or coerced you into giving up the diamonds. He gives them the diamonds he still has, says he got them from you, and all's well."

"Except for Corinne," I said.

"Except for that," Ms. Masterson agreed. "Gangs like the Flying Ghosts are unlikely to, as you said, 'forgive and forget.' Once they've got the diamonds back, they're going to want to extract some revenge for all the trouble they believe she's caused them."

"Oh," Corinne said.

Ms. Masterson took another sip of her tea. She put down the cup and looked at both of us.

"Precisely."

39

Rule #59: *While there are many instances where it's possible to see how one got into a particular situation, there are a lot more that just can't be easily explained—if at all.*

Corinne called Sung the morning after our meeting in the alley behind the restaurant. He wanted to meet her that evening near the hotel where he was staying. Corinne told me; I called Ms. Masterson. Along with Mr. Cataldi, the three of us met at Corinne's apartment.

"Neither of you are working today?" Ms. Masterson asked.

"Restaurant's closed for lunch," I said. "We're having a new electrical box installed. So we asked for the whole day off."

"Plans for your day off?" Mr. Cataldi said, looking at both of us.

"Yes," Corinne said. "I'm assuming you're going to want to go to the park where I'm supposed to meet Mr. Sung this evening."

Mr. Cataldi nodded.

"I want to go with you so I can, uh . . ." She glanced at me.

"Case the joint," I said. "And me too. I want to go along to get a look at the place."

"I'm assuming you're also going to want to go to the meeting with Sung this evening," Ms. Masterson asked me.

"I am."

"You have any objections to that?" Ms. Masterson asked Corinne.

"Do I have a say?" Corinne asked.

"Yes," Ms. Masterson said.

"I want him to come."

"Fine," Mr. Cataldi said. "He goes with us this afternoon to look things over. You, though"—he pointed to Corinne—"stay."

Ms. Masterson spoke. "We don't want to run into your Mr. Sung while we're looking the park over, or anyone else who might know you."

"Mr. Sung's seen Tucker," Corinne argued. "Up close."

"Closer than Sung would have liked, from what you told me," Ms. Masterson said.

"We were just establishing the parameters of our relationship," I said.

"Which are apparently best defined, according to you," Ms. Masterson said, "by strangling him and simultaneously threatening to crush his testicles."

"I hoped to capture his attention."

"At any rate," Ms. Masterson said. "I'm willing to take the chance that we'll be far enough away that should Sung appear, he won't be close enough to recognize Tucker. I'm not willing to take the same chance with you."

"And . . ." Mr. Cataldi said.

"And?" Corinne said.

"And Tucker's a *laowai*," Mr. Cataldi said, "and don't tell me we don't all look alike to you Chinese."

"Wow," I said. "You speak Mandarin."

"Only words I know, which I got from you, as I recall," Mr. Cataldi said.

"Only ones you really need."

I assumed Corinne was back at her apartment now, probably sleeping. Sleeping is what most restaurant people do on an unexpected day off. Ms. Masterson, Mr. Cataldi, and I sat in Cataldi's car, in the park's parking lot. It wasn't quite raining. The clouds seemed to have convened on the matter and were mulling it over.

Spatters struck here and there on the windshield. They made soft plops when they hit, barely audible. Even with the sprinkles, there were about a dozen cars parked in the lot around us. So we didn't look all that suspicious, I thought, other than if someone had noticed the three of us sitting in our car, not doing anything, which didn't seem all that normal for a park at midday.

It wasn't much of a park. A couple of acres set aside in a neighborhood of suburban strip malls, offices, chain restaurants, and hotels. It looked like once it had been part of a farm. Suburbia had crept in. On one side of the park's grassy lawn was a sprawling complex of doctor's offices. On the other side was the parking lot of the hotel where, apparently, Mr. Sung was staying.

"Think it's some kind of setup?" Ms. Masterson asked me. I thought she was being polite more than anything else in asking my opinion. I didn't think an FBI agent really needed my input. Maybe she just wanted to have a little conversation to pass the time.

"I don't have a lot of experience with that," I said.

"I think we can pretty well assume that Sung is up to something," Mr. Cataldi said.

"I don't really care," I said. "I care that Corinne might be in danger."

Mr. Cataldi nodded. "Reasonable," he said. "Can't promise you she won't be in any danger if she meets with him this evening. But you gotta figure it this way: we're looking over the meeting place ahead of time. Gives us some idea of where we'll want to be this evening when he wants to meet. We can be in a position to protect her if she needs it."

A motion off over by the hotel parking lot caught my eye. Someone, a thin woman in a bright red dress, had come out of a side entrance to the hotel and was crossing the lot, walking toward a car parked at the edge. I couldn't see her face. From the straight black hair, I was willing to venture a guess she was Asian.

She paused to glance around, searching, it seemed, for a car. I was right. Chinese.

"Off to the right," I said. Ms. Masterson and Mr. Cataldi both shifted their heads.

"Aha," Ms. Masterson said.

"Aha?" Mr. Cataldi said.

"That could be just one of the many Asian American citizens of the greater metropolitan area of the St. Louis environs," Ms. Masterson said. "Or one of the many visitors who come to this fine city each year and are staying as guests at the hotel. It could also be—what's the term you guys used?"

"*Gong-gong qi-che,*" I said. "The public bus."

"Public bus?" Mr. Cataldi asked.

"Everyone's ridden her," Ms. Masterson said. "I've gotten an interesting education in some aspects of Chinese culture."

"Corinne said that Sung had recently acquired a young female friend," Ms. Masterson said.

"Wanna bet that's her?"

"Looks the part."

"She could be his niece," I said.

"Remember last night when you said you tried to be optimistic?"

"I do."

"Congratulations," she said. "You've just gone from 'optimistic' to 'absurdly naive.'"

The woman, whoever she was, found her car, a small, tan four-door, started it, and backed out of the parking space. We watched her go.

"Would it be a good idea to follow her?" I asked.

"Maybe," Ms. Masterson said. "But then again, we're just guessing she's with Sung. And it is possible there could be more than one person of Chinese ancestry staying in a hotel in St. Louis."

Mr. Cataldi shifted in his seat and pulled a small plastic-bound notebook from his hip pocket. He flipped it open and started writing. It was the first time I'd seen either of them ever write anything down. Cops on TV shows write things down all the time.

"Got the plate," he said. "We'll call it in to the local cops. Chances are it's a rental."

I sat back and stared at the park. Ms. Masterson and Mr. Cataldi talked a little about the layout. Except for the line of trees at the rear of the park that were too far back to be of any use, there didn't seem to be any place they could hide to watch during the meeting with Sung. Both the benches were out in the open.

"Maybe I ought to be your sweetie this evening," Ms. Masterson said. Mr. Cataldi nodded. I didn't know what they were talking about. I did know, no matter what, that I was going to be with Corinne that evening.

40

Rule #29: *Like wine and cartoon characters, the best insults in Mandarin are the oldest.*

"Has anyone ever pointed out to you that you are sort of a violent person?" Corinne asked me. We were driving along Olive Street, toward the park where she was supposed to meet Sung. It was after five, still light out. The clouds had gotten thicker, but the rain had never developed past those few fat plops of earlier in the afternoon. The air was soft; the atmosphere had that kind of dreamy quality when the day's almost done.

"So far, in the short time I've known you, you've punched out a guy on the street in Buffalo, beat up a couple of other guys in front of my apartment, and now you've assaulted my ex-boss. And come to think of it, all of them are Chinese," she added. "You're violent *and* a racist."

"I worked over Mr. Cataldi," I said. "You weren't there for that."

"Sorry I missed it," she said. "So you have issues with Italians too?"

We stopped for a red light. It was rush hour. There was a lot of traffic, and we were hitting most of the lights. It didn't matter. We didn't have far to go, and we had plenty of time. My stomach was rolling. I wondered if Corinne was scared. She was good at hiding her emotions. Back at Forest Park getting chased by Eyebrows and the Curl, I'd been scared. Then, though, it was the kind of scared like when you're going down a ski slope, one that's too fast for you, one that you're hoping you're going to survive long enough to get to the bottom. That kind of scared is more about making it through the immediate moment. The sort of scared I felt now was more like when you actually take a fall on that hill and you feel something give, in your knee or in your ankle or your elbow, and you sprawl there in the snow, not moving, knowing something is wrong, something that could just be a little sprain or a twist or something that could be your elbow or your knee or your ankle, which is now bending in a direction it has never bent before; knowing that sooner or later, you're going to have to try to move, and then you're going to find out, and you're going to have to live with the consequences, whether they are just an ice pack and a couple of aspirin that evening or spending some time in the emergency room counting the holes in the ceiling tiles while the doctor tries to be reassuring. The kind of scared I was now was the scared of knowing there were a lot of variables here. Too many to control. I didn't know what Sung was up to. I didn't know if he'd have somebody else, somebody from the Flying Ghosts, along with him. I didn't know if Ms. Masterson and Mr. Cataldi would be close enough to step in if things got dangerous. I didn't know if I'd be able to handle it if they didn't. And mostly I realized that, for the first time in my life, I was scared not so much for what might happen to me but what might happen to somebody I cared about. That was a new kind of scared. I wanted more time to think it through.

The light changed. We moved forward again.

"I'm not really a violent person," I said.

"I know. I was just trying to get your attention."

"What were you going to do with my attention once you'd gotten it?"

"Later."

I wasn't sure what that meant. It didn't seem a good time to pursue it. I changed the subject.

"You're clear on everything?" I asked her. "We'll listen to whatever he has to say, but you're not going anywhere with him. We stay in sight, out in the open, where we can be seen."

Out of the corner of my eye, I saw her nod. "I still think he's going to be in a tizzy when you show up with me."

"Let him tizz," I said. "If he's telling the truth, what difference does it make if I'm there when he gives you the money he owes you?"

"Yeah," Corinne said. "Somehow I'm not thinking we're going out to dinner tonight on that money."

Sung was sitting on one of the benches we'd seen earlier in the day. He had his back to us. Two young mothers were perched on an exercise sit-up stand, watching their kids over at the playground, who were getting in a last little bit of play time before it got dark. There was a pair of miniature bulldozers with scoops mounted on short metal poles stuck into the ground, with hinges so the scoops could be swung up and down. One of the kids carefully levered the handles to drop the bucket down and bring up a shovelful of the rubber crumbles that covered the ground. With the arm of the bulldozer fully extended, he maneuvered it around slowly, deliberately, and dumped the whole bucket on the head of the other kid. The mothers were talking and didn't notice this at first. Then, when they did, they both reluctantly stood up and went over to referee.

We'd parked in the lot and were coming up behind Sung. We were only a couple of yards away from him when he turned. He looked at Corinne, then at me.

"I thought I asked you to come alone," he said in Mandarin.

"Seemed like a nice afternoon for a walk in the park," Corinne said. At just that moment, there was a low rumble of thunder far off. Maybe rain was coming after all. "We both work pretty hard at the restaurant. Nice to take a day off and go for a walk . . . after you give me my money and the explanation you mentioned."

"You're not very good at following directions." Sung was wear-

ing a pair of gray slacks and a cheap gray nylon windbreaker
zipped up over his shirt. He had on black socks and tan leather
shoes. Just like the night before, when I'd braced him out behind
the restaurant, his hair was carefully combed, oily and slick. It
looked like he spent as much time on it as Mr. Leong. Though he
had a lot more to work with.

I glanced around. One of the mothers was still brushing rubber chips out of her kid's hair. The other was bent over, lecturing
her kid. I couldn't see Ms. Masterson or Mr. Cataldi anywhere. I
heard a car door slam, then another immediately after. I glanced
over toward the hotel parking lot. Two men, both Chinese, had
gotten out of a car and were walking in our direction. Both
wore dark suits with dark ties. One was short, in his fifties, I was
guessing. Even at a distance, I could see his suit was tailored. He
walked like a man who controlled things, who was accustomed
to getting done what he wanted done, efficiently and definitively.
The other man was taller, much thicker. And younger. In his late
twenties. His suit didn't fit nearly as well. His hair was cut short,
sticking up, like a marine drill sergeant's. He carried himself with
an economy of motion. He didn't swing his arms wide or amble.
He carried himself like he was going from Point A to Point B as
directly as possible, and woe betide anyone who got in his way.
He carried himself like he wasn't unfamiliar with physical contact.

Corinne and I had come around to the front of the bench facing Sung. I stood so I could see both him and the line of trees
along the back of the park. That's where I was hoping the cav-
alry would be coming from. Corinne stood next to me. Sung saw
us looking at the pair coming up behind him. He swung around
again to see them. Then he swiveled back. He stayed seated. The
pair came up to us and stopped, maybe five feet away, facing us,
with Sung sitting between us. They looked at me, at Corinne, and
didn't say anything. Neither of us said anything. One of the kids

skidding down a plastic slide over at the play area whooped. The man with the brush cut whose suit didn't fit well—he had to be the bodyguard. The boss was Mr. Expensive Suit. Whose name, it turned out, was Ping. Sung swung around on the end of the seat and turned his head to look at Ping.

"Mr. Ping," Sung said, speaking English suddenly, "this is my assistant Wenqian." He opened his palm and lifted it in Corinne's direction. He didn't seem to remember I was even there. Or care.

"Wenqian," he said. "This is the man we stole from."

"Oh?" Corinne said. That was all. Her voice was flat, emotionless. I knew she didn't want to give Sung or Ping the satisfaction of sounding outraged. Or incredulous.

"I have spoken to Wenqian," Sung went on, like he was delivering a lecture. "I have explained that I have returned the diamonds that I took from our inventory, the diamonds that Mr. Ping and his . . ." He paused, searching for the word.

"Consortium," Ping offered. It was the first thing he said. He said it in English. His pronunciation was precise. He was probably fluent.

"His *consortium* owned," Sung went on, still in his lecturing-to-slightly-dull-children voice.

"Owned?" Corinne said. "How did they own the company's inventory?"

"I entered into a business relationship with Mr. Ping," Sung said. "He—"

"You mean you laundered money he gave you."

"I have made a number of decisions in running my business over the years, Miss Chang," he said. "I was not aware I needed to clear them with my employees."

"No need to inform your employees you're working in cahoots with criminals?" Corinne asked. Inside, I smiled. *Cahoots.*

"Criminals?" Sung sounded like he was trying to sound surprised. I got the same feeling I had when I'd first encountered him in the alley. It was like he was always acting, always trying to be something he wasn't. He sounded like an amateur actor in a local dinner theater production. He was warming up to his part, the contrite supplicant, asking for forgiveness and admonishing his partner in evildoing to do the same.

"We're the criminals here, Wenqian," he said. "We are the ones who took the diamonds and left Montreal. In point of fact," he went on, extravagantly turning both palms over to accentuate his words, "Mr. Ping has been very generous, considering what we've done to him." Mr. Sung seemed to straighten up and grow a little as he went along. It was as if he were preaching a sermon to Corinne, gently explaining what they had both done and letting her know it was time to make things right.

"I have given Mr. Ping the diamonds I took that rightfully belong to him. I would urge you to do the same."

Corinne didn't say anything.

I did.

"*Er mu bei yi,*" I said. "Sung's mother was a slave girl."

The expressions on the faces of both Sung and Ping would have been the same if I had spoken Latin instead of Mandarin. They stared at me, frozen. Ping's bodyguard, who'd been gazing off into the distance without any expression at all, slowly, lazily turned his head. He stared at me. Cold, appraising. When I first saw the Curl, from the driver's side of the car the day they'd stopped to threaten me, I'd thought his gaze was reptilian. The bodyguard had an industrial-strength version of that same look. He was looking me over the way a python would a warm little mouse. I tried not to appear too mousy. I didn't think I was sprouting a tail. Or whiskers. I did, nevertheless, feel distinctly like dinner.

"Who are you?" Again, Ping's private school elocution. He'd have been great reading the news on the radio.

I could have gone with any one of the kitchen insults we

used every day at the Eastern Palace. Vulgar, full of machismo. It would have had a lot of force. This time, though, I went in just the opposite direction. I used an insult that went back probably five hundred years. In English, it would have sounded Shakespearean. Like Henry VI saying, "Thou misshapen dick!"

But it wasn't in English. It was Mandarin. It didn't sound like much in English. In Chinese, it sounded like I was an elderly librarian, admonishing a young reader not to crease the pages of a book.

"Who are you?" Ping asked again. He looked directly at me.

"A chef," I said.

Ping turned to Sung. "You know this *laowai?*"

Sung was caught off-guard. He didn't seem exactly sure how to continue on in his dinner theater voice now that he'd been interrupted. "He's . . . ah . . . he's her boyfriend, I believe," he stammered. He tilted his head at Corinne. "He's . . . he tried to push me around when I first went to talk to her."

"I didn't try," I said, still in Mandarin. "I *did* push you around. Your balls remember it. So does your throat. Is that why you're having trouble talking now?"

"Where did you learn to speak Chinese?" Ping asked.

"I learned to speak Chinese in places where it's fairly easy to see when a person's lying," I said. "Like Sung here is doing." It wasn't the snappiest response I'd ever come up with. It worked okay, though, considering the circumstances.

Ping looked at me with an expression somewhere between amusement and disdain. His bodyguard didn't change his expression at all. It was time to keep going.

"Sung is lying," I said. "Through his teeth. You think he— what? Took part of the diamond inventory and just handed over the rest to Wenqian? I assume you know Sung, right?" Without waiting for an answer, I added, "I know he's stupid, but do you really think he's stupid enough to do that?"

"You speak Chinese very well," Ping said.

"Maybe you're just very good at understanding it," I said. I liked that. Better than the one about having learned it in places where you could tell when a person was lying. I still wasn't entirely happy with that. I let it go. There were other matters to worry about. A lot of them. The mothers were calling their kids, gathering up their stuff. I couldn't see anyone else around. Of all the people I didn't see, I especially didn't see Ms. Masterson or Mr. Cataldi. I glanced for a second at the back of the park, the only place I could figure them coming from. Nothing.

"Sung took the diamonds," I said. "He looted them from his own company. He took off with his girlfriend."

"Girlfriend?" Ping said.

"She's here now," I said. "She's staying in the same hotel as Sung, right over there."

"This is nonsense!" Sung sputtered. He stood up. I took a little satisfaction in knowing I'd been right. That had been her we'd seen leaving the hotel. Maybe I had a future in the detecting business. *Then again*, I thought, *maybe I don't have much future at all past this little meeting.*

"I've been completely honest with you," Sung went on, speaking directly to Ping as if the rest of us weren't there. "At considerable expense, I came out here and found Miss Chang and arranged for her to come here so you can deal with her. As I understand it, your people have already tried to approach her on at least a couple of occasions, with little to show for it."

Ping slowly blinked. He stared at Sung.

"I've brought you to her," Sung said. He brushed a piece of lint from his slacks. "I'm done."

"No," Ping said. "You're not. No one's done just yet."

41

Rule #48: *Decide, when things start going downhill, which is the best route to take, and take it, fast.*

Here we go, I thought. *It's all going to go downhill from here. Fast. No way it's going anywhere else.* We'd all been just sort of cruising along the crest of the hill, moving slowly without much energy. Now I could feel it in the air, feel the energy start to charge. Now the toboggan was tilting down and gathering speed, and in just a second or two, it was going to move from a gentle cruise to a runaway. Without thinking about it, I'd shifted so my left side was turned just slightly toward Ping's bodyguard. He was going to be the trouble. Most of it, anyway.

I tried to determine if the bodyguard was carrying a gun. His jacket was buttoned. If he had a gun, it couldn't have been in a shoulder holster. An amateur, my father had told me once, might carry a gun in a place he couldn't access easily. A place like his pocket, where he'd have to fish it out. Or under a buttoned jacket. This guy didn't look like an amateur. So if he had a gun, it would likely be on his right hip. His jacket was cut loosely enough I couldn't see any bulge. I tried to keep my gaze over his shoulder, like I was looking past him. That would let me see any movements, ones I might miss if I focused anywhere directly.

"No, my colleague," Ping went on, "we're not done just quite yet."

"Then talk to her," Sung said. He flicked his fingers in Corinne's direction.

"I don't need to talk to her." Ping's voice was so smooth, I could have drifted off to sleep listening to it. Except I didn't feel all that sleepy.

"I have explained it to you," Sung said in that voice again, like he was trying to explain quantum physics to a chimp. Patient, slow. "She can tell you where the rest of the inventory is." He crossed his legs and tugged his pant leg just above the knee to make the crease neater.

"No," Ping said. "I spoke with another woman who actually does know where the rest of our diamonds are."

"Who?" Sung said. He seemed to have forgotten about his pants crease. He suddenly looked concerned. His expression was like one of a predator sensing that it might, in fact, have just become prey.

"Zhen-zi," Ping said. "Your girlfriend. The one who is—as our young, classical Mandarin–speaking chef here mentioned earlier—staying with you at that hotel over there."

I started to glance in Sung's direction. I wanted to see the expression on his face. But just then a short, sharp scream chopped the air. It came from behind where Corinne and I were facing. Sung jumped, trying to uncross his leg. He wasn't successful. He started to topple. He had to slap his hand on the back of the bench to steady himself. I could sense Corinne flinch beside me. Ping's eyes narrowed slightly at the scream, and the bodyguard lowered his shoulders and relaxed. Experienced fighters react that way to unexpected noises. They don't tense up the way most people do. It wasn't much of a movement, just a twitch, as his shoulders relaxed. I saw it, though.

The scream was followed almost immediately by a quick burble of laughter. It was Ms. Masterson. I'd never heard her sound like that.

"Bernie! Stop!"

She was wearing sweatpants and a buttoned shirt with a pale green sweater over it. Mr. Cataldi was with her, in khakis and a sweatshirt that advertised Bowdoin College. Just a couple in love, out for an early evening walk in the park. Mr. Cataldi jumped at her and grabbed for her side. She batted his arm down and broke away from him, giggling. She skipped a few steps closer to us. Mr. Cataldi chased after her.

Ping didn't even turn to look at them. His bodyguard turned his head just enough to check them out. He didn't have any reason to suspect they were anything but a couple on a date. He wasn't going to let them get any closer though, I didn't think, without doing something to ensure his boss wasn't in any danger. Almost like he was floating, he came forward a couple of steps, close to me, keeping me to his left, putting himself in a position to move around me if he needed to.

It was time.

My left foot was already forward, closest to the bodyguard. I shuffled slightly with it, still leading with the left side of my body, and reached for his face. It was a feint. He was still looking at the two of them, but he must have caught my incoming strike peripherally. He snapped his head back toward me. He didn't go for the feint. He ignored my open hand coming at him and lifted his right shoulder. He was reaching under the edge of his suit coat, reaching for a gun. I made a fist with my right hand, sticking the middle knuckle out, and hit him on the inside of his right arm, just below the bicep. It wasn't a hard hit. It was enough, though, to cause his arm to go numb. I'd been hit that way before, plenty of times. By Langston. And by his uncle. Take a hit like that, well aimed, the knuckle jabbing just above the inside crook of your elbow, and you feel like you've just stuck your finger into a wall socket. He grunted. His right arm flopped, dangled. He didn't hesitate, though. His left hand came up. Fast. Like a snake's tongue flickering. I came up with my left, intercepting him, but his balance was good. His punch got through. I'd taken a lot off it. Still, it connected with my ear hard enough to set my head ring-ing. My ear felt hot. I bounced back, away from him, to readjust. He wasn't going for that. He was on me.

In a serious fight, there isn't any squaring off and shuffling around like in a boxing match or a karate competition. In a serious fight, it's about getting a hit in and then keeping in motion, keeping on top of the guy. Not giving him time to reset himself. That's what the bodyguard was doing to me. He grabbed me by the front of my shirt with his good hand. That was a mistake. I knew where one of his hands was; I only had to worry about the other one. And I knew that other one would still have been stinging at least a little. He wouldn't have a full range of motion or power in it. He jerked me to him, expecting me to resist. I didn't. I went with his pull, trying to stay light, to drift in without any resistance. At the same time, I kicked low, turning my foot in and pointing my toe, like a football kicker making a punt. The tip of my shoe caught him right on the bulge of his ankle. He was in the process of trying to head-butt me. When I connected with the kick, he grunted again. He winced; it was enough to stop the momentum of his head butt. He stumbled. His foot wouldn't hold him up. He shifted his weight to his other leg; I could feel it through his grab. Even so, he didn't let go. His weight was on me. He was dragging me down. I twisted, bringing my elbow around in a short, tight curve, aiming for his cheek. I connected a little high. His head rocked. He still didn't let go. He outweighed me by at least sixty or seventy pounds. If he could stay on top of me, I couldn't fight back. If he went to the ground, I'd have to go with him. That didn't seem like an attractive alternative. I was still trying to move at an angle against him to get off another elbow.

"That's all!" Ms. Masterson's voice wasn't giggly anymore. Probably it was tough to sound girlish and giggly when you have a Glock in your hand. Which she did. So did Mr. Cataldi, in a similar stance a yard or so away from her. "FBI," she said. Same voice. A voice that said clearly that there wasn't going to be lot of discussion about things. A voice that caught the attention of even the bodyguard, who was still leaning on me so hard that my legs were starting to quiver. He paused, froze, then reluctantly let go of me.

"Turn around!" Mr. Cataldi shouted.

The bodyguard started to follow his order. As he did, he collapsed into a heap, his leg twisted awkwardly in front of him.

"He's got a gun," I said. "Right side, at his waist."

Mr. Cataldi stepped in, and while Ms. Masterson stood beside him, her gun pointed at the bodyguard, he took a small automatic from a holster on the bodyguard's waist, then took his wrist and elbow and neatly flipped him on his back. Face pushed against the grass, the bodyguard twisted, still impassive, gritting his teeth. I didn't think his ankle was broken. I did think he was going to be limping for a while.

Corinne was standing still, right where she'd been all along. Sung, too, was sitting where he had been. His face was shiny. He was trembling a little. I sat down at the other end of the bench beside him. Suddenly I wasn't sure I could stand, not even a second or two, not any longer, and if that bench hadn't been there, I was thinking I'd be on the ground, right beside the bodyguard. I glanced over at Sung. He was staring out at something I couldn't see. I sat back. I could feel my own perspiration, collecting on my upper lip. I felt a little queasy. Then a lot. I swallowed hard. I took a deep breath, then another, then tried to think of something to distract me. I turned to Sung.

"So," I said. "How are you liking St. Louis so far?"

42

Rule #90: *Don't rush things, but don't sit on your thumbs when the opportunity's right.*

"Can I take a lie detector test?" Corinne asked.

We were in a room in the St. Louis County Police headquarters. The park we'd been in was not in St. Louis City. It was in St. Louis County. That distinction meant it was county cops who had swarmed around after the meeting with Sung had ended so dramatically. The recessed lights overhead gave off a harsh, flat glare. The room had just a bare desk and some metal chairs around it that looked like they could be comfortable for about a minute or so. We'd been there longer than that.

Corinne was talking to Detective Sydney Martin-Lourdes. She was one of a couple dozen of those cops who'd showed up at the park after Mr. Cataldi had put handcuffs on the bodyguard, then another pair on Ping. After she holstered her Glock, Ms. Masterson had pulled a set of cuffs from under her sweatshirt and put them on Sung.

"I don't think lie detectors work on Chinese people," I told her.

Ms. Martin-Lourdes's eyes snapped up. She'd been sitting in one of the uncomfortable chairs at the desk, a laptop in front of her, typing and asking us questions, then typing more.

"Sir," she said. "Ethnicity has nothing to do with the way a polygraph test works."

"He's kidding," Ms. Masterson said. She was also sitting in one of the chairs. "He has an unusual sense of humor."

"It grows on you," I said.

Ms. Masterson looked at Corinne. "That true?" she asked.

"Let me get back to you on that."

"There isn't any reason for you to take a lie detector," Ms. Masterson said. "We're pretty sure we know what's happened."

"You've solved the Mystery of the Missing Montreal Diamonds?" I asked. The queasy feeling had passed. I felt a lot better. I felt that kind of flush of relief when something's done, it's finally over, and, all things considered, it hadn't turned out all that bad. Or at least, it could have turned out much worse. Which added to the sense of relief I felt.

"We're professional investigators," Ms. Masterson said. "And . . ."

"And?"

"And Sung's 'girlfriend'"—she made those little quote hooks with her forefingers—"was surprisingly willing to talk after we picked her up at the hotel. She filled in some of the details."

"And so?" Corinne asked.

"You tell me," Ms. Masterson said. "I think you've got it figured out."

"Mr. Sung wanted Ping to think I had some of the diamonds," Corinne said without any hesitation. "My guess is he was trying to return some part of what he took, keep the difference, and blame me for having the other half."

I jumped in. "So he arranges to get Ping to come here, to confront Corinne about the diamonds she supposedly stole, and he thinks Ping's going to buy that? That's a pretty thin plan."

"Mr. Sung has a high evaluation of his own intelligence," Ms. Masterson said. "And his appeal to women."

"You mean Zhen-zi?" I asked.

"Mr. Sung's own true public bus?" Corinne added.

Ms. Masterson nodded. "Zhen-zi," she said, "turns out to be in the employ of the Flying Ghosts."

"So Ping mentioned," I said. "Just before all the excitement began."

"Yes," Ms. Masterson said. "She was working for them, cultivating a relationship with Sung to keep an eye on him."

"The Ghosts didn't trust him?" Corinne asked.

"I doubt the Flying Ghosts trust their own mothers," Ms. Martin-Lourdes said.

"Probably not," Ms. Masterson agreed. "At any rate, Sung told Zhen-zi the truth. He had all the diamonds. Once he had time to think about what he'd done, he had to realize that the Ghosts were going to try to find him. He figured if he could give back half of the diamonds and convince the Flying Ghosts that Corinne had the rest, he and his girlfriend could be off to live happily, if not ever after, at least until the money ran out."

"So Ping knew this?" I asked.

"Sure," Ms. Masterson said. "He probably knew it as soon as Zhen-zi could get away from Sung long enough to call him about it."

"So Ping didn't come to the meeting to confront me," Corinne said. It was more a statement than a question.

"Nope," Ms. Masterson said. "He came because, by pretending to believe Sung's story, he was sure to get face-to-face with Sung without Sung suspecting that Ping and the rest of the Flying Ghosts were on to him."

I looked at Corinne. "You Orientals are an inscrutable bunch."

Ms. Martin-Lourdes coughed.

"So what happens now?" Corinne asked.

"Now Sung, Ping, and Ping's bodyguard are all in custody."

"How long will that last?" I asked. "When it comes down to it, what laws have they broken?"

"None here," Ms. Martin-Lourdes said. "Not of any consequence, anyway. The bodyguard doesn't have a state permit for a concealed weapon. Small potatoes. The prosecuting attorney will likely let it slide."

"No laws broken here," Ms. Masterson said. "But the police from Canada are arriving tomorrow morning. We're holding all three of them, awaiting extradition. Once they're returned to Canada, the story will probably be different."

By the time we left the county police office, it was completely dark. A county cop gave us a ride back to the park and waited until we got into the Toyota and drove out of the lot. He gave us a quick wave as we went past him, idling his engine. I saw him follow us a few blocks, just to be sure, I assumed, that we were safe.

"You hungry?" I asked Corinne.

"I can't believe it," she said. "But I am."

We went to the Eastern Palace. This late, there were only two tables with diners. Corinne and I sat down like customers at one of the empty ones. I was right: when a restaurant closes for the first half of the day, business for the second half is always going to be off. Janet, one of the waitresses—one whom Mr. Leong had, in fact, called in on her off night to cover for Corinne—waited on us. We both ordered the same thing. *Zhou*. Rice gruel. The same dish Langston and I had prepared my first morning in St. Louis. Cold cooked rice, usually leftover rice, recooked in a pot with about twice as much water (or in the case of Li, who was running the kitchen that night, a rich chicken broth) as rice. All the liquid turns the rice into a thick slurry, soupy with a pleasant texture, one that accents whatever is added to it. In our case, we ordered it with pickled Chinese greens and a couple of dishes of chopped coriander on the side for garnish. It was comfort food, Chinese style.

We ate. We didn't say much. It was fun to be diners in the place where we worked.

"Let's go to your apartment," Corinne said when I'd parked

the Toyota on the street between our two places. We did. It was dark inside. Langston was out wherever the chefs and other restaurant workers were meeting that night after their places closed. Preferably a place where Bao Yu could tag along. We went to the front room that was my bedroom and stood next to one another, looking out onto the street. I still hadn't seen the crow. The canopy of the sycamore tree across the street was so thick with leaves, now in various hues of gray and black, shadowy in the dark, that there could have been a nest somewhere in it. I had my hands in my pockets. Corinne reached over and slipped her arm through mine and left it there.

"You okay?" I asked her.

"Nice not to have to worry about someone threatening me," she said. "How about you? How do you feel?"

I shrugged. "Surprised."

"Surprised?" Corinne said.

"Well, yeah," I said. "I figured all along you'd actually taken the diamonds."

She snorted softly. "No, you didn't."

"No," I said. "I didn't. I just wanted to get your attention." It was what she'd said to me earlier, what seemed like a long time ago but was only earlier that afternoon. Then she asked me the same question I'd asked her.

"What were you going to do with it once you got my attention?"

"'Later' is what you said."

She moved close enough against me that I could feel her head nodding on my shoulder by way of answer. Then she pivoted to face me and looped her other arm through mine.

"Yes, indeed," she said. "And right now . . ." She pressed in. "Right now is later."

43

Rule #76: *A visit to the offices of any authority figure that is so short you don't have to sit down is usually a good one.*

"This is Lieutenant Carlson, who's visiting us from the Great White North," Ms. Masterson said.

It was two days after all the excitement in the park. Corinne and I had to ask for a couple of hours off at the Eastern Palace to go the law offices of Brown, Bernson & Wilkes. Mr. Leong wasn't happy about it. Especially after he'd given us the evening off two days ago to meet with Sung in the park. He didn't grumble too much, though.

We met Ms. Masterson in the law office's lobby. We didn't have to be there. She'd called, though, and told us that Ping was asking to speak to Corinne and that while Corinne was under no obligation to do so, it might be interesting to see what Ping had to say. I thought I'd had enough "interesting" to last for the rest of the spring and well into the summer. But Corinne wanted to go.

"I'm curious about what he has to say," she told me. So we went.

The law office's lobby was larger than the entire dining room of the Eastern Palace. Ms. Masterson introduced Lieutenant Carlson, a special investigator for the Royal Canadian Mounted Police, and the local district attorney, Mr. Shannon. We stood around for a few minutes, studying the potted plants and a big frosted-glass screen that ran the entire length of the lobby. Muted pastel lights slowly ran together behind the glass, the patterns changing and flowing. Then a woman appeared. I guessed she was a secretary, even though I reflected on how sexist that assumption might be. It was right, anyway. She led us through a door—along a hall decorated with framed jerseys and other sports memorabilia from St. Louis sports teams—and into a conference room paneled in dark oak, with a thick, expensive-looking rug spread over a polished wooden floor. There were a dozen leather upholstered chairs around a table that could have accommodated a Thanksgiving dinner for most of the people in my apartment building. Although Langston and I were almost certainly the only occupants of the building who celebrated Thanksgiving.

"Make yourselves comfortable, please," the woman said pleasantly.

"Mind if I use your facilities?" the lieutenant asked her. She gave him directions. Everyone but Ms. Masterson and I sat down. I went over and leaned against one wall. Ms. Masterson stood against the other, so we were on both sides of the table, facing one another. Almost immediately, another door at the other end of the room opened silently. A tall black man came in. He wore thin gold-framed glasses, a short Afro gone almost completely gray, and a suit that, had I not been so secure in my self-image, would have made me feel shabby in my pressed khakis, light blue Oxford-cloth dress shirt, and dark blue sports jacket. Behind him was Ping. He may have been in the same suit he'd been wearing two days before in the park. There wasn't a wrinkle or a crease out of place. I assumed he'd made bail. I wondered where the bodyguard was. I wondered how *he* was walking.

"My name is Orvis Wilkes," the black man said. He and Ping both sat. "I am Mr. Ping's attorney." He nodded to the district attorney and to Detective Martin-Lourdes. "Chuck; Sydney." They nodded back at him.

Then Mr. Shannon introduced Ms. Masterson and Corinne

and me. Just then Lieutenant Carlson came back from the rest-room. Ping looked up. Just for a second, I saw surprise on his face. It was a moment, just a flicker.

"This is Lieutenant Carlson," Mr. Shannon said. "From the Royal Canadian Mounted Police."

Carlson looked at Ping. Ping nodded, almost imperceptibly.

"Lieutenant Carlson heads the Asian Gang Crime Task Unit out of Quebec," Mr. Shannon said.

Then Mr. Shannon turned back to Ping's lawyer. "Your client requested this meeting."

"Yes," Wilkes said. "But before he says what he wants to say — and let me add that he is doing so against my counsel — I would like someone here to lay out the reason he was arrested in the first place."

"You know the charges, Orvis," Mr. Shannon said. "He was involved in an attempt at extortion. He is a witness to the same. He is the employer of a person who was carrying a weapon ille-gally. He and that employee are visitors to this country. They both represent a flight risk. We also have reason to believe that he may be connected with an assault on these two" — he inclined his head in Corinne's direction, then mine — "and another man who was shot."

"Yeah," Wilkes said. He waved the back of his hand. "I know. Reason to believe. But I'd like to know just what all this is really about."

"Let me see if I can lay it out for you, counselor," Ms. Master-son said. "Your client is — we have it on the reliable information provided by Lieutenant Carlson here — in the upper echelons of an organized criminal organization called the Flying Ghosts."

Ping seemed to contemplate something in the woodgrain of the table in front of him.

"The Flying Ghosts entered into a criminal enterprise with Mr. Sung, who was laundering money for them, converting their

IGG—" Now it was her turn to glance at Corinne, then me. "Ill-gotten gains," she translated, "into wholesale diamond purchases. For whatever reason, Mr. Sung became disillusioned with the partnership. He took off with the inventory of his shop, which included diamonds that, in effect, were the property of the Flying Ghosts. Who wanted them back. Understandably. They had information, gained through a woman they had placed into Sung's confidence. The woman repeated Sung's story to them. She told them that Sung and Corinne had conspired and had each taken a portion of the diamonds. So Mr. Ping sent a Mr. Bobby Chu to Buffalo to try to find Ms. Chang."

"Allegedly," Mr. Wilkes said.

"Yes," Ms. Masterson said. "This is all alleged. I'm just laying out a possible scenario. Allegedly, Bobby Chu went to Buffalo to find Ms. Chang. He did. But he got scared off when this man"— she rocked her head at me—"got into a confrontation with him. By the time he got enough nerve to come back, Ms. Chang had left. He found out she'd gone to St. Louis. Bobby decided to take some initiative, to go after her on his own without checking in with your client, his boss."

Ping said nothing. He stared straight ahead. His tie was perfect, straight, with the dimple situated right below the knot. I could see the cuffs of his shirt, monogrammed with PMW.

"When your client discovered Bobby had taken off," Ms. Masterson went on, "he assumed Bobby had gotten the diamonds from Ms. Chang and had subsequently decided to go off on his own. So he sent two of his employees to St. Louis. They—ah—inquired about the disposition of the diamonds to Bobby. Who told them the truth. Only they didn't believe it. They beat Bobby. To death."

Ping had apparently decided that not saying anything was a reasonable course to take.

"Young Bobby no longer being a viable source of information, your client turned to threatening Miss Chang. And assaulting her. Your client and his associates were still under the impression she knew the whereabouts of the diamonds."

Mr. Wilkes nodded and said, "It's an interesting story you're telling. For a government agent, you have a marvelous imagination."

"Story gets better," Ms. Masterson said. "Mr. Sung took off. Being a romantic, though, after a few weeks he began to pine for the love of his life. So he called her. And told her where he was. Information she immediately passed on to your client. Because, in addition to being Sung's sweetie—or maybe *because* she was his sweetie—she was working for your client. Then she and Sung rendezvoused."

Lieutenant Carlson shifted in his chair, briefly covered his mouth, and blinked a couple times. But he was listening intently.

"Then," Ms. Masterson went on, "in a moment of candor, Mr. Sung explained to his love that, in fact, he'd concocted the whole story about Miss Chang's involvement. He tried to convince her that if they could throw off the blame, throw it onto Miss Chang, then your client and his colleagues would go after her."

It was so quiet in the room I could hear the low hum of the air conditioner. This was the first time it had been warm enough for an air conditioner to cycle on. Summer, almost. I thought about the winter. At Beddingfield. Suffering through that miserable cold. I was ready for the warmth.

"Leaving Sung and his girlfriend in the clear," Ms. Masterson went on. "He gave back half the diamonds, ones he'd stolen anyway, and he was left with the other half."

Mr. Shannon smiled. "Do tell what happened then?"

"I shall," Ms. Masterson said. I got the impression they were enjoying this. I was.

"Your client requested that Mr. Sung arrange a meeting, to

bring Miss Chang to a place where he could then take over and implore her to give up the diamonds."

"Which she doesn't have," Mr. Shannon said. "And never did."

"Correct," Ms. Masterson said. "Which your client already knew," she added, looking back at Mr. Wilkes. "He was actually interested in getting to Mr. Sung."

"For obvious reasons," Mr. Shannon said.

"Obvious?" Mr. Wilkes said. He leaned forward, steepling his fingers and resting them under his nose, elbows on the table. "You have laid out a very interesting scenario. It will be just as interesting to see how much of this you can prove in court. Assuming," he added, "you actually intend to file charges."

No one said anything for a moment. Then Ping suddenly cleared his throat.

"Excuse me," he said, in that same smooth and precise diction I'd heard earlier. Definitely a private school education. Somewhere in Hong Kong. An expensive one. "I assume you are recording this, so you will have a record of what I am going to say. Or"—he pointed his forefinger at me—"the Chinese chef who is not Chinese here will be able to translate immediately for you. But I would like to speak to Miss Chang in Mandarin if I may."

"Mr. Ping, again I would urge you—" Mr. Wilkes tried to interject; Ping raised his open palm. Wilkes closed his mouth, took his elbows off the table, leaned back, and put his hands on the arms of the chair.

"Okay with you?" Ms. Masterson asked the district attorney.

He pursed his lips. "Okay by me."

Ms. Masterson looked at Corinne. "You mind?"

Corinne shook her head.

Ping cleared his throat and put both palms on the table in front of him. "Miss Chang," he said. "I owe you an apology. This business got entirely out of hand."

Corinne looked levelly at him and didn't say anything.

"It got out of hand because I trusted some members of my company to handle a situation. They did not do a good job. They believed Mr. Sung, took his word for it that you were involved. After things . . . *developed,* the matter finally came to my attention. Unfortunately, this did not happen until you had been put at risk and imposed upon in some regrettable ways."

The guy's voice was mesmerizing. I figured at least some of it was complete crapola. Maybe even all of it. And I was distracted because some of the words he was using in Mandarin were unfamiliar, and I had to try to use context to get the meaning. Still, I was enjoying the soliloquy.

"When I finally became aware of what was going on, I devised a plan. I thought it would isolate Mr. Sung and allow us to confront him about the *irregularities* in the matter of our business relationship."

He dropped his gaze to the tabletop and tapped the fingers of both hands lightly on it.

"Again, unfortunately," he went on after a couple of seconds, "the plan involved using you, giving the impression to Mr. Sung that I believed his explanation. This ensured that he would be present. Do you understand me, Miss Chang?"

"I do," she said.

He glanced at me. "You following this too?"

"Most of it," I said. "Sung was using Wenqian as a" —if there was a Mandarin word for "scapegoat" I didn't know it— "person to take the blame."

He nodded slowly.

"At the same time, you were using her as a" —again, I didn't know any Mandarin equivalent for "stalking horse" —"way to get to Sung."

Ping continued to nod. When he spoke again, it was in English. "I have apologized to Miss Chang," he said to everyone in the room. "She has been very poorly treated, threatened, and assaulted. It was not my doing. But it was done by my subordinates. So I am responsible. If there are going to be charges against me, my counsel here"—he gestured toward Mr. Wilkes—"will defend me. I have considerable resources to accomplish this. In any event, however, Miss Chang will not in any way face any further contact from me or anyone in my organization."

I pressed myself back against the wall. I looked at Ms. Masterson. She pursed her lips and shrugged at me. I looked at Corinne. She shrugged, then pursed her lips. I figured those reactions pretty well summed up the morning.

44

Rule #88: *Appreciate the little things.*

We left the offices and walked a couple of blocks down the street to the sandwich shop where Ms. Masterson, Corinne, and I had met right after I picked Corinne up in Buffalo. This time we were joined by Ms. Martin-Lourdes, Mr. Shannon, and Lieutenant Carlson. We sat around a table and ordered, coffee for everyone but Corinne and me. It was late enough that the lunch crowd had dissolved.

"You haven't said anything, Lieutenant Carlson," Ms. Martin-Lourdes said.

"Corinne's lived in Canada," I said. "She could have translated the proceedings into Canadian for you."

A quick smile crossed Lieutenant Carlson's face. "Nothing seemed to need my commentary at the time," he said. I got the impression Lieutenant Carlson didn't give a lot away. I also got the impression he wasn't someone I'd want to mess around with.

"What happens to Mr. Sung?" Corinne asked. Even though he treated her like a scapegoat, some part of Corinne clearly still felt sorry for him, I thought. He'd lost everything, including a woman he thought was in love with him.

"He hasn't broken any laws in the United States," Mr. Shannon said. "We might be able to cobble something together. Try to show he put Miss Chang in a dangerous situation. Tough case to make, even if we wanted to try."

"How about in Canada?" Ms. Masterson asked.

"Ah, that would be a different story," Lieutenant Carlson said.

He took a sip of coffee and patted his mouth carefully with a paper napkin. "Technically, he's probably good for money laundering, abetting a criminal enterprise. But in light of the other aspects of the case we'll be making against the Flying Ghosts, it's doubtful the Crown Attorney will want to go to the trouble of bringing charges against Sung. In the end, all he did was take his own inventory and leave. That's not illegal."

"Might not be against the law," I said. "But I'm assuming the Flying Ghosts will not be so complacent about it."

"No," he said. "They won't. That's where it will be, as I said, a different story. We'll extradite all three back to Canada immediately. Ping is under investigation there, along with his organization, for a number of crimes."

"What about his bodyguard?" I asked.

"He'll go too," Carlson said. "On crutches. You did a number on him."

"Was his ankle broken?"

"No," the lieutenant said. "But it was pretty banged up. How exactly did you do that?"

"I got lucky," I said. Which was true. "What about Sung? Does he go back too?"

"Sung we'll take back as a material witness. Once we get him there, we're going to explain to him that his future, unless he cooperates with us in the investigation of the Flying Ghosts, will likely not be a carefree one."

"And the pair who shot Langston," I asked. "What about them?"

"They did break U.S. law," Mr. Shannon said. "We have them for the shooting in the park. Attempted homicide on your friend Mr. Wu."

Langston is going to enjoy that, I thought. I wondered if Bao Yu had seen his wound yet.

"We also like them for the murder of Bobby Chu," Mr. Shannon went on. "And since they're not U.S. citizens and constitute a flight risk, they're going to be here for a while."

"Will Ping help them?" Ms. Masterson asked.

"Ping's lawyer informs me that Ping is denying he has anything to do with them," Mr. Shannon said.

"Dicey play on Ping's part," I said. "Ping cuts them loose; what's to keep them from turning on Ping?"

"Nothing," Lieutenant Carlson said. "But they still won't do it."

"A murder and an attempted homicide," I said. "That's got to be some serious time. They're not going to give up Ping and their fellow Flying Ghosts to get some leverage?"

"Unlikely," Lieutenant Carlson said. "The Ghosts are all they've got. They're going to prison either way is how they'll figure it. They can either go as members of the Flying Ghosts, which carries some status, at least in their eyes. Or they can go in as losers who sold out their own gang."

"Not a tough choice," Mr. Shannon said.

"Right," the lieutenant said. "And Ping knows it."

"What's it do for morale in the gang, though?" Corinne asked. "How much loyalty can you inspire among your crew if they know that any of them, if they screw up, will get cut loose, left hung out to dry like these two?"

Lieutenant Carlson shrugged. "Players at the level of those two are easy to replace. They all know the rules."

"Crappy life," I said.

"True," the lieutenant said. "But in a gang like the Flying Ghosts, they have a kind of family; they have a sense of purpose, even if it's only selling drugs, being enforcers, or doing the kind of low-level stuff they do. It is crappy. But in their eyes, it's marginally less crappy than the kind of life they think they could have without being in the gang."

"So," Mr. Shannon said. He pushed back his chair and crossed his legs and folded his hands behind his head. "Some bad guys go to jail. And some badder guys go back to Canada."

"Where they're out of our hair," Ms. Masterson said.

"We've got a few we can send your way in return," Lieutenant Carlson said.

"Here's what I don't get," I said. "How did the Flying Ghosts know Corinne was in Buffalo? How'd they know where she went after she left Montreal?"

"Organizations like the Flying Ghosts deal in and rely on information to a considerable degree," the lieutenant said. "If they're involved with a legitimate business like the Wing Sung company, they make it a priority. They'd have known everything about Miss Chang and all the other employees there. Her cell phone number"—I thought of the call I'd intercepted to Corinne's phone back in Andover—"her professional and personal background. They'd have known about her parents—"

"Who are dead," Corinne said.

"I'm sorry," Carlson said, then went on, "and her friends. Any kind of information like that allows them leverage for blackmail or for control, if they need it."

"They knew about my friend in Buffalo," Corinne said. It wasn't a question. "They knew if I left Montreal, that'd be where I was likely to go."

The lieutenant nodded. "Easy to get your friend's address. Easy to send one of their soldiers to find you there."

The waitress appeared and asked if anyone wanted anything. I looked out the window of the shop. The clouds that had been covering the sky for the past few days were finally breaking.

"I'll have a cinnamon bun," I said. Corinne added another to the order, and Ms. Masterson said she was good for one, as well— and so did Mr. Shannon and Ms. Martin-Lourdes. Lieutenant Carlson hesitated and asked Corinne if cinnamon buns were as good as the bun *pommes* in Montreal. Corinne said not quite, but they were still pretty good, so he ordered one too. We ate them and watched people go by on the sidewalk outside. It was pleasant. It was as nice as things had been in a long time, not including the two nights before with Corinne. That was in a whole different category of nice.

"So," Ms. Masterson said. "Any other questions from either of you?" She looked at Corinne, then me.

"Now that you mention it," I said. "Do you remember this TV show back in the seventies, where this guy was living with two women . . ."

45

Rule #78: *When you're right, don't gloat . . . too much.*

We flew to Boston, into Logan Airport, three weeks later, Corinne and I. Langston drove us to the St. Louis Airport in the Toyota. When he remembered to, he was still limping a little for effect. I asked him, in terms of his ongoing efforts to woo Bao Yu, which was more effective: being a stoic survivor of a gunshot wound or being the best Chinese chef in St. Louis?

"Neither," he said. "Turns out she likes my dimples."

"Good thing the bullet didn't get any further over, then," Corinne said.

"Different dimples."

On the plane, Corinne took the window seat. She plugged in ear buds from her phone and turned on the music app. I closed my eyes and dozed. I'd never been able to sleep on a plane. I could put myself into a kind of stupor, in which the noises around me blended into a low white noise that I found relaxing, the voices and the engine noises and the sounds of the flight attendants. I dozed for about half an hour. Then I tapped Corinne's wrist. She was leaning against the bulkhead, eyes closed. She opened them and popped out both buds.

"What are you listening to?" I asked her.

"Antonio Soler."

"Who?"

"Soler," she repeated. "He was Spanish, Catalan. Harpsichord-ist, from the eighteenth century. He doesn't get the attention he deserves."

"He do any videos?" I asked.

"Watch," she said. "I'll do my imitation of someone ignoring you." She put the ear buds back in and closed her eyes. I waited. About three minutes. Then I tapped her wrist again.

"What?" She tugged only one ear bud out this time and only opened one eye.

"I got Carlson's explanation of how the Flying Ghosts found you—us—in Buffalo," I said. "But how'd they find us in St. Louis?"

Corinne took out the other bud and sat up. "Ariadna. A few days after you left, a guy approached her when she left her office for lunch. She described him as Chinese, bald, young."

"Bobby Chu."

"Yes. He told her he had been dating me back in Montreal. Said we'd had an argument and that he'd been thinking about it and he'd been wrong and wanted to talk to me. I wouldn't answer his phone calls; he'd come to Buffalo to try to get back together with me."

"She believed that?"

"It sounded weird, she said."

"But the guy knew who she was, knew she was your friend, knew you'd come to Buffalo. So how could his story not be straight? How could he know all that otherwise?"

"Right. He even knew where Ariadna worked. But she still didn't want to give him any information without checking with me first. So, she just told him the truth. She told him I'd met someone, a *laowai* who was a Chinese chef, and that I was going to St. Louis to be with him."

"And tracking down a prodigiously talented chef who was working in a Chinese restaurant in St. Louis would not have required the detective talent of the FBI."

"Which also managed to find you—us."

"So when Ariadna told you about meeting your so-called boyfriend—"

"I figured the Flying Ghosts were trying to get to me. So I told Ariadna not to say anything if they tried to contact her, to call the cops if they did, and I took off."

"Which is why you're weren't at her apartment when I came to pick you up?"

"I checked into that motel," she said. "And waited for you. Now can I get back to Antonio Soler?"

"Absolutely," I said. She did.

I let it go for another five minutes. She'd closed her eyes again and was leaning back comfortably on the bulkhead again. The plane banked. I could see a long, silvery thread glittering in the sun, far below, with lots of green around it. I calculated the time, estimated our flight path. We were somewhere over New York. The path of the river and the landscape; it was the Mohawk River. The same one we'd driven along last winter. On our way to Buffalo. And everything else.

I tapped her on the wrist again.

"You're pushing it," she said. Only one bud came out again this time. And she kept her eyes closed.

"One more question."

"Shoot."

"How did Ariadna know you were going to St. Louis?" I asked. "When you said she told Chu the truth, that means you'd already told her you were planning to come to St. Louis. Even before Chu came along."

She didn't say anything.

"To be with me. So you'd already decided you couldn't live without me?"

"Only one of many bad decisions I've made in my life."

I settled back in my seat. "No," I said, "it wasn't."

But she'd already pushed the bud back in and had returned to Soler.

46

Rule #67: *Fried clams always make things better.*

My parents picked us up at Logan. I was curious to see how they would handle Corinne. I was betting they would have some things they were curious about too. Like how I'd spent the winter and spring. They didn't bring it up. Not at all. I would have been mildly astonished if they had. In my family—in a lot of WASPy New England families—trivial stuff might get talked about for hours. Important stuff, though? With important stuff, you waited.

They were gracious to Corinne. They didn't hug her. Or me, for that matter. Corinne was about to learn that the Chinese have nothing on New Englanders when it comes to lack of demonstrations of public affection. Even so, I could tell right from the start that they liked her.

We didn't go home. We went through the Ted Williams Tunnel and across what is officially called the Leonard P. Zakim Bunker Hill Memorial Bridge but that some people around Boston call the Buckner Bridge, because its wide-open support uprights look like the wide-open legs of the Red Sox player Bill Buckner, who back in 1986 let a ball roll through his legs that would have won the World Series for the Sox if he had stopped it. New Englanders also have long memories. And hold long grudges.

We got out on 128 and went north, leaving the interstate for a winding road that follows right along the coast, toward Essex, Massachusetts. We went to Woodman's Clams, where, legend has long had it, fried clams were invented. My father bought dinner. Mesh baskets sagging and clattering with steamed clams. A couple of paper tubs, piled high with golden, crusty fried clams and French fries. We sat up on the top deck, overlooking the estuary that's right behind Woodman's parking lot. Corinne, as we would say in Massachusetts, tucked in. She ate like she'd been eating Ipswich clams all her life. She swished the steamers in the warm broth to wash grit from them, then dunked them in melted butter and ate them. Again, my parents didn't say anything. But I knew they were pleased. The Chinese think that being able to eat their cuisine is a sign a person is civilized. New Englanders think the same about eating steamed clams. She did just as well with the fried ones.

While we ate, my parents told us about the Indonesian sea and the boat and the people they'd met. After my mother showed him how to bring them up on their new digital camera, my father showed me photos of their trip. Then, stuffed to the point of discomfort and beyond, we drove to Andover and home. Or what had been home for a long time. I hauled Corinne's bag up to the room she'd stayed in last time and brought my own up to my room. My mother made a pitcher of lime rickeys. Not the alcoholic kind. The kind made with soda and crushed limes that are only drunk right around Boston. Woodman's Clams and lime rickeys in the same evening. They must have been happy to have me there. We sat out on the front porch, in white wicker easy chairs that spent every season but summer in the back of the garage. And then, finally, as the sun was dropping far enough to give the first sign that evening was on its way, they brought up the subject of my recent adventures.

My mother asked how it was that when they left for Indonesia, I had been a senior at Beddingfield College in New Hampshire with one semester to go until graduation, and when they had returned, I was working as a chef in a Chinese restaurant in St. Louis.

"I've been a chef for a long time," I said. "You know that."

My mother said that, in point of fact, she was less interested in how I came to be cooking professionally in St. Louis and more in how and why I had left Beddingfield. I told her it was a long story. She told me she had time. "Me too," my father said. He looked over at Corinne, who was sitting in her own chair, barefoot, her knees tucked under. She was wearing shorts, and her legs looked very good.

"Do you know anything about this?" my mother asked Corinne. Corinne told them she'd met me after Beddingfield. My father asked where. Corinne's eyes danced. She leaned forward and lifted her glass from the table. Not entirely successfully, she tried to keep a grin off her face as she said very clearly, "He picked me up at a highway rest stop."

"You've been waiting a long time to use that line, haven't you?" I asked.

"Very long," she replied. She sat back in her chair, took a sip of her lime rickey, and smiled again. At me. My mother examined a dribble of condensation that ran down the side of her glass. My father looked out across the street in front of the house. Both of them, I was relieved to see, were also trying to hide smiles.

Then my father cleared his throat. "I suppose," he said to Corinne, "it is not a coincidence that you have the same name as a Corinne Chang who is mentioned prominently in an e-mail I received recently from an FBI field officer in St. Louis, a woman named Masterson."

Corinne sat back. "That's a reasonable assumption."

"She gave me quite an entertaining report," my father said, then corrected himself, "not a report exactly. Or officially. Just informally sharing some information from one government agent to another, retired one."

"I bet it was," I said.

"Was what?" my father said.

"Entertaining."

He looked at me. "So . . . Just what the hell happened?"

I started to say that it was, like Beddingfield, a long story. But I stopped myself. If I said that, it might remind them both that I hadn't explained anything about Beddingfield and my premature departure from the halls of academia. So instead, I put my glass down on the wicker table and sat back and got to it.

"It all started because I really wanted a cinnamon bun, and I'd been driving awhile, and there was a rest stop, right around Littleton. Did you know"—I interrupted myself—"what Littleton was originally called? I'll give you a hint. It's from a Saxon word that means 'cheese farm.'"

Even with my hint, my parents didn't know. But I kept talking and got back to Corinne's story. Like the story about Beddingfield, I'd save the Littleton anecdote for later.

Rule #94: *When the rules don't cover it, improvise.*

I gave Corinne the Special Tucker Tour of Andover. We drove by Andover High School, which looked like it always had. We went to a couple of the Chinese restaurants where I'd worked. We had dinner with the Wu family. Langston's mother wanted to know if he was seeing anyone, and we told them about Bao Yu. We didn't mention the gunshot wound to his ass.

Mostly, though, we sat around at my house and read and went for walks in the evening. After life in the Eastern Palace, it was like a slow decompression period, like coming up from a deep dive in the ocean, taking it easy, resurfacing gradually. I cooked for her and my parents. After a couple of days, I asked her if there was anything she'd like to do.

"I want to go back to the Shaker place," Corinne said.

We borrowed the car again and set out the next morning. It was full, glorious summer now. The Mass Turnpike was a strip of asphalt meandering through brilliant, dark emerald hills. I told Corinne we were passing through the land of the Nipmucks, the Indians who'd originally lived in this part of Massachusetts.

"You have an impressive command of obscure facts," she said.

"Hey," I said, "I'm not the one who listens to eighteenth-century Catalan harpsichordists."

We got to Pittsfield and ate lunch at a joint there called Hot Harry's Fresh Burritos. I suggested splitting the Super Burrito, and Corinne asked if I was feeling okay and if so what was wrong with the Monster Burrito (Double Meat & Double Cheese!)? And I thought that if I hadn't been before, I just might be falling in love. Then we went to Hancock and out to the village, where we paid our admission. When we'd been there last, in the middle of winter, we'd had the place to ourselves. Today there were at least three dozen cars in the lot, along with a couple of school buses.

"Come on," she said. She took my hand.

We walked through the central part of the village and then over into the yard behind the Shakers' meetinghouse. It is a little removed from the rest of the village. It was quieter there. To the side of the house, a dirt trail cut into a thicket of maples. We followed the path, Corinne leading me, until she stopped, under the green canopy of the maples, at three granite boulders. They'd probably been sitting in that spot since a team of horses had dragged them there to clear the nearby field, when the Shakers were still working the land here. There were some smaller stones scattered around too. Corinne stepped over to one, about the size of a football. She squatted down. With her top pulled up above her waist, I could see the smooth brown of her lower back, and the top of her panties. Black.

She pulled at the stone and flipped it over, and then she had something in her hand. A clear bag, like what you'd put sandwiches in for a picnic. She straightened and handed it to me. Inside, I could see a piece of folded paper, light blue.

"Be careful when you open it," she said. "Real careful."

I was. I took the folded paper from inside and started to pull it open. Corinne interrupted me. She put one hand under mine, holding it, then brushed aside my other, the one that was unfolding the paper, and finished the job herself.

I was suddenly aware that my heart was beating. Fast.

"I'm guessing there's about a quarter-zillion dollars' worth of diamonds in here," I said. "But then again, you're the expert."

"Good eye," Corinne said. "Although your estimate is off by a little. It's more like about sixty-five thousand dollars. Give or take."

"Give or take," I said. "Which for some reason Sung didn't take when he cleaned out the rest of his own supply?"

"I think he may have forgotten about these," Corinne said. "They were a private stash he had. He must have been fairly distracted at the time."

"How did you know about them?"

"He showed them to me one day, not too long after I started working there," she said. "I think he had some vague designs about getting into my pants, and he thought it would impress me."

"Did it?"

"He kept it taped under the desk in his office," she said, ignoring my question. "He said it was a 'rainy-day fund' he could liquidate in case he needed money unexpectedly. He'd been putting aside diamonds, one from this consignment, another from that, for a long time. He did enough volume that it wouldn't have shown up in the accounts."

"How do things like diamonds not show up in accounts? It's not like filching some staples or rubber bands."

"Wholesalers in the diamond business deal in hundreds of thousands of stones," she said. "They'll send an extra one or two along to a distributor like the Wing Sung company. And distributors' inventories are constantly fluid, anyway. It isn't that hard, unless you're greedy about it, to slowly take one here and there and keep it off the books."

"So the day you showed up and he was gone," I said, "you figured out what had happened?"

"I guessed; that was all."

"And you remembered the stash here . . ." I lifted the packet.

The diamonds caught the afternoon light and twinkled like the sky's brightest stars. "And checked to see if it was still there."

"I did," she said. "It was."

"And you hid it here the day we visited?"

"Oh, no, Nancy Drew," she said. She held my hand again and used her other to fold the packet closed again. "I came down here and hid them, then went to New Hampshire and waited for you to come along."

"Complicated plan."

"*Qi wo!*" she hissed. "Of course I put it here the day you took me. What do you think?"

It was quiet. A little breeze riffled the maple leaves over our head. A catbird made a raw, mewling call.

"Technically speaking," I said, "these belong to the Flying Ghosts."

"Technically speaking," Corinne said. "Although since they weren't in the regular inventory, Ping and the Ghosts wouldn't have known about them in the first place. They couldn't have known these diamonds were missing since they didn't know Sung had them."

"*Had* them."

"True," she said. "However, since they are—what's the expression the prosecuting attorney used back in St. Louis? IGG?"

"Ill-gotten gains."

"Yeah," she said. "Since they are ill-gotten gains, and since Ping and several others of the Flying Ghosts are right now distracted by arrests and upcoming prosecutions, they are probably not in a position to accept receipt of them. So my conclusion is . . ."

"Finders, keepers?" I said.

"Unless there is a Tucker's Rule that covers this sort of situation."

"This one's in kind of a gray area, I have to admit."

She took the blue envelope from my hand and slid it back into the plastic pouch, then tucked it into the front pocket of my pants.

"You trust me with these?" I asked.

"I'm thinking we might want to use them to make an investment," she said. We started walking back to the main part of the village. Out of the shade of the maples, the sun was bright.

"Investment in what?" I asked.

She looped her arm through mine. "Well," Corinne said, "I've been to this part of Massachusetts twice now and it's lovely and all, but have you noticed one thing that's missing?"

"What?"

"There doesn't seem to be a good Chinese restaurant anywhere around here."

8/14